By Guy Portman
Copyright Guy Portman 2012

All rights reserved. No part of this book may be reproduced, stored or transmitted in any form without the permission of the author. Nothing contained herein is intended to express judgment on or affect the validity of the legal status of any term or word.

If you like this book please take five minutes of your time to post a review on Amazon.com and/or Amazon.co.uk

Follow me on Twitter **@GuyPortman**

With thanks to Marcella Dhew, Adam Riley,
Ayako Sone and my dear wife Tomomi.

Charles Middleworth

Guy Portman

One

Friday April 13th – London – Grey rain clouds have enveloped the sky and the monotonous drone of an aeroplane can be heard from somewhere above. It is raining and the masses at street level scurry for cover, heads hung forlornly, not a smile to be seen. This is the sight that greets thirty-nine-year-old actuary Adrian, as he lifts his weary eyes from the graphs at his desk and out of the sixtieth floor of the building that serves as the home of Vincent & Ernst, one of the city's premier actuary firms. Adrian however does not interpret the view in a forlorn manner; in fact he does not interpret it at all. Perhaps because it is not in his nature or just maybe because tomorrow he departs on a two day trip to Athens, one of six short breaks that he takes each year.

'It's party time,' he murmurs with as much enthusiasm as he can muster. Even for an actuary it is a particularly feeble effort. This would come as no real surprise to anyone acquainted with the industry or in fact Adrian, a man dulled by the standardisations and mundane mechanical nature of his existence. Placing both hands on the beech effect melamine desk, Adrian spins his superior zero gravity chair, complete with lumbar, lower back supports and Safco seat cushion precisely ninety degrees and rises to his feet. He gently lowers the sleeve of his grey M & S one hundred percent cotton shirt and glances at the G-9000 Mudman Casio watch that adorns his wrist.

The watch had been purchased from kbsuppliers.co.uk for seventy pounds, a real bargain. The corners of Adrian's lips rise slightly as he smirks at the thought of his two colleagues, who have recently bought what he deems to be inferior Tag Huers, for more than eight times the price. Once more Adrian recites silently the description of the G-9000 Mudman, as outlined on kbsupplies.co.uk. He had memorised the information the Saturday morning it arrived from Amazon, during a four minute break from his television viewing itinerary.

'Tough resin body, 200 metres water/mud resistant, 1/100th second stopwatch measuring to 999:59.59.99, auto calendar to year 2039, button operation tone on/off, blue backlight, countdown timer measuring up to 24hrs in 1 min increments, 5 independent alarms, 4 one time alarms and a snooze alarm, hourly time signal, low temperature resistant to -20 degrees Celsius. World time for 29 zones, including 48 cities, approximate weight is 56g; dimensions are 52mm x 46.3mm x 16.3mm.'

The corner of his lips rise further to form a genuine smile of contentment, both at the genius of his purchase but also at the prospect of tomorrow's indulgence, a Canon EOS-1D Mark IV. Adrian lowers his eyelids and tentatively licks his lips, as the features, as outlined on digital-newworld.com appear before him. Just like on the day he had first read them, one month previously.

Canon EOS-1D Mark IV:
- 16.1 MP APS-H 27.9mm x 18.6mm CMOS sensor
- Full HD (1080p) movies with manual control
- 3.0" Clear View II LCD with Live View mode
- Shutter speed: 30-1/8000 sec (1/2 or 1/3 stop increments)
- Dimensions 156 x 156.6 x 79.9mm

- Weight (Body Only): Approx. 1180g

Several minutes later, Ethel, the most senior female actuary in the firm, on noticing Adrian clearing his desk remarks,
  'Adrian are you off already? But it's only 18:33.'
  'Yes I must be going, packing to do and travel insurance to organise,' replies Adrian, who then adds in an excited tone,
  'Insurance Options have a new annual multi trip package.'
  He is oblivious to the fact that Jenny one of the secretaries' groans audibly from two desks down and Ethel's smile evaporates instantaneously, to be replaced by a rather startled expression. Adrian continues. 'If you are planning to travel a few times a year then an annual policy offers both convenience and value for money.' He inhales deeply before continuing. 'Insurance Options annual multi trip cover includes:
1). Winter sports for free from 15 up to 22 days.
2). Travel as many times as you like over a year – maximum trip durations range from 50 to 90 days.
3). Up to 3 under 18's included free per insured adult.'
  'Well that's not much use to you is it, I assume you're going alone or have you made another friend in that internet forum of yours,' exclaims Jenny taking delight in placing Adrian in a potentially embarrassing situation.
  'If you would allow me the opportunity to outline the remaining features, you would understand why Insurance Options annual multi trip cover is my package of choice.'
  'Very interesting, I'll bear it in mind for our family trip to Disney in November,' says Ethel.
Adrian does not take the hint from Ethel to stop and continues. 'Where was I, oh yes,' he states gleefully. 'There are four levels of cover, so it is a simple matter to pick the right policy for your needs. One receives cover for emergencies, personal belongings, travel delay, personal liability and legal costs, in addition to much more.'

A now scowling Ethel uses this interlude to change the subject. 'Well have a great time and we'll see you next week.' Adrian accepts the invitation to shut up without further ado and after taking a sanctimonious glance at Ethel's inferior Gul Micro chrome analogue watch, he departs, deep in thought about its inferiority to his own.

He trots out of the office and across the lobby, presses the down switch for the elevator with the thumb of his right hand, and then proceeds to wipe it on his Irish linen hemstitched handkerchief, to eradicate any germs. Moments later and he's off, whooshing down the sixty floors before walking through the marble hall and out through the revolving doors. With his early departure from work - he usually leaves the office at nine or even ten p.m. - and with nothing of particular note on Sky Plus for several hours, Adrian decides to be unusually adventurous and go to his local public house for a pint.

Social interactions have become fairly infrequent events for Adrian in recent years. His wild university days, which were really not that rebellious, lie far in the past. Adrian has spent the majority of the last decade and a half creating algorithms to estimate the probability of occurrences such as death, sickness or loss of property and the value of insurance policies based on these findings. This arduous and rather dull work has been achieved with consummate ease, for Adrian is both diligent and intelligent.

A little over an hour later Adrian arrives at The George. He pushes open the door and walks over to the bar. The pub's air is stale and musky, the carpet a heavily stained garish purple. To the left of the long wooden bar is a fruit machine with luminous lights that flare incessantly.

Adrian, his heavily built six foot one inch frame now leaning against the bar, takes sips from a pint of Kronenbourg whilst he inspects each feature of his Nokia phone in turn, relishing its slim design and full touch glass display. He begins to recall some of phone's characteristics, mouthing them silently. 'Fully integrated social networks, free GPS navigation, and 8MP camera.'

He would have recalled many more of the Nokia features had he not been interrupted by a tapping on his shoulder. Turning he is surprised to see Cedric, a printer and daily frequenter of The George.

'Did your colleagues like the business cards?' asks Cedric. Tilting his head towards Cedric Adrian replies, 'I think so yes. Can't say I was however overly impressed with their gifts. Take this pen for instance.' Reaching into the inside pocket of his grey single breasted, one hundred percent wool suit, Adrian takes out an antique effect silver pen, before continuing. 'Absolutely useless, not yet four months old and it is already all but broken. I cannot understand why manufacturers still insist on using tungsten carbide for the rotating ball when brass or steel are superior alloys and no more expensive.'

Cedric does not respond. Adrian takes this as an invitation to continue. 'The business cards were exquisite and a truly remarkable example of the photo lithographical process; I must congratulate you.'

The previous November in this same pub Cedric had shown Adrian some examples of the business cards his company had recently designed. Impressed by the craftsmanship, Adrian had promptly ordered some as Christmas presents for his senior colleagues. On opening their gifts they had appeared rather bewildered, for they already had business cards and felt at any rate that they made rather impersonal presents.

'Yeah thanks, they've been selling alright this year,' says a smiling Cedric, mildly embarrassed by the flattery.

'Bet they have. I am a big fan of photolithography myself but must also confess to being quite enthused by electron beam lithography and nanoimprint lithography.'

Cedric is quite taken aback, for he is accustomed to the standard compliments of the, 'oh isn't that paper shiny,' or, 'the letters look nice don't they' variety.

'I find nanoimprint lithography a novel method of fabricating nanometer scale patterns, quite ingenious and practical with its high throughput, resolution and low costs,' continues Adrian, in a rather condescending fashion.

'However do you believe that this is the future of printing, or…' Adrian utilises the pause here, in a futile attempt to build suspense and then adds, 'interference lithography.'

Cedric opens his mouth as if to reply but Adrian placing his index finger to his lips, emits a gentle 'sssh' noise and then says, 'the benefits of using interference lithography are obvious….'

Cedric chuckles but a cold stare stops him in his tracks and he stands upright as if to attention.

'The quick generation of dense features over a wide area,' continues Adrian. 'Without there being a loss of focus and its ability to be used for patterns that would take too long for electron beam lithography to generate. However its limit to patterned arrayed features is an obvious drawback as is the addition of non-optical effects, such as secondary electrons from ionizing radiation.'

Cedric now somewhat alarmed blurts out, 'nanoprint lithography.'

He then waits quivering for Adrian's contemptuous reply, however it is not forthcoming. Adrian is silent, his balding head tilted upwards as he delights in the extent of his printing process knowledge. Cedric uses this opportunity to provide evidence for his answer. 'Because umm nanoprint lithography is more flexible and needs err less expertise.'

'Yes indeed,' quips Adrian.

'Err Stella was it,' asks Cedric.

'Kronenbourg.'

22:30 – The George's atmosphere is increasingly raucous and jovial. Adrian and Cedric are on their sixth pint of the evening and Adrian's cheeks have reddened somewhat from their cumulative effect. Cedric takes a memory stick from his pocket, holds it aloft with one hand and exclaims, 'this contains some of our new templates for next year.'

'I would very much like to see them.'

'Umm possibly another time, must be getting back to mother,' replies Cedric, who at forty one years of age is still living at home.

'It won't take long; I only live round the corner in Shipley Street.'

Cedric agrees and off they set, Adrian in his earnestness almost breaking into a jog. On entering the house, Adrian scurries across the hall and into the sitting room, snatches the memory stick from Cedric's outstretched hand and inserts it into the Presario laptop.

'Don't suppose you've got any beers?' enquires Cedric.

'No I don't keep beer in the house. However there is some vintage edition single malt whisky.' Without further ado Adrian goes into the kitchen, grabs two glasses and the whisky from the drinks cabinet before pouring it and adding some ice cubes from the freezer.

Within a minute the templates are appearing on the computer screen. Cedric wishing to explain the first template begins to speak. 'It's a ...,' but is interrupted by Adrian with the words, 'let me do my own investigations.' This is followed by a pause of no more than two seconds.

'This is obviously an example of nanoprint lithography, and as for this, it has been created using electron beam lithography has it not,' says Adrian, who then remarks,

'Pleasing to the eye if a little amateurish.'

Cedric goes along with Adrian's observations, uncertain himself in every instance, which method was utilised.

Half an hour later Cedric is snoring loudly from his position hunched on one of Adrian's Burlington leather lounge chairs. To Adrian's consternation Cedric is dribbling onto one of its large curvaceous arms. He awakens suddenly and glances at such speed at his watch; Adrian is unable to discern the manufacturer, let alone the model.

'Fuck its past midnight, mother will be worried.' With a cursory good bye he's off into the night.

Adrian looks at the Mudman G-9000 and in his weary state does not dwell to savour any of its features but merely to check the time. Reclining on the Burlington leather sofa he turns on the Sky Plus control and watches the Panasonic fifty inch 3D television come to life. A commercial for Vizio televisions appears on the screen. Adrian turns his head to the side in disgust and mutters, 'it's far too late at night to be witnessing such tacky merchandise.' He laughs aloud as he compares his Panasonic to the inferior Vizio and then switches channel. A short time later he shouts 'yes' very loudly, clenches his left fist, punches the air and exclaims,

'Only nine hours to go.' The nine hours he is referring to is the amount of time there is to elapse before the collection of the Canon EOS-1D Mark IV.

A squalid slum appears on the television's screen. Adrian, unsure where it is assumes that it is either Sugar Mountain in Manila or perhaps Jakarta. Citing the injustices of the global economy and its unrighteous policies, a more sombre mood descends upon him. With his arrogant self-righteousness, materialism and almost autistic grasp of human relationships, Adrian often appears devoid of typical emotions; this however is not always the case. For if one were to observe him very closely, there are points in time such as now, evidence that Adrian is not entirely estranged from others in his behaviour. A small smudge on his logarithmic graph paper at the office, caused by a single tear, days after the death of his dear mother also bears testimony to this.

A combination of the late hour and consumption of alcohol has left Adrian fatigued and he stumbles up the flight of stairs to bed. So exhausted in fact is Adrian that he does not linger with the bed light on, to delve into one of his manuals, as is generally his habit. He is asleep within a minute of his balding head hitting the microfiber orthopaedic cervical neck support pillow. The room is silent, apart from occasional muffled snores.

03:00 - Adrian's brow is damp with sweat and his body is twitching nervously. Dark ominous clouds are circling his now tortured mind and from somewhere far in the distance a drone is audible. The clamour, its origin unexplained is growing persistently louder, more threatening and chaotic. Far ahead the distinctive outline of a person is visible, its arms and legs stretched outwards; an impression suspended in the air. Moments later the figure is enveloped by a mist of tenebrous nebulosity, only for the cloud to surge onwards revealing the figure once more. In spite of his subconscious state there is a determination in Adrian to find out who this distant ghost like figure is and he struggles forward through the sky towards it.

The infernal clamour continues to increase in volume and is reaching almost deafening proportions now. Adrian is confused and fearful; his breathing coming in fitful gasps. The figure approaching yet closer, reveals itself to be a middle aged man, clad in a tan brown two piece suit.

Adrian despite his apprehension finds himself approaching the man, calling out to him as he does so. The noise is now so loud that Adrian is forced to clasp his hands to his ears. It is a sound that he has never previously encountered, a diabolical roar, senseless, unrecognisable and increasingly terrifying. The dark and threatening clouds loom around Adrian, who panicking crouches to the ground and screams in fear, his adventurous spirit crushed by these alien inhospitable surroundings. Engulfed in terror he wails incoherently for what seems like an eternity.

Sometime later Adrian becomes aware that he is back in the bedroom. His rapidly beating heart resonates through his body as he reaches for the bedside light switch. The fear only begins to subside once the room is immersed in light. All is quiet now, save for the chirping of a robin in a neighbouring garden. Turning the sodden pillow over, Adrian lies down, still breathing rapidly. Though shocked at the traumatic nature of the dream, he rationalises that the whole fearful episode is a result of an excess of alcohol. Despite this, some lingering dread results in him spending the remainder of the night sleeping fitfully, with the bedside light left on. On awakening later that morning, Adrian sits up and peers around the room cautiously, before admonishing himself for drinking so much the previous evening. Recalling the fact that today is the day he collects his Canon EOS, normality is restored instantaneously.

Three hours later - Adrian clambers out of the taxi, stuffs a twenty pound note in the hand of the driver and then heads off at a trot in the direction of Premier Electrical Goods. Asad, the shop's proprietor is stooped in the corner of the store, loading one of the display shelves with new lenses.

'Hello, I am here to collect the Canon EOS-1D Mark IV,' greets Adrian on entering the premises.

'It arrived early this morning,' replies Asad, as he rises to his feet. Adrian smiles broadly and punches the air with his clenched right fist in triumph. Though having met Adrian on a number of occasions in the shop, Asad appears bemused by this display. Walking over to the front desk, Asad picks up a cardboard box and tentatively begins to remove the tape that is securing its lid.

'I will deal with that,' instructs Adrian, grabbing the box from Asad's grasp and feverishly clawing at the tape with his finger nails.

After ripping open the FedEx box and the bag contained therewith, he catches a first glimpse of the Canon EOS's matt black compact body. Pulling it from the open bag, he holds it up towards the light and inspects it. This is the first time that he has actually clasped a Mark IV in his hands and he marvels at how so much ingenuity could be packed into a mere one thousand, one hundred and eighty grams, not including batteries. Meanwhile Asad paraphrases the terms and conditions of purchase. In spite of his usual meticulous attention to detail, Adrian ignores Asad, and instead paws through the manual with his right hand whilst the other clasps Canon's latest offering to his breast.

The manual is to remain open for the entire duration of the taxi journey home, as Adrian memorises the features, relaying them back in his mind and checking them against the functions on the camera's display panel. He is particularly impressed by the information pertaining to photographing in low light, so much so that he reads the information aloud.

'Low Light Shooting - Thanks to the EOS-1D Mark IV's exceptionally wide ISO range of 100 to 12800 – expandable up to an incredible ISO 102400 - shooting need never stop even in the darkest of conditions.'

Four hours later - Adrian is standing in the check-in queue for British Airways flight B7310 to Athens. He is wearing a beige safari jacket with numerous pockets. This tiresome, rather lengthy interlude allows him the opportunity to scan his fellow travellers' baggage. Whilst he does this he reminds himself of the features of his own Samsonite Pro-DLX. These appear in his mind as bullet points:

- Organised interior is provided with elastics, dividers, etc to keep the case well organised.

- Removable camera shuttle is a padded compartment designed to carry your laptop computer and help protect it from shocks while travelling.

An hour and a half later, Adrian is on the aeroplane awaiting take off, looking slightly perplexed and rather angry. In the next seat is an overweight boy munching loudly on pretzels. However the cause of his consternation is not this but rather the on-board announcement that is being relayed to the passengers:

'The following electronic devices may not be used during takeoff or landing: portable music players, portable computers, and cellular phones, which should be in the off position and stowed away.'

Adrian wonders what leisure pursuits are left available to him, as he is not in possession of a book. Then remembering the Canon EOS, his hand shoots up into the air, at the same time he shouts out to an air hostess stood in the aisle way, a couple of yards in front of him. 'Excuse me it is acceptable I assume to familiarise myself with my new camera, after all it is impossible that it could affect the electromagnetic
interference either of the on-board equipment or ground based networks.'

'You can't take photos at any time on the flight I'm afraid,' replies the air hostess.

'Why of course,' responds Adrian. 'I meant only to remind myself of the features on the navigation display.'

'Put it away or we'll be forced to confiscate it until landing,' retorts the air hostess, who then turns curtly and walks away down the aisle.

The three and a half hour flight passes largely without incident, save for when Adrian pulls up the window shutter and is met by a view of closely knit clouds. He shudders as recollections of last night's fearful nightmare comes flooding back and slams the shutter closed. Despite the protestations of the overweight child, his mouth still full of pretzels, it is to remain so for the duration of the journey.

17:00 - Athens airport – Adrian, passport in hand is awaiting the arrival of his luggage.

17:41 – Adrian is standing at the entrance of the majestic Athenaeum TransGlobal Hotel, smiling contentedly as he gazes up in wonder at the colossal structure. Slowly inhaling, he fills his lungs with Athens's notoriously polluted air. 'What a choice,' he murmurs aloud seconds later. A porter with a large moustache approaches with the intention of collecting his luggage. Immediately recognising Adrian to be English, he greets him:

'Good evening Sir, please I takee bag.'

Bringing his index finger to his lips Adrian silences him and slowly yet purposefully with both hands clutching the Canon EOS, proceeds to raise it upwards. It is as if he were the captain of a World Cup winning football side on first clasping the trophy and holding it aloft to the heavens. The preparation for the Canon EOS's baptism has been fastidious, the ideal format having been set on the bus. Exposure control, program ae auto, anti-blur, natural light, portrait, landscape. With two quick clicks on the zoom out control, the majestic main tower of the Athenaeum TransGlobal is perfectly positioned on the camera's screen.

'One, two, three,' whispers Adrian. The flash instantly illuminates the screen. He stands motionless, revelling in the moment.

Minutes later and Adrian is standing in the centre of his room. The porter on attempting to explain how to use the various in room facilities is once again silenced and departs clasping his measly tip, a one Euro coin, mumbling obscenities under his breath. Standing with his arms outstretched Adrian slowly rotates three hundred and sixty degrees, surveying the room as he does so. A smile adorns his face, as he savours the décor and furnishings.

As with every hotel Adrian has visited over the last decade or so, he feels the need for an inspection, to scrutinise every aspect of the room thoroughly. Removing the Compaq Presario laptop from the suitcase, he places it on the bedside table and then opens one of its Excel spreadsheets. As with all prior inspections it begins with the dimensions of the room, which he grades a four out of five; he never gives fives. After this he proceeds to move onto the more specific aspects, the wallpaper, furnishings, electrical appliances, towels and the like.

'Pleasant enough wallpaper, yes I agree a plain purple bordering on lilac is a satisfactory choice for a room which benefits from an abundance of natural light. I will give it a three,' states Adrian aloud. In spite of it being dark, he has already noted the room faces east. The data is entered. The figures are then inserted into a Dijkstra algorithm, an unimaginably complicated process that most mortals could not even begin to comprehend, it looks like this:

```
1  functionDijkstra(G, w, s)
2    for each vertex v in V[G]            // Initializations
3        d[v] := infinity                 // Unknown distance function from s to v
4        previous[v] := undefined
5    d[s] := 0                            // Distance from s to s
6    S := empty set                       // Set of all visited vertices
7    Q := V[G]                            // Set of all unvisited vertices
8    while Q is not an empty set          // The algorithm itself
9        u :=Extract_Min(Q)               // Remove best vertex from priority queue
10       S := S union {u}                 // Mark it 'visited'
11       for each edge (u,v) outgoing from u
```

17

```
12          if d[u] + w(u,v) < d[v]        // Relax (u,v)
13              d[v] := d[u] + w(u,v)
14              previous[v] := u
```

Dinner at the Athenaeum TransGlobal as with all TransGlobal hotels is a delight. The cuisine is aimed at the hotel's largely business clientele and varies only marginally across the TransGlobals' vast chain. Tired solitary businessmen are seated at a number of the tables drinking wine. A jovial middle aged couple studiously reviewing an Athens tour book is the only evidence of any kind of family life. Adrian feels at ease in this five star business environment, for although on vacation, he appears as a business visitor and therefore does not seem out of place without family or friends in attendance.

Adrian orders roast duck with caramelised red onion and juniper. On the dish's arrival at the table, he leers over it with the Canon EOS and then zooms in to capture the culinary delight. The waitress witnessing this incident stifles a giggle and flees to the safety of the kitchen where she laughs hysterically. Having consumed the meal, Adrian tentatively dabs his lips with his napkin and then slips a one Euro coin onto the silver plate containing the bill. The waitress emerges. Noticing the tip her humour dissipates instantaneously.

Dijkstra algorithm analysis provides the post dinner entertainment. Periodically Adrian takes sips from a glass of Angostura eighty percent proof rum, a product of Spain and a quite superior example, he concludes. He is reaching for the bottle to pour a second glass when recalling the nightmare from the previous night he returns the bottle to its resting place.

Adrian turns on the room's LCD Panasonic television complete with ultra wide viewing angle. A BBC World documentary on the subject of Penicillin has just begun and Adrian as a test to himself attempts to remain one step ahead of the narrator. Sitting in an upright position, he scrutinises his mind in a calm, deliberate and determined manner. This is a test worthy of his majestic intellect. He inhales deeply and then begins; 'Penicillin is a widely used antibiotic agent; it is derived from the Penicillium mould. Penicillin's molecular formula is R-C9H11N2O4S, where R is a variable side chain.'

A minute and a half later this information is imparted by the narrator. Adrian in his customary manner clenches his fist in victory and punches the air in delight. 'It was in 1928 that Sir Alexander Fleming observed that colonies of the bacterium Staphylococcus aureus could be destroyed using the mould Penicillium notatum,' he continues confidently.

Eager and smiling broadly, he awaits validation and then repeats the clenching of the fist, this time with an additional victory jig around the bedroom. By eleven p.m. the documentary has finished and a contented lethargy has engulfed his fatigued body; sleep finds him shortly thereafter. The only sound is the barely audible whir from the Zwicker air conditioner and the occasional buzzing of a lone mosquito. The hours pass; 12:00, 01:00, 02:00.

02:47 – Adrian appears restless, his breathing agitated and his brow speckled with dots of sweat. His mind is no longer a tranquil dormant void, as he finds himself floating through a sky, rapidly filling with sinister rain clouds. At the same time an incessant drone reaches him, growing persistently louder by the second. In the distance partially obscured by the clouds, a figure appears. Adrian trembles uncontrollably and attempts to turn and flee, there being none of the curiosity in him of the previous night but through no want of his own is involuntarily drawn closer to the figure. Fear turns to panic on the realisation that this eerie figure is the same man in the tan suit from the previous night.

Adrian desperately continues to attempt to halt his progress but to his dismay his efforts prove to be in vain and he floats ever forward. The man remains slightly ahead of him, as they begin to descend slowly downwards towards the infernal clamour. Holding his hands to his head Adrian screams uncontrollably but it is to no avail and he continues to descend, all the while the ominous commotion increasing in volume and intensity. Moments later he is below the cloud level and descending still.

What appears to be flat ground lying far beneath him is drawing closer now, as the racket continues remorselessly. As the descent continues unabated, his semi-conscious mind becomes aware that beneath him is not flat ground at all but a myriad of tiny dots growing steadily closer and more distinguishable. Moments later and they are no longer dots but an impenetrable mass of human faces, which stretch for what seems like eternity in every direction, peering up at the sky as they wail incoherently. Yet closer the petrified Adrian is drawn, hovering now not more than fifteen metres or so above them. Wide-eyed with terror he continues to wail, a hideous mindless sound that is lost in the commotion of the multitude below.

A loud knocking sound awakens Adrian and he sits bolt upright in the bed, drenched in sweat and gasping desperately for air as he turns his head rapidly from side to side.

The knocking continues and a faint voice can be heard. 'Hello you ok? Guests saye very noisy.'

All is quiet now save for the savage beating of his heart. The panic begins to subside somewhat on the realisation that he is in the hotel room. Reaching to his left he turns on the bedside light.

'Jesus Christ what was all that, it must have been a dream but...'

The voice of the porter in the hallway interrupts him. 'Hello, hello why scream, is everything ok?'

'Everything is fine thank you; it was merely a bad dream,' replies Adrian in as calm a voice as he can muster.

'Ok very good, goodnight sir,' replies the only slightly reassured voice. The light remains on, as Adrian's heart continues to thud rapidly and his breathing remains accelerated. Questions bombard his anguished bewildered mind. Each one he whispers aloud in a muffled fearful voice, as they appear in his now disjointed chaotic mind.

'How can that just be a dream? Why two nights in a row? It was so real? Who is that man? Who are all those people? Why these nightmares when I am calm and on holiday? Why was I floating? How is this rational thought?' Adrian does not have time to contemplate an answer for any given question before he reels off another, his rational thought processes in disarray. As the minutes pass, his heartbeat gradually slows and pace of breathing subsides. An hour and a half later he is asleep once more.

Early the next morning Adrian is laying on the king sized bed, gazing out through an opening in the curtains at a brilliant blue sky. He sighs wearily, satisfied that all is safe now and that normality has been restored. It is the very same sensation that people have felt since the time of the Neanderthals when experiencing the comfort that is dawn and its salvation from the perils of the darkness.

Even though weakened both physically and emotionally, he is ready for the rigours of the day having consumed a continental breakfast. On the king sized bed, Adrian places items he deems necessary for the forthcoming adventure, a visit to the famed Acropolis. He scrutinises the items and then places them in his olive drab Maxpedition Pygmy Falcon II backpack. The items are:

1). A small hand towel
2). A World executive city guide to Athens
3). A pocket map of the city and surrounding areas
4). A 10cl bottle of Evian

5). The Canon EOS-1D Mark IV

08:20 - Adrian crosses his arms across his chest, each hand holding on to the opposite shoulder strap and he's off. Though it is early in the year, the thermometer rises steadily and he is soon perspiring from the exertions of the ascent to the Acropolis. The first stop is the Propylaea, next the Pinacotheca, followed by the temple to Athena Nike and then the remnants of the Erechtheon. With each stop comes a relentless clicking of the Canon EOS; each scene being captured in a myriad of different settings to be analysed later that day.

10:30 - Adrian is standing in front of the Parthenon. The temple's great Doric columns tower above as he scurries around capturing every conceivable image with the Canon EOS; the friezes, metopes and pediments that had filled the pages of his childhood text books. The constant exertion of the morning's sightseeing is beginning to fatigue him; his pace slows and the unremitting clicking begins to wane. He is about to sit down for a minute or so to recuperate sipping water and studying the city guide when something catches his attention.

To the right of one of the Parthenon's columns, about twenty metres or so away from his position stands a family of four. The family consists of a mother, father and two young children; a small girl with pigtails and a boy of five or so, who is drawing circles in the dust covered stone at his feet with his index finger. It is not any of the family members that have drawn Adrian's attention however but the item slung casually over the father's right shoulder; a camera but not any old camera. 'Highly unlikely,' mutters Adrian to himself, 'not a Canon EOS-1D Mark IV, they only came on the market days ago, must be another model, a Canon 30D or a 40D perhaps. It is just too bloody far to be certain. If only I had brought my Swarovski binoculars.'

He makes the decision to approach closer and then slightly hunched begins to edge forward towards them, slowly yet deliberately, as a hunter would on stalking a red stag in the Highlands of Scotland, not wanting to draw attention to himself. The family remain oblivious, seemingly in awe of the majestic Parthenon and he is soon no more than eight or so metres away. 'Just too far out,' exclaims Adrian before concluding that another two point five metres should be adequate to discern the model.

Crouched and silent, the approach continues. The father turns slightly, about twenty degrees or so and is no longer broadside, the outline of the camera becomes obscured. Adrian, having reached the neighbouring pillar stands with his back against it, planning the final approach. Turning anti- clockwise round the column he tiptoes forward; the family are no more than four metres away but are still too far. Then it dawns on him to zoom in using his own Canon EOS; he scolds himself at his slowness of thought in realising this.

Patiently he raises the EOS, not wanting any sudden movement to disturb his prey. The mother though has spied the crouching Adrian out of the corner of her eye and whispers to her husband, who is admiring the Parthenon's spectacular metope. 'What's that very strange man just behind us doing? He keeps getting closer.'

The husband turning around glares at Adrian and then blurts out to his wife, 'must be one of those bloody paedophiles, quick children let's go.'

All four are running now down the steps of the temple as Alpine chamois might on being alerted to the hunter in their midst. Adrian stands upright and sighs deeply, 'I'll never know now,' he exclaims lamentably.

The Acropolis is followed by a visit to the beautiful neoclassic building that serves as the National Archaeological Museum, ranked among the top ten museums in the world. Departing the museum a few hours later, Adrian glances at the G-9000 Mudman and is surprised to see it is almost three p.m. A wave of spontaneous trepidation resonates through his body at the thought of the approaching night. Attempting to forget this lingering concern he saunters off to the Atelier Spyros Vassiliou, eager to inspect the gallery's lithographs. In anticipation of these, the perils of the night are forgotten.

20:03 - Adrian is in the hotel restaurant taking sips from a glass of Cabernet Sauvignon whilst scrutinising the menu. He speaks quietly to himself as he rationalises his choice:

'One course will be adequate, a restful night's sleep is the priority, absolutely no cheese or chocolate. Veal escalope, yes indeed.'

23:03 - Adrian is transferring the last of the day's photographs from the EOS's memory stick to the laptop.

23:41 - Adrian is asleep, snoring gently and contentedly. The bedside light is left on.

02:45 - He awakes alarmed, subconsciously aware that this is the approximate time the previous night that the ghastly nightmare had begun. Reassured to find himself in the hotel room, he yawns wearily and turns his ponderous frame to the side. The window is slightly ajar and a gentle warm breeze is causing the curtains to flutter softly. Adrian yawns again and stretches his tired body. Eyelids flicker briefly and then sleep finds him once more.

03:10 - Dark menacing clouds are encroaching on the tranquil enclave that had been Adrian's mind up to this point. If awake he would no doubt have passed it off as a change in the weather but he is not.

The noise reaches his ears, barely discernible yet familiar. Clasping his hands to his ears Adrian moans softly but it is to no avail. That same infernal clamour as evidenced during the previous two nights is increasing in volume by the second. Staring out inanely, Adrian views with distress the tenebrous storm clouds heavy with rain rushing through a foreboding sky. The myriad of faces appear far beneath him, their wailing terrifying and unintelligible. A distant figure is approaching ever closer; Adrian becomes aware that it is the man in the tan suit from the previous nights and that he is speaking, in a quiet yet earnest tone. Somehow he can hear the words even above the sound of the lament emanating from below: 'It's me Charles, Charles Middleworth,' says the man. Adrian stares at the man in shock, unable to respond.

'It's me Charles, remember now,' continues the man.

Adrian awakens panic stricken, sitting up in the bed struggling for breath. He shouts out 'Canon EOS, Canon EOS, Canon EOS, Canon EOS,' continuously in a very loud voice, attempting to cling to this bastion of rationality and logic in the face of the unexplainable chaos he has just witnessed. A voice is calling out from the other side of the door, 'what is it sir, open door, open door.'

Adrian does not respond. Motionless he stares sobbing at the lilac coloured far wall. The banging on the door continues unabated. A short time later it stops and there is the sound of a key turning in the lock; then the door opens. Three people enter. The porter from last night, the hotel manager and a third, a heavily muscled member of the hotel's security team with a large badge pinned to his lapel. There is a look of grave concern on all three of the men.

'What has happened here, what is the problem,' enquiries the manager.

Adrian in terror jumps from the bed and rushes for the door screaming inanely, fearful that these people are members of the multitude from the dream minutes earlier. Held back by the security guard, Adrian struggles desperately to free himself from the vice like grip, shouting 'GET ME OUT, get off I must get out of here,' as he does so.

'Calm now, calm down,' says the manager, beckoning with both hands in downward motions.

'Why such noise,' asks the porter.

The security man stands steadfast and silent, holding Adrian securely by the arms, as he continues to try and free himself with ever feebler efforts. Gradually it dawns on an ashen-faced and timid Adrian what has occurred and he confesses,

'It was another nightmare,' in an apologetic tone.

'This is unacceptable; the guests have been upset for a second night,' says the manager sternly, pointing accusingly at Adrian. 'You will spend the rest of the night in a ground floor room, away from the other guests'.'

Adrian leaps out of bed, packing his possessions at a furious pace, as the three men look on. Then it is down to the windowless ground floor room where he is left to his own devices. So distraught is he that these frightful nightmares are continuing each night and are now impinging on reality that he is too terrified to sleep. He wonders why that man Charles Middleworth keeps appearing in his dreams. For he is quite sure he has never come across anyone bearing that name and with a near photographic memory, this is something that he can be quite confident of.

15:00 – The Next Day – Adrian is on a flight back to Heathrow. Earlier that day during check out, his much valued TransGlobal club card had been confiscated and his name entered onto the hotel chain's blacklist. The same list that contained the names of guests caught smoking marijuana on the premises, or had brought back undesirables to their rooms. Not only did Adrian raise no argument, he also did not even inspect the bill in his haste to depart. Had he done so, he would have noted that he had been charged for four cans of Fanta Orange from the room's mini bar that he had not drunk; at the exorbitant rate of five Euros a can.

Adrian, his head resting disconsolately against the window beside him notices a misty canopy of grey swirling nimbus clouds some way beneath the plane. He pulls the window shutter down.

Two

The ground floor study does not benefit from an abundance of natural light, as a result of this and the lack of ventilation it has a rather stale musky aura. A legion of small dots of dust and tiny threads of fluff cascade slowly downwards; visible only as they pass the illuminated circle of light that surrounds the antique ceramic desk lamp. The wallpaper is brown and nondescript, the dark purple curtains slightly frayed. A mahogany desk, the room's centrepiece, is covered in small piles of bound papers and files, some of the papers are tattered around the edges. An austere looking elderly gentleman with angular features and closely cropped grey hair is sat at the desk conversing on the telephone, with the owner of an employment agency named Percy.

'We appreciate the applicants are not, at the high level you require and that we endeavour to supply you with,' says Percy.

'I know you're trying,' replies Colin.

'There just aren't any suitable applicants out there,' remarks Percy.

'I appreciate that believe me.'

'We must be a dying breed Colin.'

'I concur; it's the decline of the church and family values I say.'

'Sure,' replies Percy. 'Do any of the résumés look promising?'

Colin fingers through the résumés on the desk, selects one, holds it up for closer analysis and remarks, 'I require someone young, keen to learn, well educated and presentable.'

'Yes go on,' says Percy.

'It's a good solid profession with high earning potential.'

'Well people have to die.'

'Then why Percy is the industry attracting people like Kurt,' continues Colin. 'Kurt lists his interests as Megadeth, Bauhaus and The Hurting. No idea what they are, I can only assume Megadeth, spelt incorrectly I might add is the term coined by Herman Kahn, the military strategist in his book Thermonuclear war to describe a million deaths. How on earth can that be an interest?'

'Megadeth are a Goth band Colin,' replies Percy struggling to stifle laughter.

'Not Goths again,' replies Colin. 'Virtually every other job application I receive these days is from one. How do you know about Megadeth anyway Percy?'

'My daughter Beatrice listens to them,' says Percy, his voice now taking a sombre tone. 'She only wears black now and she's umm; well she's threatening to become a vampire.'

'Oh no how beastly, I'm so sorry,' says Colin, who makes the decision not to explore the issue further, as he does not feel it appropriate, although he is intrigued. Instead he picks up another résumé from the desk. 'Another candidate for some unknown reason sent in a photo of himself,' he remarks. 'Pale as a ghost, purple Mohawk, facial piercings with what appears to be a bone through his nose. It's just intolerable.'

'God only knows, these Goth adolescents are all over Lyme Regis, it's a bloody disgrace,' replies Percy. 'If only there was still national service.'

'Why is it that they are so keen on death anyway?' asks Colin.

'It's the usual scenario,' responds Percy. 'Adolescents wanting to rebel and the death thing; well it's a taboo isn't it?'

'Come to think of it Percy, don't think I've seen an older Goth; suppose death becomes less appealing the closer you get to it.'

'I haven't seen an old one either,' says Percy.

'Maybe they die young from not seeing the light of day.' Colin considering what Percy has just told him about his daughter feels immediately remorseful about this statement. The discussion continues for several more minutes. At the end of the conversation Colin hangs up the telephone and looks down at the desk. The image of the Goth with the Mohican and facial piercings stares up at him. He grunts in disapproval, turns the offending image upside down and brushes it beneath a pile of papers; normality is restored instantaneously. The phone is ringing, Colin answers it.

'Good afternoon Colin Raven.'

'Hello father it's me.'

'How was the holiday?'

'It was err, interesting,' replies Adrian, who then adds, 'I'm planning to come and stay next weekend, if that is convenient.'

'Why of course. Your brother will be here with Natalia, will be a good chance for us all to get together.'

'I will arrive Friday at seven p.m., bye.'

Colin places the receiver down and reclines back in the antique wooden chair, somewhat puzzled as to why Adrian was so uncharacteristically uncommunicative. Reaching the conclusion that the reason must have been that he was busy, Colin bends forward picks up the pile of résumés from the desk and feeds them into the Ativa paper shredder at his feet.

A wood pigeon is cooing softly in the beech tree at the end of the garden. Small pointed brown sticky buds are visible at the ends of the tree's slender twigs that protrude from the beech's branches like skeletal fingers. Adrian oblivious to the joys of spring is perched on an Ikea garden chair, preoccupied with the horrors of recent nights. Weary and feeling of a delicate disposition, he sips tap water from a porcelain mug. The Canon EOS-1D Mark IV lies forgotten, forlorn and partially submerged in the grass at his feet. With no rational coherent understanding for the nightmares, Adrian is deeply distressed, particularly with the forthcoming night and the potential horrors it could yield.

On Adrian's lap are an array of small packets of medicines, they are for the promotion of sleep and the relieving of anxiety. The non prescription varieties had been purchased from the chemist that day whilst the more potent ones originate from the bathroom cupboard. Benedict, Adrian's younger brother had previously had something of a dependency on prescription drugs and had left them in the house, the previous year. One of the boxes has a large ominous black X and a detailed description at one end. Adrian reads the name aloud, pronouncing each syllable deliberately, 'N-o-r-m-i-s-o-n.' He then outlines the drug's characteristics from memory in his mind. They appear as bullet points and look like this:

- Normison is branded Temazepam.
- Formula $C16H13CIN2O2$
- Acts as a Gamma-aminobutyric acid modulator and anti-anxiety agent.

He is concerned that the consumption of Temazepam will impair his alertness and concentration. With work the next day this is not an ideal scenario. However after reflecting once more on the events of recent nights, Adrian takes the last remaining two pills from the packet and swallows them with the aid of a gulp of water.

22:00 - Adrian is collapsed on the sofa, his head resting on its soft eiderdown cushion. Though awake his eyes are barely open, he is drooling slightly. Reaching out with one arm, he attempts to clasp the television controller on the floor in front of him, but in his listless state is soon defeated by the physical exertion of the activity.

An empty whisky tumbler, its contents having been downed some hours earlier lies dejected on its side. Next to the tumbler is a half empty bottle of Cardhu single malt whisky, its base sunk into the soft blue carpet. The reddish brown contents appear to Adrian to be swelling as the sea might on a blustery day. His weary and addled mind, a combination of fatigue, Temazapam and whisky makes this uncertain and he continues to stare at the bottle, trying to ascertain if this is indeed the case. As he focuses on the liquid, Adrian recollects on the beautiful clear morning, the frost still clutching at the grass, when his father, Benedict and he had visited the Cardhu distillery, two years previous.

'Cardhu is a Speyside distillery in Morayshire,' murmurs Adrian in a quiet voice. 'Founded in Eighteen- twenty-four by John Cumming and currently owned by Diageo. This particular bottle, dated November, Two thousand and three, is from the very last batch of single malts produced, prior to the distillery commencing with vatted malts.'

Adrian would have continued with some complex chemistry relating to the formation of malt whiskies, had the combination of Temazapam and alcohol not brought a halt to the proceedings, resulting in him losing consciousness.

Only the faint ticking of the Seiko kitchen clock and the sound of Adrian breathing slowly and deeply, interrupted at intervals by muffled snores, are perceptible now. It is as if Adrian's lethargy has contaminated the surroundings, for the air is heavy and still.

03:09 – Adrian becomes subconsciously aware that he is descending through a sky clustered with clouds of the vertical cumulonimbus variety, as often witnessed prior to a sudden deluge. Emanating from somewhere far below a sound is discernible, an unremitting incoherent roaring that increases in volume with each passing second. The outline of a man appears in the distance, partially obscured by the clouds and approaching closer. Within a minute or so it reveals itself to be the tan suited figure from recent nights, Charles Middleworth. Even in his dormant state Adrian is able to recall the name.

The great swathes of faces of the chaotic multitude appear in the distance beneath him, at first as a congealed hate-emitting mass, but as Adrian continues to descend their individual features become distinguishable. These are different people than the previous night, yet they are equally pernicious, the huddled figures irate and irrational. An old man with piercing green eyes, his features contorted in anger stares upwards. To his left an emaciated woman with tortured features and rabid irksome eyes, her head swathed in a purple shawl, speckled with dots of soot and grime. The din is deafening, Adrian holding his hands to his ears once more is lifted from his slumbers by the shouting and agonizing wails all around him.

Awake now and back on the sofa still screaming, his eyelids remain firmly shut for almost a minute, before the realisation dawns on him that he is back in the sitting room. Anxious and sweating profusely, he sits upright and looks around the room, each breath coming in quick succession, mouth agape in horror.

Some minutes later having regained a modicum of composure, there is astonishment and anxiety in equal measure that having taken twenty milligrams of Temazepam only hours earlier, how such a vivid terrifying nightmare could have occurred. There is anger that this member of the benzodiazepine family has not adhered to its stated purpose, as a potent anti-anxiety medication. Adrian reaches out and grabs the bottle of whisky from the floor, unscrews the top and takes a large gulp. After which the thought occurs to him that he is at the mercy of a force he cannot comprehend and therefore is unable to control. He lies back down on the sofa and repeats 'Canon EOS, Canon EOS, Canon EOS...,' repeatedly for quite some time. Eventually sleep finds him once more.

11:00 - The Next Day - Despite the hour it is as if it were night, for the sun is notable only for its absence, concealed behind a blanket of impenetrable cloud. Inside the office of Vincent & Ernst, Adrian's desk is littered with all manner of paperwork; letters, graphs, insurance policies, and print outs of complex mathematical tables and algorithms. Adrian rests his heavy head in his hands and sighs wearily. The episodes of recent nights and the lingering after effects of the Temazepam are not compatible with complex mathematical analyses and he is struggling to maintain concentration. Leaning back in the superior zero gravity chair complete with lumbar, lower back supports and Safco seat cushion, he looks across at the framed print on the far side of his desk. The picture is of James Dodson, a renowned eighteenth century mathematician, actuary and insurance industry innovator. Usually if struggling to maintain concentration, a momentary glimpse at the severe features and glistening eyes of Dodson would inspire Adrian and his work rate would reach a feverish pace. On this occasion though there is no renewed vigour.

A shrill voice begins to call his name repeatedly from a neighbouring desk, the sound excruciating and invasive. The voice belongs to the office secretary Jill, the only member of the office's staff Adrian actively dislikes. 'Yes,' responds Adrian after the fifth repetition of his name.

'You're very quiet today,' says Jenny. 'How was your holiday?'

'It was err, interesting,' replies Adrian, struggling to find words to describe the trip.

'Did the multi trip insurance come in useful?'

'No, not on this occasion,' states Adrian. 'But it is always best to have multi trip insurance cover and not to need it than to need multi trip insurance cover and not to have it.'

He then proceeds to pull a couple of sheets of paper from the top of the pile in the in-tray on his desk; they have numbers scrawled in pencil across them. 'Oh yes,' murmurs Adrian to himself, 'the life expectancy tables for asbestos poisoning sufferers in Northumbria.' Rapidly he scrutinises the numbers, a simple task for an actuary of Adrian's brilliance, even in his current condition. Within a minute the decision has been made to use the formula $Lx + t = (1-t) Lx + t\, lx+1$ for the likelihood of death.

Next Adrian opens a new Excel spreadsheet on the computer, saves it as NorthumbriaAsbestosMortality1.xl and begins to type using only his right hand the column headings, in a bold, Times New Roman font, size sixteen point five. He is at the point of entering the formula in column D when he is interrupted once more by the piercing high pitched voice of Jenny. The sound of which causes Adrian to press his thumb so hard against the pencil clasped in his left hand that it snaps in two.

'Adrian what's 700x7-64?'

Adrian grits his teeth in annoyance and then replies '4836!'

Jenny and the temp she sits next to, whose name Adrian can never remember, giggle. It is a common occurrence in the office for Jenny to test Adrian on his mental arithmetic, as she revels in the fact that he is always able to answer instantaneously. Not that she interprets it as a positive thing but rather that it reinforces in her mind the aura of Adrian as an oddity, which she finds most amusing. Adrian for his part finds the questions so simple that they do not distract him from his work. Today however is different.

'Adrian!' exclaims Jenny yet again.

'What now?'

Jenny would have been wise to sense the tone in Adrian's voice but she does not and asks, 'I was just wondering what 17x32-7 is?'

Adrian rises to his feet and marches over to her desk, where he now stands, towering over her. Jenny looks up at first surprised to see Adrian there, then in fright on seeing the veil of animosity that has descended upon him. 'Here is a question for you, an easy one,' says Adrian. 'Even you should be able to calculate it. 16x8.' He then counts to three and asks, 'well what's the answer?' No answer is forthcoming; Adrian taking this as invitation to continue says, 'might I ask what you are doing working in an actuarial firm when you don't even know your times tables.' Jenny does not respond. Instead she cowers in her seat and begins to sob.

Some of the other members of the office having heard the shouting are now standing around Jenny's desk. Adrian walks back to his own desk, sits down and resumes work. His bewildered colleagues stare after him and then return to their own desks, without a word. Ethel passes Jenny a box of tissues and tells her not to worry, putting a reassuring hand on her shoulder as she does so.

13:06 - Adrian is in the process of leaving the office for lunch when Ethel stops him as he walks past her desk. 'Is everything alright Adrian?' she asks in a concerned voice.

'Good thank you. The Northumbria mortality tables are now completed.'

Not wanting anyone else in the office to overhear Ethel whispers, 'what was all that with Jenny? She was in quite a state and has gone home.'

'She was being annoying,' responds Adrian casually.

'So you attacked her for not knowing her sixteen times tables.'

'Well err, yes.'

'Most people learn times tables up to times twelve not sixteen Adrian.'

'Possibly, but regardless she was affecting my pattern of thought.'

'I can appreciate that, but it's not like you to lose your temper and well what happens if she now walks off claiming discrimination or something,' says Ethel. 'You know as well as anyone the litigious nature of working life these days.'

'Ridiculous, for shouting at her.'

'You were intimidating her,' replies Ethel, standing up as she does so and looking at Adrian sternly. 'There's no place for that kind of behaviour here.'

'I must disagree with your definition of intimidation,' states Adrian. 'For my understanding is that it is to force into or deter someone from an action by causing fear and...'

'It was overly aggressive behaviour,' interrupts an annoyed Ethel.

Adrian gets no further than 'But...,' before he is interrupted again.

'We're both senior members of staff and on a level here, but in addition to our normal workloads, I look after employee relations and you're in charge of selecting software.'

'Yes about the software, I recently came across...'

'Not now,' rebukes Ethel angrily, who then continuing in a more consoling tone says, 'if you've got a problem with staff, speak to me. I'm on your side.'

'The probability of her taking action is negligible,' remarks Adrian.

'How do you know what the probability of someone taking a certain course of action is?' responds Ethel, her voice betraying displeasure once more.

'Well if you took x to be Jenny...'

'See you at the meeting this afternoon,' interrupts Ethel before sitting down.

Walking towards the lift, Adrian is acutely aware that the nightmares of recent nights are now affecting his working life. This is a worrying turn of events, for he takes pride in maintaining professionalism and composure at all times whilst at work. Above all he hopes that the unsettling algorithmic proof uncertainty that has descended upon his life is temporary.

On exiting the building, Adrian is met by the full force of an unremitting deluge that forces him hurriedly towards the shelter of Spitalfields Market. He is not alone in seeking shelter there. The market is a bustling mass of workers on their lunch breaks, desperate for some respite from the torrential downpour. They mill around talking on their mobiles, amongst themselves or simply amble about inspecting the food stalls. This is the sight that greets Adrian as he weaves through the bustling mass of rain sodden bodies moving in every conceivable direction.

Now huddled amongst the mass of people on the market floor, Adrian begins to feel increasingly claustrophobic. The multitude of voices all around him seems as one unintelligible commotion, increasing in both volume and intensity with each second. It is as if he is no longer in the familiar surroundings of Spitalfields Market, where many hundreds of lunch breaks had been spent, but rather once more in the midst of a nightmare. Adrian clasps his hands to his ears. The umbrella falls to the ground. He starts to run, pushing and shoving suited business men, women and tourists as he attempts to flee the hostile surroundings. They are angry and shocked in equal measure, a business man shouting and shaking his fist, a secretary screaming as she is crudely shoved aside.

Escaping the market offers no reprieve; for as he looks upwards, dark ominous storm clouds are visible racing through the sky. Adrian's hands drop down from his ears and he sprints across the wet stone pavement, ignoring the risk of falling on its slippery surface. On reaching his office's building, he swings open its glass door, enters the lobby and cowers inside, struggling to regain his breath. The security guard and receptionist, alarmed to see him huddled behind the door, look at each other inquisitively, as if expecting the other to respond in some way. The receptionist, a tall young woman wearing a plaited skirt, makes the decision to take the initiative and says 'excuse me, is there a problem?'

Adrian does not respond and stares back at her. Standing to her full height to give her voice added resonance, she adds,

'Sir is everything alright?'

Adrian blurts out a barely coherent, 'yes yes it's fine.' With this he hurries across the marble floored lobby, enters the lift and presses the button for the sixtieth floor. On the way up Adrian makes the decision that a visit to the doctor is necessary.

16:40 - The purr of a high performance vehicle can be heard from somewhere in the distance. Seconds later the elegant and perfectly proportioned sleek that is the Aston Martin V8 Vantage S convertible comes into view, exuding a regal air as it glides effortlessly down the country lane, courtesy of its four point seven litre engine and 430bhp of controlled aggression. The Vantage's unparalleled superiority is only too evident to its incumbent, thirty-nine-year-old property developer Theodore Miller, as it passes a Vauxhall Corsa coming in the opposite direction. Behind the Vantage's vinyl steering wheel Theodore sneers at the Corsa's lack of grace and garish blue coat.

16:43 -Theodore pushes his handmade loafer clad foot on the brake pedal. The Vantage responds effortlessly, cruising to a halt opposite Ramsbottam village church.

Lowering the tinted sound proofed window, Theodore closes his eyes and tilts his head upwards, perforating his nostrils to the outside air. Not in the manner of someone enjoying the crisp country air but as a wolf might in the

Russian winter taiga, on revisiting an ailing moose, to sense whether it is time to strike or to return when the moose has deteriorated yet further. One single lingering whiff fills Theodore's nostrils.

Attuning his senses, Theodore reviews the findings from his only previous visit to the church, a Sunday service some months earlier. Sitting detached at the pew, as the vicar read from Jeremiah, his inquisitive nature had been drawn to the high beams and thick walls of the church's impressive interior. The very next thought that entered his mind was that the space would be ideal for converting into luxury apartments and the more he dwelled upon it, the more it appealed. Jeremiah's wise words were no longer audible to him as he scrutinised the aged congregation scattered sparsely amongst the pews. Noting that the church, once the bastion of life in the village was in morbid decline, Theodore had smiled broadly, exposing his ivory white teeth.

The driver door opens upwards in a curvaceous arc. Theodore slides his lithe body out of the full grain leather interior and into the open. Within a few steps he is standing in the church's graveyard scanning the headstones of the graves. As he does so he reads out the year of demise inscribed on each, in a quiet yet purposeful voice, '1912, 1915, 1879, 1872, 1922, 1877, 1899...'

Within a minute the task is completed and he is sitting once more behind the Vantage's vinyl steering wheel, satisfied that the graves are so old as to be all but forgotten and that his plan for the church is gaining momentum. For now however there are other ventures to attend to, but he will return. Taking out the BlackBerry from the inside pocket of his velvet jacket, he types an entry for two months hence. It looks like this:

2011/6/17 Wednesday
09:00
10:00

11:00 'Contact lawyer - check legal status of stiffs'
12:00

Theodore places the BlackBerry back inside the jacket pocket, yawns widely and then runs both hands through the curls of thick black hair that adorn his head. At the same time he inspects his reflection in the rear view mirror. There is concern that his usually tanned complexion has lost something of its lustre and that there is the unaccustomed sight of small shadows beneath the eyes, a consequence of troubled sleep of late. The BlackBerry is vibrating. Theodore removes it from his pocket and presses the accept call button.

'Yes?' enquires Theodore curtly.

'This is Colin speaking'

'Colin how are you?'

'I was phoning on the off chance that Anastasia and you are available for dinner at mine this Friday?' continues Colin. 'Benedict and your sister-in -law will be here, as will Adrian.'

'Adrian?' says Theodore; unsure as to whom Colin is referring.

'My other son. You've met him on numerous occasions.'

'Adrian, yes of course,' says Theodore, who does now vaguely remember having met him. 'We'll free up the time, how's seven-thirty?'

'Seven-thirty it is.'

On hanging up Theodore sighs, for his previous experiences of interactions with the Raven family have been insipid affairs and he can think of no reason why this dinner will prove otherwise. As he turns on the ignition, Theodore reminds himself of the fact that for every adversity there is the seed of an equal or greater benefit. He is acutely aware that the relationship with Colin, his sister-in-law's father-in-law, is one that needs to be cultivated. Not only due to the family connection but also because Colin is a former town councillor and as such could be a useful ally in any future construction plans in the local area.

Meanwhile Colin, sitting in his study, polishing the lenses of his spectacles with a white linen handkerchief, is also not overwhelmed by the prospect of an evening with Theodore and his wife Anastasia. He reminds himself that as with so many things in life, it was an act of duty to invite these new additions to the family for dinner, and that duty and pleasure do not always go hand in hand.

Three

The sitting room's usual orderliness is no longer apparent. For the carefully stacked papers on the table, neatly patted-down cushions on the settee and rug pulled taut so as to be without a single bump have been replaced by an all together more chaotic scene. Blue Rays, medicinal packets and beer bottles are strewn across the floor and the now emptied bottle of Cardhu single malt whisky stands erect, its base submerged in the carpet, in the same position in which it had been discarded the previous night. Adrian is slouched, lethargic and despondent in the superior zero gravity chair, complete with lumbar, lower back supports and Safco seat cushion. It is in fact identical to his office chair and looks rather out of place in a home environment.

Today is Adrian's second day away from work, the longest period he has been removed from the office other than for holidays in his entire fifteen year career. Even when his mother died two years previous he had returned to work the very next day, only for his colleagues to insist he go home. However Adrian is still in no state for work. Even though dearly hoping for a return to his enthusiastic rational state, each night has yielded further horrors. Reclusive, he has spent the last two days and nights locked away in the house with the curtains drawn. The only conversation had been a call to the office, advising them that he would not be returning quite yet; the excuse a family illness. The lying made him feel somewhat guilty but this he deemed preferable to what explaining the true reason might yield.

The previous night in an attempt to find a solution to the nocturnal woes, Adrian had set his Casio alarm clock at regular intervals of fifteen minutes. This he believed could be a possible solution; his theory behind this is the well known fact that dreams only occur when rapid eye movement (REM's) are present. These occur at intervals, usually three to five times each night. Generally they are under ten minutes in duration though there have been recorded instances of up to an hour. By having the alarm clock set at fifteen minute intervals, Adrian had deemed it probable that by artificially disrupting the sleep pattern in this manner, REM's could be reduced thus leading to the cessation of dream content.

Secondly and potentially more significantly the alarm clock ringing would disrupt any REM's that were causing protracted nightmare sequences at that given moment. This theory had Adrian hopeful, convinced that this could be a viable solution. However it failed, for although there were fifteen minute intervals when he slept contentedly, there were others when the multitude's clamour was more deafening than ever, as he soared terrified through a dark sky, accompanied by the ghastly interloper, Charles Middleworth.

The Nokia is ringing. Adrian timidly raises the device to his ear.

'It's customary to speak when you answer the phone,' utters a voice at the other end of the line. A momentary lapse follows. 'Anyway just bought Quest for Modernity IV: Barbarians. There are two improvements just as I envisioned. New scenarios and more of the usual, wonders, civilisations, leaders etc, it's really good.' There is a brief pause followed by, 'what no questions?'

'What do the Barbarians look like?' asks Adrian unenthusiastically several seconds later.

'Like Barbarians of course, the usual array of Huns and Goths, they've even got ones with bright coloured plumage in their hair, right up your street Adrian. Got some great cheats already, how to double your gold at the beginning and some treasure unit protection ones as well,' adds the voice. There is a pause of a second or so and it starts again.

'What so excited you're lost for words? This weekend at dad's we'll get on it. Ah I nearly forgot its Natalia's birthday this weekend and she wants something big, surprise her.'

The phone line goes dead. Adrian leaning back in the superior zero gravity chair rubs his tired eyes with the palms of his hands. Usually there would be at least a modicum of excitement over a new addition to the Quest for Modernity series. A game that he and his brother Benedict, who had just been on the telephone played for hours online, though rather less since Benedict had married his Russian internet bride.

(Note: Quest for Modernity IV: Barbarians is a kingdom building/military strategy game that continues in the same vein as its predecessors, Quest for Modernity I, II & III. Though mythical in nature, the game is loosely based on the era when our foraging ancestors ceased their nomadic existence and began to advance towards modern ways. The object of the game is to create an empire and defend it against external forces. At the beginning of the game you are allocated a small band of foragers. From these humble Stone Age beginnings you are required to lead them to world dominance. Credits, which are accrued according to performance, can be allocated as the player/s sees fit for the following activities, (forest clearing, farming, irrigating, building work, excavating, storing supplies and developing an army). The game shifts continually between real time and an accelerated time frame (one second equating to one day).

Adrian's tormented mind briefly focuses on Natalia's birthday present but is defeated by it almost instantaneously, for he is quite unsure what to buy her. Natalia's interests as far as Adrian has ever been able to fathom are limited to expensive items that other people are aware are expensive. He recalls the wedding gift he had purchased Benedict and Natalia; the Netgear ReadyNAS NV+ ND4450 server. Some of the Netgear's features appear in Adrian's mind and he recites them aloud, but with none of the usual relish.

- '4 Hot Swappable 500GB HDD
- DRAM 256 MB of RAM installed
- Host Connectivity - Gigabit Ethernet
- Data Link Protocol Ethernet, Fast Ethernet, Gigabit Ethernet'

The logic behind this choice of gift had been meticulously planned, for the Netgear ReadyNAS combined a measure of exclusivity and a reassuringly expense price tag; with a retail price of six hundred and fifty pounds, inclusive of VAT. Despite this Natalia had looked at Adrian with disdain and said nothing when he had asked her at a later date if she had liked the gift.

Returning to the present Adrian shouts, 'I don't need this now.' Grabbing an empty beer can from the coffee table, he scrunches it up and hurls it against the wall, before once again becoming preoccupied by more pressing problems; the disintegration of his life and encroaching insanity.

(Note: Natalia had met Benedict seven months earlier online at the dating site www.RussianAngels.co.rs, where he had registered as a member for a fee of seventy Euros a month. Natalia and her older sister Anastasia had spent their formative years in poverty in Nizhny Novgorod, (population - 3.3m approx, location - 255 miles east of Moscow). Anastasia however was now firmly entrenched in the United Kingdom, with her English husband, Theodore. Now in a position to facilitate her sister's aspirations, she had vetted the potential suitors. Natalia had been most unenthusiastic about the aged Lotharios who made up the majority of her suitors and it was an extraordinary and most fortunate coincidence when Benedict had registered an interest. For not only was he far closer to her own age (Benedict is thirty-five and Natalia will turn twenty-nine this Saturday) than the others but he hailed from only five miles away from Anastasia's Hampshire home. In addition to this Theodore and Anastasia were satisfied that the Raven family were reasonably wealthy and held a degree of influence in the local community).

15:57 – The waiting room is full of people, old and young alike. A frantic mother is attempting to placate her wailing baby by cooing in a soft voice whilst waiving a small teddy from side to side, a few centimetres from its flushed, tear-streaked face. This proves to be in vain; it is as if the baby is aware of the tetanus jab it is about to receive and cries ever louder, struggling violently to escape the clutches of the belt securing it to the pushchair. With all the chairs having incumbents, Adrian has been forced to stand; he is anxious and unsure as to what benefits this consultation will provide. For no apparent reason he begins to murmur almost silently the names of hypnotic drugs: 'Estazolam, Triazolam, Midazolam, Zolpidem, Zaleplon, Doxylamine...'
He would have kept reiterating the names of hypnotic drugs for quite a while longer had he not been interrupted by the voice of a nurse, who has just entered the room clasping an appointment list in her left hand. 'Adrian Raven, Adrian Raven.'
'Yes over here.'
'Step this way please,' instructs the nurse, pointing towards an open door at the end of the corridor that adjoins the waiting room.
The room is bathed in light, but it is not a reassuring welcoming glow, rather an inhospitable institutional glare, as so often present in the sterile confines of hospitals, schools and other bureaucratic buildings; a luminescence that leaves one naked and exposed.
'Please take a seat,' instructs doctor Dr Shah, as she swivels her chair towards Adrian.
Adrian sitting down, fails to notice that the chair is almost identical though slightly inferior to his own superior zero gravity chair. Dr Shah swivels her chair around towards the

desk again and glances at Adrian's medical history on the computer screen in front of her.

'It's nearly two years since your last visit; you've been keeping well then,' remarks Dr Shah. 'What is the problem today?'

'Well essentially.' Adrian pauses briefly here, not entirely sure how to phrase his complaint, before continuing in a rather hesitant fashion. 'I have been suffering from nightmares of the most extreme nature.'

'Ok, are they affecting your sleep patterns?' asks Dr Shah.

'Yes, they are frequent and severe, affecting my sleeping hours and alarmingly beginning to impinge on my waking ones as well.'

'Well have you had any severe upheaval or stress in your life? A personal issue perhaps or work related problems.'

'No,' states Adrian categorically.

'Relaxation and stress-relieving activities can be helpful in relieving symptoms of this nature,' says Dr Shah. 'You might find breathing exercises, visualisations and guided imagery to be advantageous. There's a useful website, www.stressrelievers.org.'

Dr Shah writes down the name of the website on a pink post-it note and hands it to Adrian. He takes it from her outstretched hand but offers no comment, instead looking at her in a rather bemused fashion. Inspecting him with large hazel eyes Dr Shah immediately notes from his expression that Adrian wishes to be prescribed medication. She had witnessed this same bemused look on innumerable occasions. Patients on visiting the doctor often do not feel they have fulfilled the expectations of their visit, unless prescribed some form of medication. Offering no further comment she scrawls something on another post-it note, hands it to Adrian and says, 'try this.'

Adrian, who had been anticipating that it would contain the name of some miraculous remedy is disappointed to see the words Chlor-Trimeton scrawled across it, for he is acquainted with the fact that this is the brand name for chlorpheniramine; a mild antihistamine.

'This is not suitable,' states Adrian. 'The severity of these episodes demands something more potent than a mild antihistamine.'

He then waits in the anticipation that she will write out a prescription for another drug. Dr Shah, a stern non-compromising expression upon her countenance says nothing. In an attempt to persuade her Adrian continues. 'I have tried Normison in the hope that a benzodiazepine gamma-aminobutyric acid modulator would be a solution. It was not and I deem it impossible that a much milder antihistamine could provide any tangible benefit at all.'

Dr Shah having often witnessed similar outbursts from the drug dependent clamouring for prescriptions concludes Adrian is a drug addict, exhibiting classic symptoms of such; curiosity and a professional knowledge of prescription drugs and an enthusiasm whilst describing them. Spinning back around in the chair, she presses the background tab on Adrian's record. Benedict's name appears with details of his numerous visits to the surgery, complex medical issues and numerous prescriptions for all manner of medicines from the period when he was living at Adrian's house.

'In the family,' she thinks to herself as she swivels in the chair towards Adrian once more.

'Book another appointment if your symptoms have not improved in a week, goodbye.' She turns adroitly away from him and back to her papers, leaving Adrian no room for further discourse. Disgruntled he departs, clutching the post-it note forlornly.

Adrian trudges home drenched and shivering from a relentless downpour that had begun ominously the moment he left the surgery. The adverse weather conditions only add to the sense of impending doom. A car speeds past, sending a wave of muddy cold water splashing onto the pavement, soaking Adrian to the point of saturation.

It's three a.m. and the clamouring of the multitude is beginning to wane, growing fainter with each passing moment. The cantankerous acrimonious faces turned to the heavens are becoming obscured and blurred beneath a thickening mass of cloud, as Adrian finds himself floating through the air accompanied by the tan suited, non-descript Middleworth.

Sometime later Adrian becomes aware that he is sitting in a car behind a steering wheel with three spokes and a thin rim. A pair of large fluffy dice attached by a string to its roof oscillate from side to side. On either side of the vehicle people scuttle past; there are women in tweed skirts and men in flannel suits.

After turning into a larger road, the traffic clears and the car accelerates. The dice sway ever quicker and the monotonous drone of the engine increases in volume. There is a metallic rattling noise emanating from the back of the vehicle, audible even over the sound of the engine as the speed dial climbs steadily. A large bang resonates through the vehicle. Moments later thin plumes of noxious dark smoke begin to envelop the interior as flames lick the fabric of the seats and roof.

Adrian awakens coughing uncontrollably. It is some time, the exact amount of which he is no position to calculate before the realisation dawns on him that it was a dream. As the fear begins to subside, Adrian lying in bed rues the additional misfortune of another frightful nightmare plaguing his sleeping hours. Having never experienced a fire in a car or been involved in a professional capacity with calculating the risk of such occurrences and having never given thought to the matter, read or watched programmes on the subject, Adrian is perturbed as to why he has been dreaming about a car fire. For a full hour he lies awake, attempting to rationalise this harrowing ordeal before sleep finds him once more.

Four

Small flocculent clouds are drifting gently through a blue sky. Adrian travelling down the country lane in the back of an ABC minicab is preoccupied with his own issues and notices neither the sky nor the baby rabbits playing blissfully in the long grass of the fields. The overzealous driver is speeding a full fifteen miles an hour over the speed limit, a habit Adrian deplores. Considering last night's dream this is of particular concern but there is some consolation in the thought that the destination will be reached quicker and no mention of it is made to the driver.

The minicab pulls to a halt outside a large manor house. Clambering out of the vehicle clutching a Samsonite overnight bag, Adrian having made the decision to omit a tip hands the driver the eight pound fare and then walks slowly up to the front door. He is about to knock when it opens and his father emerges smiling. 'Adrian, you're early, where's your car,' greets Colin, tapping Adrian lightly on the shoulder with the finger tips of his right hand, in what is a rare moment of affection.

'Evening father,' says Adrian as he enters the house and places the bag on the hall's fading Persian rug. 'The Renault is being serviced.' This is a lie, for he does not wish to go into the real reason for its absence. On noticing Adrian's jaded appearance, the smile evaporates from Colin's face.

'You look pretty awful,' he exclaims. 'Not entirely dissimilar in fact to a corpse that came into my possession last week.'

Adrian considers his response carefully and then says, 'had a mild, err, illness and have been absent from work the last two days.'

'I take it you've been to the doctor,' says Colin, pointing accusingly at Adrian with the index finger of his right hand.

'Yes, case of insomnia apparently, nothing to be unduly concerned about,' responds Adrian, wishing to placate his father, for whom illnesses had become something of a sensitive subject since Doreen his wife and Adrian's own mother had unexpectedly been taken ill and died.

They sojourn to the drawing room where they sit drinking Lapsang Souchong tea from dainty porcelain cups whilst nibbling on slices of organic carrot cake from the patisserie in town. Adrian talks about his time in Athens, omitting mention of the nocturnal incidents. Colin outlines in great length the alterations that have been made to the house's Thomas Turner of London grandfather clock (circa 1860).

'Where is Benedict?' asks Adrian several minutes later.

'Your brother's with Theodore and the girls, they should be here in about,' Colin checks the time on the J&T Windmills traditional English watch that adorns his wrist before adding, 'eighty-five minutes.'

Adrian wishes it were only Benedict and his father attending dinner. Briefly he mourns the disintegration of the family unit, caused by the untimely death of his beloved mother and the arrival of Natalia. The thought of Natalia reminds him he has forgotten her birthday present; he makes a mental note to find an expensive bottle of wine from the house's cellar.

Its eight p.m. and the chiming of the Turner grandfather clock reverberates through the dining room. Colin, Benedict, Adrian, Theodore, Natalia and Anastasia are sitting at its mahogany circular table, dining on braised beef goulash.

'Nice clock, very nice. Is it a Lavezzi?' Theodore's question is directed at Colin, who is sitting next to him.

'No it's a Turner of London,' replies Colin.

'You should check out the Lavezzis',' continues Theodore.

'I am aware of them,' replies Colin sardonically. The tone evident in his voice should have caused Theodore to cease this topic of conversation but he continues regardless.

'Bought a Lavezzi last month actually, the weights are in gilt brass and the dial's brass fusion with roman numbers printed over a white aluminium relief. It's quite something.'

'A quite amazing clock,' adds Anastasia glancing in Colin's direction, at the same time caressing her long golden hair. Her accent is a carefully cultivated one, identical in fact to England's nobility, without a hint of the Russian peasant tones of her youth.

Colin taking a sip from his glass of Cabernet Sauvignon wine offers no further comment on the subject, for he considers the concept of white aluminium relief on a clock to be both vulgar and ostentatious. Lamenting the invasion of what he considers inferior foreign models, he looks up from his plate at Anastasia and Natalia, who are talking loudly in Russian to each other, oblivious to the others in attendance.

Theodore and Benedict, sitting two places to Colin's right, are in animated conversation about a forthcoming construction project Theodore is planning in the south of Spain, which Benedict will be involved in. Benedict bending forward in the cushioned dining chair, his lean frame pressing against the rim of the mahogany table, periodically taps his fingers on the table's surface, as if this will hasten the process of thought.

Meanwhile Adrian's attention is focused on the framed black and white photograph on the wall next to the Turner grandfather clock and is inattentive to the proceedings. As far back as he can remember the picture has been hanging in this same position. It is of a funeral procession led by a horse drawn hearse; Adrian's grandfather severe and stoical standing at its side. As Adrian's attentions continue to dwell on the picture the thought occurs to him that although having not followed the family tradition, due to a desire to avoid the unpredictable and uncertain nature of death, that he is somehow unwontedly through his dreams being drawn back towards it. Adrian is alarmed that his mind, until so recently capable of only logical processed thought could now conceive such an illogical and vague concept.

All conversation has ceased and the only sound is the clinking of cutlery and the barely audible ticking of the grandfather clock. Colin through the corner of his eye is watching Natalia performing peculiarities with her fork, as she rotates it in her fingers whilst tentatively licking the gravy from the pieces of meat and vegetables impaled thereon. The vulgarity of the woman disturbs him immensely and not for the first time there is amazement that God would conceal such a coarse and conceited creature within such a fine frame.

Anastasia breaks the silence with the announcement, 'I am buying new wallpaper.'

'Really what kind,' responds Benedict, enthused by the possibility of a topic of conversation that they can perhaps all participate in.

'How about white to go with the Lavezzi?' remarks Colin.

'Would show up the dirt don't you think,' responds Theodore drily.

'I must have the highest quality,' continues Anastasia.
Natalia asks, 'where you buy?' These are the first words she has uttered in English during the meal.

'We're undecided,' continues Theodore, 'but have a few places in mind.'

Adrian returning his attentions to the proceedings asks,

'Anastasia, I take it you are acquainted with Marquees?'

'More wine anyone' interjects Theodore, who has feared Anastasia finding out about Marquees since she had first proposed the need for new wallpaper, a month earlier. This effort at a distraction proves futile however. Anastasia merely glances acrimoniously at her husband and bids Adrian to 'resume'.

'Marquees is the most exclusive wallpaper retailer in London, if not the entire world,' continues Adrian.

Theodore now seething mutters, 'Adrian' spitefully under his breath.

'Marquees is located at 7 Sloane Street, the postcode is SW1 7WR, I forget the telephone number but it starts 0207 373,' states Adrian.

'Tell me more,' orders Anastasia impatiently.

Adrian now has the attention of the entire table with the exception of Theodore, who stares morosely at his plate.

'The wallpaper is divided into five ranges,' states Adrian.

'Brother I never took you for an interior designer,' interrupts Benedict, pressing in animated fashion once more against the rim of the table.

Natalia looks at her husband wrathfully, at the same time bringing the long and perfectly manicured diamond ring clad index finger of her left hand to her lips, to prevent any further outburst.

'They were a client,' replies Adrian. 'The reason for this is that their products are not catered for by off-the-shelf home contents insurance policies due to their high value, which has resulted in Marquees offering their customers bespoke wallpaper and curtain insurance cover.'

'Interesting stuff Adrian,' says Colin before taking another sip from his glass of wine.

'Indeed it was, take the algorithm for the risk of fire, Cov (X small, X large) =...'

Anastasia interrupting him mid-algorithm demands, 'Describe the wallpaper to me?'

'There are five ranges, namely the French nineteenth century papiers paints panoramiques, Chinoiserie, Persian silk laced range, the eclectic range and ...' Adrian pauses.

'And the other,' pleads Anastasia unable to wait. The usual contempt she holds for Adrian having deserted her; she gazes longingly at him with beautiful emerald eyes.

'The Chinese panoramiques,' adds Adrian, enjoying this rare moment of female attention. He then proceeds to regale his audience with further intricate details regarding Marquees's choice of textiles.

As Adrian continues the detailed description, Theodore pours himself another glass of wine and gulps it down sombrely. He had heard the rumours of multi-millionaire bankers having been presented with their Marquees bill courtesy of their wives, first incredulous but on confirming the amount with the shop, their complexion turning a sickly green. In his current financial predicament, he is aware that a trip to Marquees presents a serious threat. Although not of a religious disposition, he mumbles a prayer to some as of yet unknown deity, in the hope that Anastasia will forget about Marquees; he is not hopeful however. This unfortunate turn of events, allied with the nightmares that continue to plague his sleeping hours, he deems most unfair.

As the dinner draws to a close, another silence is broken by Natalia screaming 'prezzies, prezzies,' in a high pitched tone. Colin departing the dining room is unsurprised by the fact that one of the few new words that Natalia appears to have learnt reflects her narcissistic tendencies and secondly that it is a colloquial term.

Later that evening, Colin places the crystal wine glasses in the Zanussi dishwasher dejectedly but remembering the long awaited trip to Egypt the following week, a degree of enthusiasm is restored. Natalia and Benedict will be staying in Colin's house for the foreseeable future, until the builders have completed renovating their own property, to Natalia's exact specifications. There are plans for a home cinema, indoor swimming pool in the basement and no doubt thinks Colin to himself, a garish Lavezzi clock in white aluminium relief.

Saturday and Sunday's waking hours were for the most part spent in relative harmony. There were games of Quest for Modernity IV: Barbarians with Benedict that would last for up to an hour, before being disturbed by Natalia demanding attention. At other times there were walks in the woods that surround the house and periods spent in the garden admiring the daffodils, crocuses and irises, an abundance of colour in the wide flower beds.

These pleasures of the day contrasted with the nocturnal hours when the deafening roar of the multitude would become audible, as Adrian floated alongside Middleworth through a menacing sky. These fearful episodes punctuated by visions of the explosion in the car, as smoke and flames engulfed its interior. Each time Adrian awakening in panic would cough and splutter, as if the smoke were real and then lie trembling with fear, awaiting the onset of sleep; the blight of his existence.

Late Sunday afternoon, prior to the departure for London, Adrian had been in the kitchen alone when he heard the name Charles Middleworth being whispered time and time again, from somewhere behind him. Ignoring it, he had instead focused his attentions on a graph in the business section of The Times newspaper, outlining recent fluctuations in global silver prices. The whispering however persisted unabated, until he became quite uncertain whether the voice was a figment of his imagination. Having endured this torment for some minutes, he turned off the air ventilator above the oven and it had stopped, as quickly as it had begun.

It is now Sunday evening and Adrian is back in London. The Canon EOS-1D Mark IV is on the table in the sitting room, attached via its UBS cable to the Compaq Presario laptop. Adrian is analysing photographs of the Athens trip on its fifteen point six inch screen. With some images he enhances the colour correction by a fraction of a point and with others marginally alters the tone details.

The Parthenon appears on the screen, the majestic structure bathed in the early morning sunlight. Adrian gazing in wonder at the picture concludes it is perfect and that for once Adobe Photoshop's array of photograph enhancing features, such as mask densities, colour enhancement and exposure alteration options are null and void. Pressing the print button authoritatively, he waits, as the image is ejected by the HP Business Inkjet Printer.

Adrian marvels at how the Parthenon has survived, in spite of the trials and tribulations of history. Some of the destructive events the monument has endured appear in his mind as bullet points, in chronological order. They look like this:

- 1687 -Venetian mortar.
- 1801 - Pillaging of sculptures by Earl of Elgin.
- Present - Photochemical smog, (primary pollutants: nitrogen oxides, hydrocarbons, carbon monoxide) (secondary pollutants: ozone and organic nitrates).

To Adrian, the edifice to rationality and progress that is the Parthenon provides a beacon of hope in this time of adversity and there is a determination that like this monument, he too will survive and prosper.

Five

07:50 – The Following Morning – At the Train Station – Adrian's complexion is pallid and lacklustre, shadows are visible under the eyes and from his head tufts of hair stick out haphazardly in all directions. There is an announcement over the tannoy; the seven-fifty-three to London Bridge has been cancelled. Closing his eyes, Adrian yawns widely.
08:11 – Due to the seven-fifty-three having been cancelled, the train is twice as full as usual. Crammed in the midst of a crowd of weary commuters, Adrian recalls the multitude from the previous night and is immediately apprehensive.
08:15 – Steadfastly concentrating his attentions on the screen of the G-9000 Casio Mudman, he counts down the minutes and seconds until arrival, as they pass like an eternity.
08:41 – Adrian rudely pushes commuters out of the way in his haste to escape the train.

Entering the office, Adrian attempts to get to his desk unnoticed.

'Morning Adrian, great to have you back,' greets Ethel in a manner far too enthusiastic for eight-fifty-nine on a Monday morning.

'Great to be back,' replies Adrian, rather unconvincingly.

Papers are stacked to such a great height in the in-tray, its fragile structure appears ready to collapse, that the slightest tremor will bring the whole precarious stack crashing down.

The email inbox provides no reprieve and it seems like an eternity to scroll down from the latest arrival to the last read email. Working steadily with a meticulous eye for detail, Adrian is temporarily distracted from his problems.

It is only later that morning whilst working on an algorithm for the likelihood of fire at a new shopping mall in Trent that matters start to go awry. The word 'fire' triggers images of the fire in the car from the recurrent dreams, which now emerge in his mind in all their vividness. Recollections of the metallic clattering noise emanating from the boot, the heat and smoke. Once more his breathing comes in fitful bursts, as the ghastly memory of the frightful episode engulfs his mind. Fleeing to the bathroom he douses his face in cold water and then marginally refreshed, returns with trepidation to the desk.

Lunch time is approaching and although there is a welcoming blue sky outside, Adrian is reluctant to leave the office and return to Spitalfields Market. For the previous visit weighs heavily on his mind and there is a lingering concern that this once favourite haunt will never be quite the same again. Rotating in the Safco chair with lumbar support precisely one hundred and eighty degrees, he looks out through the tinted window and down at the bustling mass of people sixty floors below emerging for their lunch breaks. There is anxiety, for the view is reminiscent of the nocturnal descent through the clouds towards the multitude bellowing unrelentingly below. Spinning the zero gravity chair aggressively back round to face the desk, Adrian decides that lunch will consist of confectionery, purchased from the office's vending machine.

The hours pass quickly; so engrossed is he in a probability table that evaluates the probability of negligence in various retail sectors. The fire probability table for the shopping mall in Trent remains at the bottom of the pile of papers.

16:00 - The report now complete, Adrian reclines in the Safco chair and emits a sigh of relief, as the deadline is the following morning. This only leaves the matter of getting three copies printed, two to be hard-bound for the client and one for internal use.

18:00 – Adrian is sifting through the mountain of emails in his inbox, deleting some and utilising Outlook's flag feature to prioritise the remainder in a variety of colours, when as during the previous day he becomes convinced that he can hear the name Charles Middleworth being whispered from somewhere behind him. Glancing at the G-9000 Mudman Casio, he notes the time is 18:00:15. At 18:03:36 silence prevails.

19:07 - Only Adrian remains in the now deserted office, in a relentless pursuit to complete yet another report.

21:03 – A portly security man in a blue uniform appears in the office. Adrian, bleary-eyed looks up from his papers and makes the decision that the inevitable return home can be delayed no longer.

That night with his iPod playing whale music, Adrian had effortlessly surrendered to sleep. The notion of whale music had at first seemed a very strange concept, as with there being hundreds of genres of music; Adrian deemed that it was unnecessary to seek more from the natural world. However having visited www.whalemusicwonders.com, a website he had come across through a link on the stress relievers website that Dr Shah had written the name of on the post-it note she had handed to him in the surgery, his hopes had been aroused. The description of the music contained words that were certainly promising, for example, 'harmonious', 'relaxing', 'invigorating' and 'stress relieving.' Indeed the first few hours of sleep that night prove to be most agreeable and it is as if Adrian is with the contented whales, singing and dining on krill in the warm clear waters of The Pacific.

In the early hours of the morning Adrian begins to twitch agitatedly, his features now etched with tension. The cause for this subconscious consternation is the wailing of the multitude, whose intrusion has impinged upon the tranquil enclave that had been his dormant mind. Though the melodious outpourings of the Leviathans are still being played, they do not eradicate the sound but rather merge with it, creating an onslaught upon the auditory senses that increases voluminously with each frightful second. Moments later Adrian finds himself floating beside Charles Middleworth through a storm cloud congested sky. The great swathes of faces that appear far below seem to span for affinity in all directions. At first as a single wrath-emitting mass but as they draw nearer their individual features become distinguishable.

Adrian awakening sits bolt upright in bed and looks around wildly in all directions. Though aware within several seconds that he is in the bedroom, the piercing screams continue unabated, high pitched and chaotic. Convinced that he is still asleep, Adrian jumps from the bed and begins to kick and punch the bedroom wall with a rabid ferocity, in an attempt to awaken. Some seconds later becoming aware that the incessant noise is emanating from his head, he proceeds to run around the house in an ill-conceived attempt to escape it. This proves to be in vain and the incessant high pitched assault on the auditory senses remains. The exertion concludes in the sitting room, where he collapses to the carpet, holding his hands to his ears whilst banging his head relentlessly against the floor, wailing all the while. Discovering the wires protruding from his ears, he claws at them feverishly and the din stops instantaneously. Remembering the whale music brings a surge of relief.

Within a minute Adrian has clambered up off the floor and is returning to the bedroom when he is startled by the shrill ring of the door bell. Approaching the door silently, he peers tentatively through the peephole. Two uniformed police officers, a male and a female, are standing in the entranceway. For several seconds Adrian stands motionless, peering out at them through the peephole. The bell rings again, resonating through the hallway. Adrian opens the door. As he does so the police officers take a step back, as if bracing themselves.

'Good evening officers, how might I be of assistance?'

'We've had a complaint of a disturbance from the neighbours; is everything alright?' asks the female officer in a concerned manner. While she speaks her colleague peers around Adrian into the interior of the hallway.

'Fine but thank you for your concern,' says Adrian. 'It was merely err, a slight commotion caused by some dreams; well nightmares actually. Thanks again and goodnight.' Adrian begins to push the door closed but the male officer prevents this from occurring by placing his foot against it.

'We're going to take a look inside,' exclaims the female officer authoritatively. Adrian considers asking them to produce a search warrant but concludes that this will only delay matters and reluctantly ushers them inside. Within a few minutes they are satisfied that nothing sinister has occurred and leave. Adrian is dismayed that the dreams are once again impinging on waking reality and he returns to bed as sombrely, as if he were going to his own coffin.

07:05 - The beeping of the Casio GQ50-1D alarm clock announces the start of another day. Though exhausted Adrian clambers out of bed and prepares for work, for despite the horrors of the night, the mundane mechanisms of the day persist.

To Adrian's relief the train is remarkably empty and he is able to rest in moderate comfort for the entire duration of the journey. An hour later and Adrian is in the meeting room waiting for the start of the fortnightly internal meeting. Checking the time on the Casio Mudman, Adrian notes that it was supposed to start seven minutes earlier. At the internal meeting all matters Vincent & Ernst are discussed, from new clients to updates on the cleanliness of the office fridge. Adrian dislikes the banality of the event, preferring to be at the cutting edge of actuarial work, analysing data and writing algorithms. He struggles to remain awake, so fatigued is he from the cumulative effects of disrupted sleep. It is towards the end of the meeting, during the fridge cleanliness update that Adrian becomes convinced that he can hear the name Charles Middleworth being whispered repeatedly. Attempting to ignore it, he focuses his attentions on the matter at hand. This proves in vain however and the whispering persists, much to his chagrin.

At the conclusion of the meeting Adrian remains in the room, on the pretence of clearing up his papers. Once everyone has departed, he scours it systematically, searching for the potential source of the sound. Within seconds he has deduced that the only object that could possibly emit any sound is the Daikin air conditioning unit. Clambering up onto the conference table, he presses his ear to the ceiling suspended unit. There is a faint continuous humming sound being emitted by the device. He had been under the impression that the Daikin is supposed to be silent when on indoor operation mode, FTK/XS, as it is currently. Clasping his papers under one arm, Adrian leaves the room, cursing the Daikin under his breath as he does so.

There is evidence of a renewed vigour in Adrian, as he sits upright and purposeful in the Safco chair, navigating the keyboard of the Intel PC with consummate ease. Perhaps this is due to the double espresso he had drunk moments earlier. A thought unconnected to his present task of clearing the in-box occurs to him and despite the relative urgency of completing the clearing of the emails, Adrian minimises Outlook and leans back in his seat, deep in thought. There is the realisation that it is of paramount importance to attempt to gain an understanding, if one indeed exists, of who Charles Middleworth is and why this man is embedded within his own subconscious. The matter of the multitude and the car fire will have to wait. As during his previous reflection on the matter, Adrian is convinced that he has no connection to anyone bearing this name. It is now a matter of attempting to prove this conclusively. Through achieving this he hopes to prove that Charles Middleworth is an irrelevancy and as a result his subconscious obsession with him will cease once and for all.

Reaching into the inside pocket of his suit jacket, Adrian takes out the antique effect silver pen with the tungsten carbide rotating ball and spins it on the surface of the desk. By the time the pen has stopped moving, having completed a few degrees shy of three rotations, Adrian is deliberating on whether the Gaussian elimination method[1], as first proposed by Karl Friedrich Gauss, a famous nineteenth century mathematician could prove a beneficial method for analysing this matter.

On further thought however Adrian concludes that this would essentially be overkill, as it is too convoluted a method and at any rate the data he is likely to be collating will be of the non-numerical variety. Instead the decision is made to use a method that was designed for the purpose of making logically sound decisions; The Rational Planning Model. Nine minutes and thirteen seconds later Adrian has finished designing it, in Word 2010, it looks like this:

---

[1]Gaussian Elimination is the systematic application of elementary row operations to a system of linear equations; the purpose being to convert the system to what is known as the upper triangular form. Once this has been completed, back substitution can be utilised to find the answer.

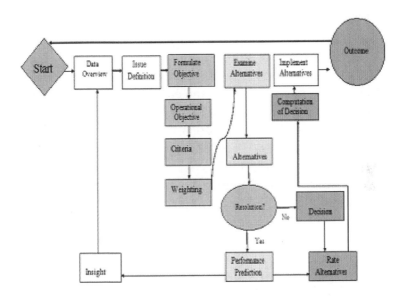

Next Adrian sets about the task of attempting to collate the information to insert in it. This starts at the most basic level, by typing Charles Middleworth into the Google search engine. The search returns no results for a Charles Middleworth, though there are two entries for a Betty Middleworth, winner of the nineteen-eighty-five Northumbria Home Baker of the Year award. One of these links contains a short video of the prize giving ceremony. He decides against viewing it.

Adrian is not surprised to find that the name Middleworth exists, for he is already aware that during The Middle Ages, Midlers' were people who worked in the centre of a populated area. Variations of this name are quite prevalent in The United Kingdom today. Almost silently he begins to whisper names beginning with Mid, 'Middell, Midell, Middler, Middleweek'.

It is at this juncture that Adrian decides to enlist the help of Franklin Meager; a data analyst/programmer at The National Archives office in Surrey. Franklin Meager is a childhood friend of both Adrian and his brother and had resided a few miles from the family home. From an early age the three of them had spent virtually every available minute of their spare time on the house computer. Their friendship had been forged during this revolutionary period in computing; beginning with the era of the Commodore 64, through to the Commodore SX-64 and in later years the Atari Portfolio and Amiga 3000.

In recent times however relations with Franklin had been soured somewhat by Franklin's increasingly odd behaviour; however needs must. Franklin has access to information on every inhabitant of The United Kingdom; born from eighteen-seventy-six to the present day (excluding illegal aliens) and Adrian reluctantly concludes that this is the logical next step in his exploration. He types a message to Franklin's personal email address.

....

Subject: Charles Middleworth
Dear Franklin,
I have a favour to ask. I require information on any individual(s) by the name of Charles Middleworth. Please report back to me on the findings (i.e. address/date of birth/immediate family/registration details regarding birth and death).

Thank you in advance for your assistance in this matter.

Regards
Adrian
....
A little over ten minutes later a response arrives.

....
Tues, April 24, 2011 at 11:24 AM, Franklin Meager <meagerfranklin@gmail.com> wrote:
Subject: Charles Middleworth

Hiya Adrian,

Great to hear from you, how are things? I'm fine and enjoying life! Unfortunately I can't provide assistance with your request for information, as it's not a family member. We're quite strict on privacy these days! Data protection act etc. If the information is not in the public domain, there's not much that can be done, sorry.

Let's meet up! There's an Alpha meeting Friday evening, come down, you'll love it. We discuss the meaning of life and all kinds of other interesting subjects. Let me know?
Love and peace

Franklin
....

Adrian thumps his fist on the desk, disgusted that after all the favours that have been granted to Franklin, by both he and his family down the years that he refuses to do this one small thing. In defiance of his disgust, Adrian types a measured response.

....
Subject: Charles Middleworth
Dear Franklin,
It is with great reluctance that I am forced to remind you of the fact that you are indebted to my family and me. Please consider the below points with due diligence:
i). One month residing rent free in my house the year before last.
ii). Vile pornographic literature left therewith and found by my mother when she came to stay (this was our final time together prior to her illness).

iii). Discounted (50% off) funeral for your uncle Frank last year (note: my father awaits outstanding payment at your earliest convenience).

iv). A near decade of weekends spent on the Raven family computer, (Circa 1982-1992).

v). Not admitting to owning those disturbing videos (1987). Instead falsely accusing my eleven-year-old brother of being the proprietor.

Regards

Adrian
....

A little over an hour later a response from Franklin appears in the in-box.

....
Tues, April 24, 2011 at 12:34 PM, Franklin Meager <meagerfranklin@gmail.com> wrote:
Subject: Charles Middleworth
Adrian,
It's a shame you have allowed these matters to fester so! Come along to Alpha Thursday night 19:30 at St Patricks Liverpool Street as my guest, it'll be a wonderful opportunity for you to start to come to terms with your issues.
There's one Charles Middleworth in the system:
Born: 1st January 1930
Birth Registered: Nottingham
Died: 5th November 1969
Death Registered: Nottingham
Marital Status: Single
Parents: Cornelius Francis Middleworth and Reena Cecil Middleworth (formerly Reena Drake).
Siblings: Only Child

Love and Peace

Franklin

(p.s. delete this email from your inbox and your deleted items)

....

Adrian surmises that there cannot possibly be any connection between himself and Charles Middleworth. After all he was only born in nineteen- seventy-two. Though relieved that no information has been brought to light that might link him to Charles Middleworth, Adrian remains at a complete loss about his subconscious obsession with the name. He types another email to Franklin.

....

Re: Subject: Charles Middleworth
Franklin,
Could you please confirm Middleworth's former address and cause of death?
I will attend the Alpha meeting on this one occasion.
Regards
Adrian

....

Intermittently through the day whilst scrutinising a logarithmic chart or preparing a probability table, Adrian is sure he can hear the name Charles Middleworth being repeated continuously.
16:02 - An envelope icon appears on the computer screen, signifying the arrival of an email. It is from Franklin:

....

Tues, April 24, 2011 at 16:01 PM, Franklin Meager <meagerfranklin@gmail.com> wrote:

Re: Re: Subject: Charles Middleworth

Hiya Adrian,
Fantastic news can't wait to see you! Please use the following information responsibly.

Address: 5 Newgate Road, Nottingham NG17 5YO.
Cause of death: Car fire (Category 7ii: mechanical failure in the engine compartment, Verdict: Accidental).

Love and Peace

Franklin
....

Adrian stares at the screen in disbelief and then shouts 'No' very loudly, before bolting from the Safco chair, through the office, out into the corridor and down the emergency stairs; all sixty floors of them.

Six

That very afternoon in the thriving metropolis that is London, another of Hampshire's progeny is also facing adversity. For at the very moment Adrian is fleeing from the office building that serves as the home of Vincent & Ernst; three point one miles away in Sloane Street, Theodore is entering Marquees.

The previous evening; as the Lavezzi clock with white aluminium relief finished chiming for nine o'clock, Anastasia declared that the visit to Marquees would be taking place, the very next day. Theodore, who up to this point had been enjoying his dinner of lobster thermidor, instantaneously lost his appetite. That night Theodore once again slept fitfully, though on this occasion he reasoned on awaking in a cold sweat, there was due cause.

On entering Marquees, Anastasia and Theodore are ushered to a large floral patterned sofa, where they now sit; taking sips of oolong tea from delicate porcelain cups. Theodore is trembling incessantly, which results in several drops of tea spilling from the cup in his hand. A young female shop assistant with plaited hair opens the Marquees wallpaper catalogue on the walnut table in front of them.

Turning to the first page, she begins her delivery. 'This delightful pastel blue is engraved with the finest Indian silk and is a Marquees classic.' After pausing for precisely two seconds, she continues. 'The story of this particular example is that Marquees's founder, Sir Alfred Elkin, had been searching for years for a blue that would capture the essence of the spring sky, which he would view fondly through the glass of his beloved orangery at the family's stately home, Stanmore house...'

'Next,' quips Anastasia.

'Very well madam,' replies the shop assistant turning to the next page. 'Might I introduce you to this quite exquisite white, a timeless classic from our Chinoiserie collection. This has proven to be most popular with Europe's nobility. Rumour has it that Louis IX on seeing the sun reflecting on Chamonix's snow...'

'Can't you just leave out the silly narratives,' intrudes Theodore. 'You're not reading bed time stories to children.'

The startled shop assistant gets no further than saying, 'our clients...,' before Anastasia cuts her off.

'We will have stories for the wallpaper I like, not the others. Next.'

'Certainly madam,' replies the shop assistant, who is at the point of turning the page when Anastasia pointing in the direction of a most intricate section of material on the far wall exclaims, 'I like that.'

'That is from our most exclusive hand painted Chinese panoramiques collection,' responds the shop assistant, before daintily pressing her tongue to her index figure and opening the Chinese panoramiques section of the catalogue. Theodore moans despondently and looks up at the ceiling.

Anastasia gazes longingly at the picture on the page in front of her; depicting a magnificent triple-gabled circular temple, complete with silk clad courtesans and robed monks. Beside the temple are rice paddies, where peasants in straw hats toil, and forests, complete with sika deer, black crested cranes, Chinese monal pheasants and Sichuan jays. In the background, majestic snow capped mountains loom imperiously, interlaced with gushing streams that cascade down their precipitous slopes.

'This Chinese panoramique,' states the assistant, 'is original Ming Dynasty, lovingly restored. This particular piece dates from the early seventeenth century and captures the idyllic west Szechuan rural life, as viewed from the imperial palace. Hand painted by the emperor's most skilled artisans, who came from as far away as the Korean peninsula. If you look at the wall to your right, you can appreciate the exquisite nature of the work; no two parts are identical.' She then sighs contemplatively.

'We'll take it,' states Anastasia.

'What about the pastel blue, it would match the curtains and cushions we bought last month,' implores Theodore, in an attempt to convince his wife to choose what appears to be a less expensive option.

'NIET,' rebukes Anastasia coldly, turning to her native tongue, as so often the case when scolding someone for refusing to give in to her every whim. A sharp callous tone, no different from the niets' she uttered in her youth on the wastelands of Nizhny Novgorod, when having sucked off a punter, who rummaging through their pockets, had pulled out not the agreed eighteen rouble fee but merely fourteen or fifteen, before attempting to make up the difference by adding a packet of cheap Troika cigarettes or a half empty bottle of low grade vodka.

Theodore's shoulders slump dejectedly and he stares morosely at the ground. Several seconds later the assistant, who is relishing Theodore's discomfort enquires, 'how many square feet will you be furnishing Sir?'

'The whole house,' warns Anastasia, pointing a menacing finger inches from his face.

'The whole house,' responds Theodore incredulously.

Anastasia nods.

Theodore mutters, 'three thousand and fifty-three square feet.'

'Sorry I didn't quite catch that,' replies the assistant.
'Three thousand and fifty-three!' bellows Theodore.
'That better be all the walls,' states Anastasia.
'Yes, excluding the cellar and attic.'

The assistant scurries off to prepare the quote. Theodore prays that China were mass producing this stuff during the era of the Ming Dynasty and it is not as expensive as it appears to be, but he is not hopeful.

The moment the assistant returns to the desk, Theodore grabs the envelope from her grasp and crudely rips it open. His eyes open wide in horror, his heart misses a beat and if he were to have looked at his reflection in one of Marquees's mirrors, he would noted his complexion's greenish tinge.

£100 + VAT per sq ft
3053 sq ft * £100 = £305,300 (Excl: VAT)
Total: £366,360

A trembling Theodore hands the assistant his unlimited spend credit card.

Several minutes later the payment has been processed and Theodore is returning the credit card to his wallet when the assistant asks, 'would Sir be interested in our bespoke wallpaper insurance cover?'

'No Sir would not,' replies Theodore, turning abruptly and marching out of the shop, cursing Adrian under his breath as he does so. So incensed is Theodore by the enormity of the bill that he quite forgets to contact his bank manager that afternoon, to discuss making some recommended alterations to his portfolio, which is now his only source of income; at least until the next property venture is under way. Anastasia stays inside the shop to arrange the delivery of the wallpaper. Several minutes later she leaves haughtily, without even a cursory goodbye.

Torrid intrusions have continued to punctuate the nights relentlessly. Skies congested with surging tenebrous storm clouds, bulging with animosity. Adrian flailing helplessly in their midst, abandoned by the custodian that is gravitational pull and now at the mercy of a sinister force, that is not governed by the laws of physics. Of Charles Middleworth, unhindered by the criterion that regulate sleeping and waking hours, he transcends them both, as an interloper, from which there seems no prospect of escape.

Each night the visitation of the unremitting anguish that is the multitude, this ghastly abomination, wailing incessantly; voluminous outpourings that violate the auditory senses. So too the visions of the car persist, the innocuous rattling sound from the boot, the detonation followed by the frightful fire and the purpurescent toxic smoke engulfing its interior.

Friday afternoon sees Adrian motionless on the sitting room's Burlington leather sofa, in a state of repose. In the darkness that is his semi-conscious mind, float luminous disjointed algorithms, which appear without even the slightest adherence to mathematical reasoning and represent nothing but floundering, random threads of nonsensical matter. Parentheses upside down, equal signs placed haphazardly, whilst the numbers and variables are clustered together chaotically and represent nothing but meaningless bunches of unintelligible folly. These algorithmic mutations sway and surge in a seemingly arbitrary manner, for as they are unrestricted by any force of nature, they act only on their own compulsion.

With having not returned to the office since the horrors of Tuesday, the day times serve merely as self-deprecating interludes; listless, unproductive hours spent languishing in the abyss that is now an existence, seething with hopeless introspection. As for the prospect of hope, it seems but merely an apparition, fading in the miasma, which threatens to obscure all beneath its fog of relentless despair.

The material instruments, for so long embraced with an enthusiastic zeal, are now forgotten, as if suddenly obsolete. Be it the G-9000 Casio Mudman hidden in the darkness beneath a shirt sleeve or Canon's revolutionary offering, the EOS-1D Mark IV sitting abandoned on the table, its matt black surface being encroached upon by tiny specks of dust. The Nokia lies discarded in a tracksuit trouser pocket, its array of sophisticated features ignored.

Adrian awakens, forces his weary bulk into a sitting position and blinks several times, as his eyes become accustomed to the light. From within one of the tracksuit trouser pockets, the Nokia begins to beep. The sound is the alarm signifying that there is an hour and a half until The Alpha meeting; he had agreed to attend. As he reluctantly rises and struggles upstairs to prepare to leave the house, his tormented mind turns once more to the still unexplainable reason for his connection to the deceased Charles Middleworth.

An hour and a half later - The interior of the church is brightly illuminated, courtesy of an array of ceiling lights, which beam down luminous rays and warmth in equal measure. From the whitewashed walls hang framed paintings of a religious nature. They are pictures depicting Christian symbols, such as the cross, the Holy Spirit and the Trinity, all of which are covered in great swathes of bright colours. From a young age Adrian had become familiar with the austerity of traditional Church of England Christianity, this however was something quite different, more lively and extroverted.

One of the paintings portrays the Holy Spirit as a white dove flying through a dark foreboding sky, Adrian looks away. Turning his head in the direction of the near wall, his focus falls on a painting dominated by a draped empty cross, the ends of which are triangular; Adrian assumes that it must depict the Trinity. Below the painting is a verse from 1 Corinthians 15:54. 'When the perishable has been clothed with the imperishable, and the mortal with immortality, then the saying that is written will come true. Death has been swallowed up in victory.'

Adrian slowly whispers the words aloud, aware that they are somehow relevant, though he is not quite sure how. Despite this he savours the verse's positivity.

A stream of people are pressing their bodies through its narrow door, chattering eagerly amongst themselves as they do so. Most appear to be young professional types, in their twenties and thirties. Minutes later and the room is a hustling mass of humanity. Adrian is becoming uncomfortable now, for despite the welcoming nature of the room and the happy contented people; their close proximity and the voluminous nature of the proceedings remind him of the wailing multitude, which plague his sleeping hours. He is considering leaving when a bedraggled and breathless Franklin appears next to him.

'Hi Adrian sorry I'm late somebody under a train at Bank,' greets Franklin, perching his cumbersome frame on the adjacent chair.

Adrian is at the point of offering a response when a woman of forty or so, standing on a raised platform near the front of the church begins to speak. 'Firstly welcome everyone; it's truly wonderful to see so many of you here this evening. For the benefit of our guests, my name is Theresa and I am an Alpha course organiser.'

Adrian notes that she is wearing what could best be described as an ethnic ensemble. It consists of a wool cloak on which depictions of llamas had been woven and a woollen hat with a large bobble on top, which hangs down over the ears and has the same llamas printed across it. He considers it to be an outfit that an ancient Inca would have worn; which he finds disturbing.

For some reason that Adrian is quite unable to fathom, clapping begins from the back of the room, growing persistently louder and more eager. Adrian looks across at Franklin, who appears to be enjoying himself immensely; he is smiling broadly and standing on tiptoes to garner a better view of Theresa, as she continues to talk. 'Sure I used to go to church when I was a child with my parents but I never really understood the whole Christianity thing and stopped going in my late teens. Five years ago I was invited to an Alpha meeting and I have been here ever since.' Theresa pauses momentarily and then adds, 'do you know what Alpha has given me?'

A number of those in attendance raise their hands in the air, hoping to be chosen to answer just as small children do in class; Theresa ignores them. Adrian desperately wants Theresa to reply that she has overcome some terrible psychological ordeal. Perhaps like him she has been plagued by terrifying nightmares, waking visions and some other worldly connection with a dead person and that Alpha provided her the means to escape this torment. He is not hopeful however and her answer confirms this. 'Before I was unsure about my place in the world and who God is. But Alpha has made Christianity relevant to my life and has allowed me to focus on my existence.'

Now adamant that Alpha can offer no respite from his current predicament, Adrian looks despondently at the floor. He is envious of Theresa and others suffering from predicaments like not being sure how to pray, or is God real and how can he guide us. Adrian wishes he too were affected by such minor concerns.

A short time later they divide into groups of twelve, their chairs all facing inwards in a circle, to discuss some of these pressing issues touched upon earlier. The group leader is a plump, animated middle aged woman in a floral dress, whose role it appears to Adrian is to encourage the group's exchange of ideas; her name is Molly. She appears to Adrian to be identical to the numerous other plump and animated middle aged women of a religious persuasion, he had come across running stalls and organising events at the Church fetes and jamborees of his youth. Molly proceeds to continually mention God's relevance in the modern world and how Alpha embraces science and allows Christianity to be relevant today. It is evident to Adrian that whilst she mentions words like philosophy and science, they are to her all inclusive terms. Evolutionism, empiricism, rationality and Newton seem to be of little concern, all replaced with an enthusiastic evangelical zeal.

Adrian is paying scant attention to the proceedings and is instead reflecting on his own issues when unannounced Molly addresses him directly. 'Well you've been very quiet today, obviously happy taking in all this information. Do you have any questions?'

'I find your use of the term science to be inadequate for this discussion,' responds Adrian. 'Surely earlier attempts to reconcile Christianity with science; the most prominent example being Newtonian mechanics are in stark contrast to later attempts to reconcile Christianity, with say relativity or evolutionism.'

Molly looks extremely confused and despite looking around desperately for assistance from the group, it is not forthcoming and she is forced to respond. 'Well not sure who Newtonian is, but mechanics is making things and so is evolutionism, so it's all the same,' answers Molly gleefully yet wholly inadequately; her skills more akin to the baking of macaroons than solving the complexities of the universe. Adrian moans abjectly and looks up at the ceiling in dismay. He is sorely disappointed, having expected from Theresa's earlier address that the Alpha course, which purports to offer a revolutionary understanding of God and the meaning of life, would combine scientific endeavour with Biblical teaching.

A fervent discussion amongst the group members ensues. Franklin quite openly discusses some of his sexual deviances and how he is attempting to overcome them through prayer. Ordinarily such a topic of conversation would have disgusted Adrian's conservative inclinations, but in his present predicament it barely registers. Momentarily he considers discussing his own issues with the group but decides against this course of action, for he is quite unsure how to initiate a discussion on a subject of this nature. There is one topic of conversation however that does arouse Adrian's interest; the subject of which is purgatory. So intently does he listen when the subject is broached that he does not notice the corner of one group member's lips curling upwards in a snarl, at this inherently Catholic concept being mentioned, in what he feels to be a Church of England setting. For purgatory, this place of post-mortem temporal suffering seems somehow relevant to his dreams, in part due to the fact that the multitudes appear to resemble lost souls. In customary fashion though on a highly uncustomary subject, bullet points appear in Adrian's mind. They look like this:

- Intermediary physical location of the multitude (neither the traditional concept of heaven above or of hell below).
- Universal anguish of multitude.
- Aged appearance of majority of multitude (percentiles impossible to calculate).
- Presence of deceased Charles Middleworth, (DOD: 5/11/69).

This thought pattern is so illogical and unscientific that it startles Adrian, yet the notion remains, as he is acutely aware that dreams respect neither logic nor scientific rationality. Placing both hands on the back of his head, he mutters 'Jesus,' in a despondent fashion.

'Do not use the Lord's name in vain,' admonishes Molly sternly.

Wishing to avoid any further confrontation with Molly, Adrian makes the excuse he is going out for a cigarette, despite not being in possession of any. Franklin shouts after him, 'see you out there in a few minutes.'

Sitting on the damp stone steps at the front of the church, Adrian stares ahead into the darkness of the forecourt and beyond to the road and the shafts of light emanating from the cars, as they speed past, spraying sheets of water onto the pavement. If you were to study him very closely, you would notice tears forming in his eyes, for there is fear that his adherence to scientific rationality and logic is under threat, from an unexplainable and sinister force. A thought reveals itself, as it does so he begins to state it aloud. 'It is almost as if Charles Middleworth was …'

People are emerging through the narrow door of the church, chattering amongst themselves; the noise of which distracts Adrian. Franklin approaches, doing up the zip of his raincoat as he does so. 'Wow that was amazing,' he remarks. 'What's the matter with you?'

'Oh nothing just wet from the rain,' responds Adrian, wiping tears and rain water from his cheeks with the sleeve of his poly cotton lined fleece anorak.

The two of them continue to converse on the church steps, cowering under Franklin's umbrella. Twenty minutes later they depart for the train station; Adrian clutching two hundred and forty pounds in twenty pound notes from Franklin to put towards his uncle's funeral costs.

On the train home, Adrian decides to go to Hampshire the next day, as he is keen to escape the cycle of morbidity that life in London has been in recent days.

Seven

The Next Morning – Adrian is in the back of an ABC mini cab, travelling from Falgate train station to the family home, on this occasion well within the speed limit. Weary from another night intruded upon by Middleworth, the multitude and the car fire, he stares blankly out of the window at the hedgerows, fields and The River Tenton meandering gently along the valley floor in the distance.

Two ornately decorated three metre tall stone columns come into view on the right side of the lane; they signify the start of someone's drive. Each column has an immense Venetian streaked black marble ball atop of it. On noticing the columns, Adrian's inquisitive nature is in evidence, if only for the fleetest of moments. Although only viewing the columns for approximately two seconds, Adrian noticing the columns rolled volutes surmises that their inspiration must have been the Ionic columns of ancient Greece; in addition to this he correctly identifies the balls as being Venetian black marble. He concludes that one would expect to come across columns of this ilk in Hollywood or Monaco, for they appear very out of place in this rural environment. These columns mark the start of Ramsbottam Hall's drive, the proprietor of which is Theodore Raven. Adrian, having never previously visited the property is unaware of this.

At this very moment at the end of the drive in Ramsbottam Hall's principal bedroom, Theodore is asleep on its four poster bed mumbling incoherently, his features etched in angst; for he is in the midst of a nightmare. The nightmare is terrifying and vivid, not dissimilar in severity in fact to one of Adrian's own. A short while earlier the ordeal had begun with Theodore finding himself somewhere in the dark inhospitable bowels of the earth, with several irate mosquitoes darting about menacingly above his head. These few mosquitoes have now been joined by a great swarm of the vile insects, which descend upon his being as a cloud of voracious, incessant buzzing; enveloping Theodore and penetrating his skin with their narrow proboscises. In a futile attempt to prevent the attack, Theodore's hands flail wildly in front of him. He awakens, screaming deliriously and his hands continue flailing for quite some time.

A little over eight minutes later the mini cab is turning into the front driveway of the Raven family home. As it does so, Adrian looks upwards into the large elm trees that line the driveway and observes the leaves fluttering in the breeze. The moment the mini cab is stationary he clambers out of the vehicle, removes the Samsonite Pro-DLX suitcase and overnight bag from the boot, gives the driver ten pounds and approaches the front door. He places the suitcase on the door mat and pulls the brass door handle forcefully; the door opens. Natalia is standing in the middle of the hall. She says 'hello,' in a cold, unwelcoming tone. Adrian responds in the same manner and stands motionless on the carpet, whilst Natalia examines him suspiciously, as she is wary of this threat to her husband inheriting Colin's estate in its entirety.

Standing in the dull light of the hallway, the house seems strangely unfamiliar to Adrian. The reason for this is not only the presence of the malignant new addition to the household. For without family in attendance the house seems merely an empty shell, devoid of warmth and intimacy. It is as if even here in his family home, this ever present feature in his life, the unexplainable and incomprehensible lurk.

'Where's Benedict?' enquires Adrian, breaking the eerie silence.

'In study,' replies Natalia curtly.

Adrian walks through the hall to the study door and opens it. Benedict is perched on his father's chair behind the mahogany desk, leaning forward in animated fashion whilst he types feverishly on the keyboard in front of him. A ballpoint pen protrudes from his mouth, as if it were a cigar.

'Adrian good to see you,' says Benedict, standing up as he does so. This action results in the pen falling from his mouth to the desk below.

'Good morning,' replies Adrian.

Benedict, inspecting his brother through the thick lenses of his spectacles remarks, 'you look tired and thin.'

Adrian is about to respond when Benedict says, 'let's get beers from the fridge and get started on Quest for Modernity.'

Natalia, who is standing in the doorway emits a groan, turns adroitly and walks off swearing in Russian.

Within a minute the two brothers are drinking beer as they wait for Quest for Modernity IV: Barbarians to load on the new Hewlett Packard computer's twenty-seven inch screen, Benedict had persuaded his father to purchase, days prior to his departure to Egypt.

Despite Adrian's usual relish for the Quest for Modernity series and the obvious marked improvements with this new version, such as the enhanced modernity builder tool bar, he struggles to concentrate. Fatigue and ongoing concern over the now seemingly permanent feature of the dreams and his connection to Charles Middleworth, prove to be not conducive to forming complex strategic plans. Several times he is chastised by Benedict for basic strategic errors, such as failing to erect adequate numbers of defensive balustrades or forgetting to build storage facilities and irrigation ditches.

They are an hour and thirty-three minutes into the campaign when Natalia appears in the doorway bearing a malevolent scowl. Adrian and Benedict are unable to hear the outburst that follows her arrival, due to the game's electronic Gregorian chant theme tune, which is being played at a high volume. It is however evident to both brothers as they behold Natalia's furious gesticulations that the gaming session has reached its conclusion. They hurriedly down the remainder of their beer and then toss the empty bottles into the frayed brown leather bin next to the desk. Benedict picking up a half consumed box of Belgian truffles from the desk, hands them to his brother with the words, 'they're yours, you'll like them.'

Adrian wanders out to the garden alone, and down to the bottom of the lawn, to the old oak tree where he and Benedict had in their childhood regularly swung from a tyre, attached by a piece of rope to one of its branches. This almost daily routine had come to an abrupt end shortly after Adrian had turned eleven, when having taken a particularly long running jump at the tyre, the branch had snapped mid flight and he had fallen to the ground, resulting in a fractured fibula. Adrian's fondness for the tree has remained however and it is here that he rests against the familiar gnarled trunk, devouring the remainder of the Belgian truffles and staring out at the silver birch trees and the mass of bracken in the wood below. After finishing the truffles, he reaches into the left pocket of his blue corduroy trousers, takes out the folded yellow post-it note Dr Shah had given him at the surgery, tentatively unfolds it and then reads its contents, in a calm and assured voice. 'www.stressrelievers.org.'

Despite the unfortunate experience with the whale music, Adrian decides to revisit the website. Returning to the house, he enters the study just as The Turner grandfather clock in the dining room begins chiming for midday. Sitting down in Colin's leather upholstered chair, he types www.stressrelievers.org into the web browser on the computer screen in front of him.

One of the more prominent links on the home page is for yoga; a well documented stress reliever. Adrian clicks on the link and a list of yoga's potential benefits are revealed. They look like this.

- Invigoration
- Vitality
- Relief of fatigue
- Relaxation therapy
- Anti-aging benefits

Though aware that yoga will not shed any further light on the Charles Middleworth issue, he is eager to indulge in any activity, which has even the remotest possibility of alleviating his troublesome sleep.

That evening as the three Ravens dine on rigatoni with a mascarpone sauce, prepared by Benedict, with Adrian acting as an assistant (Natalia does not cook); Adrian decides to bring up the subject of yoga. He is immensely surprised when Benedict announces that he is something of an expert on the matter. From Adrian's experience, Benedict had previously never failed to ridicule anything that swayed even marginally from the mainstream. However as he listens intently to his brother, it begins to make sense why yoga has proved an exception to this rule.

'Never thought I'd partake in yoga,' remarks Benedict.

'You know better than anyone that alternative lifestyle choices and me don't usually mix.'

It had been at the beginning of last year when Benedict's morphine addiction had reached its nadir that he had been forced reluctantly to seek refuge at a rehabilitation centre. It was there that he had been introduced to the merits of yoga.

At first he had steadfastly refused to participate in what he regarded as an activity that was both a non-masculine pursuit, as well as being mystical holistic nonsense. However after weeks of persuasion he relented and attended an introductory class. For the following six months he had indulged in yoga on a regular basis.

'Don't get me wrong,' states Benedict. 'You won't ever find me sporting long hair or wearing silly yogi outfits.' Benedict skewers two pieces of rigatoni on his fork and swallows them instantly before adding, 'but I would argue conclusively in my case at least that yoga aids the relaxation of the mind and body, in addition to being quite an enjoyable pastime.'

As Benedict goes on to explain in intricate detail his experience with yoga and its benefits, Adrian ponders on whether there are perhaps similarities between his own adversity and Benedict's morphine addiction. All the while the Thomas Turner grandfather clock ticks quietly in the background and Natalia fidgets impatiently with her new iPhone. Benedict mentions that he had on one occasion quite recently when staying at the house attended a yoga class on a Monday evening in Falgate. The two brothers agree to go the following Monday. Natalia refuses Benedict's overtures for her to join them, much to Adrian's relief.

That night as Adrian slept on the Miracoil bed with spring system beneath the framed picture of Isaac Newton; he dreamt. Once more he found himself floating through the sky alongside Charles Middleworth towards the wailing multitude far below, their distressed faces turned upwards towards the heavens. In the early hours of the morning Adrian is behind the wheel of the car when he is aware of a large bang, within moments smoke and flames are enveloping its interior. So vivid is the nightmare that he awakens coughing and rubbing his smoke irritated eyes. Lying awake in bed he struggles to comprehend his subconscious obsession with Charles Middleworth and his demise in the car fire; someone he had never even heard of until so recently.

The following morning finds Adrian in the kitchen sipping tea from Colin's Funeral Care Insurance centenary mug. Having just devoured his second cheese and ham four egg omelette, he is feeling slightly nauseous. Following Benedict's comment the previous day about him looking thin, Adrian had weighed himself on the bathroom scales and had been alarmed that his weight had dropped from the usual one hundred kilograms to ninety two point four. Looking at the reflection of his heavily built six foot one inch frame in the bathroom's full length mirror, there was no doubting he looked somewhat emaciated and that it appeared his hair had thinned somewhat.

Having finished his tea, Adrian remains in the kitchen, capturing images on the Canon EOS of the three deteriorating tulips in the vase on the kitchen table that Colin had put there prior to his departure for Egypt. After each photo, Adrian inspects the image and then proceeds to alter the light contrast function by a single increment before repeating the exercise. This activity that until so recently would have yielded so much joy no longer absorbs him fully, for with his mind preoccupied with troubling matters it has lost something of its lustre. Several minutes later he abandons the camera on the window sill and leaves the room, his mind turning once more to the unexplained and unwelcome intrusion of Middleworth.

Monday afternoon - Adrian is pushing a trolley down aisle four of the Sainsbury's supermarket in town. He is alone. Benedict and Natalia had dropped him off on their way to the opticians (both Benedict and Natalia are short-sighted. It has previously occurred to Adrian that this is all they share in common). Stopping half way down aisle four, Adrian begins to compare the sugar content for the three brands of

Alpen cereal currently in stock. He is reaching for the final box when out of the corner of his eye, he notices something. The object of his attention is a man, his back turned towards Adrian, as he ambles at a leisurely pace in the direction of the Weetabix, a shopping basket hanging limply from one hand. Turning his attentions from the Alpen, Adrian scrutinises the man's appearance with mounting concern. He is of average height, slightly built, clothed in brown, with a thinning palate.

Deciding that a closer inspection is required, Adrian despite his misgivings decides on an act of temerity. Discarding the trolley, he jogs round to aisle five, where the conserves, sugar and flour are to be found. He then advances all the way to the end of aisle, where he peers around the shelf containing the powdered ChocoMilks. The man is still some distance away, ambling slowly towards Adrian down aisle four, perusing the sugared cereal brands to his right, quite unaware of Adrian.

It is not until the man has passed the Weetabix and Freddies cereals that Adrian is certain that it is not Charles Middleworth. For he is too old, appearing at least a decade and half older than his nemesis would have, at the time of his demise. In addition to this he sports a prodigious, crescent shaped chin, quite unlike the unremarkable one possessed by Middleworth. Returning to the trolley, Adrian takes two boxes of the Alpen containing the highest sugar percentage from the shelf, places them in the trolley and heads towards the checkout.

It is now evening and Benedict and Adrian are driving to the yoga class in Benedict's Lexus LS 600h.

'Yoga's good,' exclaims Benedict on turning out of the lane and onto the main road. 'But it's not as easy as it looks.'

'Benedict,' says Adrian several seconds later.

'Yes.'

'Do you ever remember dreams?'

'Sometimes yeah, why?' responds Benedict somewhat defensively.

'What is their typical content?'

Benedict turns the steering wheel to the right, narrowly avoiding a small rabbit that has ventured onto the road. Adrian grips the door handle with his right hand so firmly that his knuckles whiten.

'Well the usual stuff, about chicks and things like that,' replies Benedict having straightened the steering wheel.

Adrian does not reply.

'Between you and I,' continues Benedict, 'occasionally and I mean very occasionally I, umm, dream about computers.' He falls momentarily silent and then adds, 'and sometimes about mother.'

Nothing more is said until they reach Tatchin Junction at the edge of the rapidly expanding commuter town that is Falgate.

'Benedict, are you err, acquainted with the name Charles Middleworth?'

'No' says Benedict. 'Never come across anyone with that name.'

'Are you certain?'

'Yeah quite sure,' replies Benedict, accelerating forwards as the lights turn green. 'Why?'

'No reason.'

Several seconds later Adrian says, 'Benedict ...'

'Jesus Adrian what is this forty questions!' interrupts an annoyed Benedict, as he clicks the indicator to the down position, before tapping his fingers impatiently against the steering wheel, as he waits for an opportunity to turn into the driving area at the front of what had once been Falgate's Methodist chapel. This rather drab looking building is now utilised for a myriad of activities, ranging from childcare day centre to hosting Alcoholic Anonymous meetings and on Monday evenings yoga classes.

They enter the building through its small wooden door and are met by the sight of large blue mats covering the entirety of the floor space. To Adrian, the mats appear identical to the ones he had come across in PE lessons during his school days. Removing his Adidas Terrex Fast X FM trainers, he places them neatly at the side of the room and begins performing light stretches on one of the mats. Three lycra clad women and a man enter the hall and they too start stretching. Several minutes later Benedict appears sheepishly from a room at the rear of the hall. He is wearing a fluorescent yellow outfit with a matching head band. At the very moment Adrian is about to pass comment on his choice of apparel, Benedict anticipates it. 'I know but Natalia insisted on it, say no more.'

By the time the class has begun, there are eleven people in attendance. The yogi, who is sitting at the front of the room in characteristic cross legged yoga pose, offers a brief introduction. Adrian is rather disappointed that the man appears nothing like how he had imagined a yogi to look. Not only is the yogi named Matt but he is also white (Adrian had been under the impression all yogis are of Indian extraction). The middle aged Matt possesses a portly physique, neatly combed greying hair and a monotone voice. It occurs to Adrian that Matt resembles a chartered surveyor or an accountant. The class takes the form of the yogi Matt demonstrating a series of techniques. Each technique is described in a monotone by Matt, as if he were reading from a computer manual.

First up is Halasana. This entails lying on one's back, legs brought back over the head with the tips of the toes touching the ground behind. Benedict as most of the other members of the class performs this simple beginners' technique with a consummate ease. After much straining, face reddening from the effort, Adrian too is able to successfully achieve the Halasana pose, if only for a second or two at a time. Putting this success down to the amount of time spent sitting on superior zero gravity chairs, complete with lumbar and lower back support, he waits eagerly for the next demonstration.

'Can't wait to see you attempting Dhanurasana or Ustrasana,' whispers Benedict in flawless Halasana pose, on the adjacent mat. The next position requires one to lie stomach down and to reach behind, grabbing both feet and arching back, ideally so only the stomach is in contact with the ground. It is known as Dhanurasana or the bow position.

Matt issues a word of warning. 'This is an advanced move so please don't try it if you're not confident.'

Benedict contorts his body effortlessly into the desired position, his head turning from side to side to accept the applause of the other students. They too then attempt the technique, with varying degrees of success. Adrian determined not to be outdone by his brother, takes a big breath, his face reddening once more, as he futilely tries to clasp his feet with his hands. The pain is ferocious but he dismisses it and arches his back yet further. There is a loud cracking noise, followed in quick succession by a piercing shriek. Benedict laughs aloud, as Adrian lies on the ground groaning. Sitting out the remaining techniques, Adrian instead performs some light stretches alone. To his surprise, by the time the class has finished, the pain has largely dissipated.

On the return journey home having just passed Tatchin Junction, Adrian asks, 'why are you still wearing that headband?'

Benedict removes it from his head with his left hand, throws it onto the back seat and says, 'that class was just what I needed after the stress Natalia's been giving me lately.'

Adrian considers it most uncharacteristic of Benedict to bring up subjects of a personal nature. Fearing that Benedict is going to ask his opinion of Natalia, Adrian fidgets nervously, but the question is not forthcoming.

Instead Benedict asks, 'how long are planning to stay at dads?'

Adrian briefly considers his response and then replies, 'in all likelihood a few weeks, I need, a, err, break from work.'

'Sure,' replies Benedict. Though curious as to why Adrian has deserted his actuarial duties, he decides against exploring the issue further, presuming from his own personal experiences that this could be a sensitive matter. Benedict had lost the majority of his clients from what had been a very lucrative IT security consultancy business, as a result of his morphine addiction.

Benedict is talking about a new property venture Theodore is planning in Spain and that he plans to have a role in. He mentions that Adrian's assistance with this would be appreciated. Though Adrian responds in the affirmative, he is all but oblivious to the conversation, for his thoughts have turned to Charles Middleworth and the impending night.

Eight

Adrian awakens reinvigorated from a night, which for the most part had been comparatively restful. Notwithstanding several episodes during the early hours of the morning when finding himself floating beside Middleworth, the multitude clamouring below and in the car with the rattling sound emanating from its rear, followed by the detonation and resulting smoke and fire.

Rising from bed, Adrian puts on his dressing gown and heads downstairs. There is a carefree abandon in his gait that not even a degree of stiffness in the lower back and hamstrings, courtesy of the yoga class, can nullify. Having consumed two bowls of high sugar Alpen cereal and with little of note to keep him occupied, he decides to indulge in some house work.

A little over an hour later, Adrian now dusting in the sitting room, moves the ceramic vase from the table by the window and is greeted by the sight of a book being utilised for the purpose of a mat. The book is entitled 'Solving Problems through Courage and Fortitude – a step by step guide', written by Bartholomew Thomas PhD, MBA. Adrian's previous experiences with literature that embraced the solving problem theme had been from the IT and actuarial science perspective; more often than not incorporating complex logic and binary code. Intrigued as to its contents, he opens it.

Dr Thomas's belief was that issues can only be resolved by confronting them with prompt and assertive action. This philosophy is demonstrated in 'Solving Problems through Courage and Fortitude – a step by step guide,' with examples taken from everyday life. At the conclusion of each narrative, the steps that led to the successful solving of the problem are listed. Having read the introduction, Adrian scans the book's contents page, in the hope that there is one on the subject of overcoming nightmares or unexplained visitations by dead people; but there are none. Undeterred, he decides to read it anyway, rationalising that with eighty pages; an average speed of twenty seconds per page will allow him to complete the exercise in only twenty-six minutes and forty-two seconds.

Over the course of his reading, Adrian discovers that Dr Thomas insisted upon the necessity of creating a simple statement that facilitates assertive action, towards the goal to be achieved. The goal is evident to Adrian; to rid his subconscious of those thoughts facilitating the dreams and obsession with Charles Middleworth. But it is not until the book has been returned to its role of vase mat that he is able to formulate the statement part. Steadfastly ignoring the algorithms and mathematical logic that appear in his mind, Adrian decides upon a statement, remarkable for its simplicity. 'Drive to Nottingham and tour the city by car.' This is to include a trip to Newgate Road, where Charles Middleworth had lived. The thought is both terrifying and contrary to previous efforts, to ignore the irrational and peculiar fixation with the deceased Charles Middleworth. Acknowledging that to date this has proved to be an ineffective strategy; there is a glimmer of hope that confronting the matter in this direct courageous manner, might just be a first step towards solving these issues. The book advises that the next step is to vocalise the action. Adrian repeats it three times, in as calm and composed voice as he can muster.

'Drive to Nottingham and tour the city by car. Drive to Nottingham and tour the city by car. Drive to Nottingham and tour the city by car, including visiting Newgate Road.'

The sense of fear increases with each vocalisation of the proposed act. Energised by the prospect of a potential path to redemption, Adrian turns his attentions to the steps necessary for the completion of this task.

Online that evening, Adrian discovers that Sir Bartholomew Thomas was the author of ten bestselling self-help books, a motivational speaker and sat on the board of an international charity. A moot note however was that he had met his demise, as a direct result of abandoning his step-by-step philosophy to problem solving. In the autumn of nineteen-sixty-nine, Sir Thomas had attempted to clamber over a gate whilst partridge shooting in Spain. In his haste he had forgotten to formulate a step-by-step plan and two errors had been made. Firstly he had failed to unload the weapon prior to mounting the gate and secondly he had slipped whilst dismounting it, resulting in the discharging of the shotgun and near obliteration of his head. Adrian vocalises what he regards as being the correct procedure for this action.

'1). Unload shotgun.
2). Place cartridges in pocket.
3). Hold shotgun securely with less dominant hand.
4). Mount gate.
5). Climb over gate.
6). Dismount gate.
7). Once firmly entrenched on ground, reload shotgun and proceed.'

Though the procedure seems remarkably straightforward, Adrian is not to be discouraged by Sir Thomas's act of folly; appreciative of the fact that people do not always practice what they preach.

09:13 -The Next Morning
Adrian and Benedict are standing beside the Lexus LS 600h saloon. Benedict is explaining in intricate detail the car's capabilities and functions.

'As you well know the LS 600h is the world's first car to have a fully integrated hybrid powertrain,' says Benedict.

'Yes I am aware of this,' replies Adrian, finding this detailed explanation increasingly tedious.

'Now it may have the emissions and fuel consumption of a six cylinder vehicle, but don't be fooled by this. The LS 600h is incredibly powerful. Take the acceleration for example, nought to sixty-two miles per hour in six point three seconds.'

Not wishing to delay the inevitable, Adrian clambers into the car's leather clad interior.

'The eight inch colour electro multi vision touch screen is perfection,' continues Benedict, leaning through the open door and pointing at the device. 'Climate control, navigation and audio, you name it, everything is controlled from here.'

The tutorial finishes and Benedict hands the car keys to Adrian. Expecting another lecture on the temporary extra driver insurance Benedict had organised the previous evening, Adrian waits silently, but it is not forthcoming. So he bids farewell, pulls the driver door shut, takes a deep breath, turns the key in the ignition and he's off, winding effortlessly down the country lanes.

10:27 - Somewhere between Junction fourteen and fifteen on the A1, Adrian becomes aware of a rattling sound. It is emanating from somewhere in the back of the vehicle. The sound is so faint that he dismisses it as a product of his imagination and concentrates resolutely on the road ahead. The noise persists. Adrian attempts to reassure himself it is merely illusory, but this proves to no avail. Images of the car fire from the recurrent nightmares emerge in his mind, in all their harrowing intensity. Hurriedly he recites the safety features of this latest Lexus offering, as relayed by Benedict earlier that morning, in an effort to pacify his mind.

'Airbags frontal airbags side impact airbags knee protection anti-lock brakes traction control.'

The noise continues relentlessly. Refusing to surrender to the irrational thoughts tormenting him, Adrian turns on the car's Alpine stereo system. Instantaneously the car is filled with the sound of Metallica's song Fuel, courtesy of 105.2 FM, a Midlands heavy metal station. The rattling noise is no longer audible over the frenetic drum beat. Over the forthcoming minutes however, the sound of the drums has the effect of Adrian becoming uncertain whether it is merely the drumming and not also the rattling noise from the rear of the vehicle. That the two separate sounds are no longer distinguishable, having now merged as one. Distressed, his brow damp with sweat, Adrian twists his head around and peers into the rear of the car, in an effort to locate the source of the problem. Turning back to the front, he is met by the sight of a white transit van, looming ominously close. Stamping on the brake pedal, a collision is narrowly avoided. The stereo is turned off; the tinted electric window lowered a couple of centimetres.

No sooner has he done this than the unmistakable odour of smoke reaches his nasal cavity, growing more noxious and acrid with each passing second. Panicking that the engine is overheating; Adrian pressing his foot on the brake pedal, enters the slow lane, lamenting the fact that there is no emergency lane on this section of the A1.

After what seems an eternity, the emergency lane appears. Turning into it, Adrian opens the passenger door and turns off the ignition whilst still moving, then hastily exits the vehicle the moment it stops. Scrambling across the asphalt to the safety of the grass verge, he runs up the embankment and collapses to his knees at the summit. A lorry driver taking an impromptu break watches Adrian bemused. The car does not explode. Adrian sitting on the bank is aware that the odour of smoke remains, its source somewhere in the distance behind him. Rising to his feet and cursing the day Charles Middleworth had trespassed upon a previously benign existence, Adrian proceeds to scrub the mud from his corduroy trousers, using a chequered cotton handkerchief, with the aid of some water from a puddle.

On returning to the Lexus, Adrian opens the boot and the source of the rattling sound is revealed. The offending item is a small metallic bin, decorated garishly with podgy cherubic angels clasping trumpets. 'Natalia!' shouts Adrian, aware that his brother would never have purchased such an abhorrent item, if left to his own devices. He gets back in the car, takes a deep breath and then turns on the ignition. Driving cautiously at no more than twenty miles per hour, he leaves the Lexus at the first opportunity; Worksop train station's car park. The decision is made to complete the remainder of the journey by train.

13:53 - Small drops of rain are being driven against the thick window of the Virgin Pendolino intercity train by forceful gusts of wind. The derelict Victorian buildings along the railway line and the more modern structures behind them appear somewhat familiar to Adrian. Turning his head away from the view, he stares at the brightly lit ceiling of the train carriage. There is dismay at the fact that the intention to travel to Nottingham by car has failed. Though he acknowledges that it had been a reckless decision to attempt to do so, considering the car related nightmares of recent weeks. He wishes life were as it used to be and that he were sitting on the Safco chair, with lumbar support in Vincent & Ernst, contentedly devising and analysing algorithms.

The train glides to a halt. Adrian gets off the train. As he walks towards the exit, he formulates a plan that allows him to delay the inevitable. Firstly to gain an overview of the city by wandering around for an hour or so and after this to make his way towards the vicinity of Middleworth's former address. The imprecise, vague nature of the plan distresses him somewhat, as he walks out with trepidation into the city that had been Charles Middleworth's earthly abode.

15:11 - The Kings Arms - Adrian takes a large gulp from his pint of Kronenbourg. During the last hour he has set sight upon the castle perched on the hill and Nottingham Council House, with its two hundred foot high dome. The pub is remarkably similar to others he has frequented in the past, the frayed nicotine stained curtains, the peeling white paint on the walls or the ageing drinkers and mangy old dog with droopy eyes lying on the cheap red carpet. Taking another gulp from the Kronenbourg, even larger than the first, Adrian realises that the beer is stale and assumes it is likely leftovers from the brewery.

His attentions fall on a haggard looking man, with tired sullen features, dark hollowed eyes and sagging wrinkled skin, slumped in a jaded wooden chair on the other side of the bar. He is reading The Racing Post. There is something familiar about this man, though Adrian is unsure as to why. Taking another gulp of beer, Adrian scrutinises the man's features, before reaching the conclusion that his familiarity must merely be his resemblance to the numerous other aging people of a certain social disposition; he had come across in public houses, on the tube or queuing at the post office.

The man now aware of Adrian's attention is bearing an expression of extreme displeasure, his upper lip curling upwards in a grimace, his head turned menacingly towards him. 'What you lookin at?' shouts the man.

Adrian ignores him, in the vain hope that it is someone else in the pub that has incurred his wrath. The man rises from the chair and approaches closer; vengeful eyes bearing savagely on Adrian.

'What de fuck you lookin at?' shouts the man.

'Who me?' asks Adrian in an innocent and unassuming tone.

'Yeah you faggot.'

'I was merely in a conundrum,' replies Adrian. 'And err was absent mindedly looking in your direction...'

'Conundrum?' replies the man, who is now only four or so metres away.

'A conundrum could best be described as a question for which only an answer of a conjectural nature can be made,' responds an alarmed Adrian.

It is evident that the man is not impressed by Adrian's grasp of the English language. He is very close now; his gaunt face a web of lines, each wrinkle forming a deep trench across the sagging skin. The man raises his still half filled glass and throws it forcefully in Adrian's direction. Adrian ducks to avoid it. It smashes against the wall, sending small shards of glass flying through the air. 'Fight, Fight, Fight!' screams an emaciated toothless crone sat in the corner by the fruit machine. The man approaching yet closer begins to raise his withered hands from his waist. Adrian flicks out his left foot in the direction of the man's groin. He groans and doubles over, but then begins to straighten, steadying himself for an assault on Adrian's person. There are shouts of 'fight' and 'get him Dave!'

Grabbing his Vincent & Ernst umbrella, Adrian swings it back in an arc and brings the handle crashing into his adversary's chin. One of the Dave's few remaining teeth flies through the air and he slumps backwards hitting the ground with a thump. Engulfed with guilt, Adrian is considering an apology, when he sees other customers rising to their feet with sinister intent.

Adrian flees across the red carpet, through the door and out into the street. Certain that they are in pursuit; he continues in his flight, turning down the street on his left, before taking a right and then another left. All is silent now, save for the pattering of rain on the asphalt and the sound of cars someway in the distance. Bent forward, hands on knees, Adrian is struggling for breath, when he notices a street sign on the other side of the road. The name of the street is Newgate Road. He reads it a second time in disbelief. Though aware that Newgate Road was in the vicinity, he had not known its location in relation to The Kings Arms. With the magnitude of the fact that he is now standing in the very place where Charles Middleworth had lived, the incident at the pub is instantly forgotten.

Newgate Road is a narrow street, lined on both sides with terraced, two storied red brick Georgian properties; quite typical in fact of many provincial English cities. The rain has stopped and the street is remarkably quiet. Only the drone of an airplane in the distance is discernible to Adrian, as he begins to slowly advance towards the property that had been Charles Middleworth's home. He counts down the numbers of the houses on the opposite side of the road, in a faltering voice, 'nineteen, seventeen, fifteen.' The pace slows yet further and is now little more than a shuffle, as Adrian delays the inevitable. 'Thirteeeen, el-e-v-e-n, n-i-n-e, s-e-v-e-n'.

Five Newgate Road is an unassuming property. A large vine coils up its front, obscuring much of the red brick beneath its dark green leaves. The window frames are a freshly painted white, in contrast to the peeling paint of its unkempt neighbours.

Adrian's heart beat is rapid and his breathing frenetic, as he stands staring at the house of the man that from the grave, is threatening his very sanity. Unsure as to how to proceed or what illogical reasoning has led him to being here, Adrian remains stationary. He briefly considers returning to the train station but rationalises that having come so far, he should investigate the property further.

Pizza takeaway menus are strewn across the pavement. They are for a local pizzeria, Planet Pizza, and have pictures of a variety of pizzas masquerading as planets from our solar system. Adrian picks up a number of the soggy menus, with the intention that should people notice him; they will simply assume he is delivering takeaway menus and pay no further attention.

A teenage girl is pushing a pram on the other side of the street. Seconds later she disappears from view. Satisfied all is quiet, Adrian approaches the gate of Five Newgate Road. The house's lights are off and there is no sign of life visible in its darkened interior. Adrian opens the gate, tiptoes up to the front door, bends down and peers through the letter box. Junk mail is strewn across the beige carpeted hall floor. A smiling pepperoni pizza masquerading as Mars, stares up at him from a Pizza Planet takeaway menu. Further forward and to the left of the junk mail items is an envelope. Adrian tilting his head at an awkward angle struggles to make out the letters, which he reads aloud in a faltering voice. 'I-r-e-n-e M-i-d-d-l...' Adrian recoils backwards and then hastily retreats towards the gate. On reaching the gate, he attempts to compose himself by taking several deep breaths. Acutely aware that this is the only place that could yield any clues to his as of yet unexplained association with Charles Middleworth, he intrepidly approaches the ground floor front window to his right and looks inside. The room is congested with an abundance of settees, chairs, coffee tables and a number of china Prince Charles spaniels, of nearly knee height. On the wall are several water paintings, one of which depicts a meadow and a windmill.

To the right side of the house is a small gate, bolted shut with a chain and a large padlock. Behind the gate is a path, hemmed in somewhat by the neighbouring property. Clutching the umbrella and pizza menus in one hand, Adrian clambers over the gate and then proceeds gingerly down the path.

The back garden consists of a minute and perfectly manicured lawn, surrounded by a high wall. There is a small patio that leads up to the back door; it is covered with flower pots, in a variety of sizes. Crouching down, Adrian approaches the ground floor window closest to him. Once satisfied that there is no one inside, he peers in. It is the house's kitchen, in the middle of which is a rectangular table surrounded by four wooden chairs, a fridge, a washing machine and an oven.

Two cautious steps bring him to the patio. Another step and he is alongside a window. Looking through the window, the first object that catches his attention is a small wooden cuckoo house hanging from the far wall. The clock has a circular maroon face with gold dials and a red painted roof. At one end of the room is a small television, at the other a desk, covered in piles of paper and books. To its right is a table, on top of which are three photographs. Adrian's attentions fall on the first, a framed picture of a portly curly haired lady, one arm draped affectionately over a black Labrador dog. The second is of two boys in school uniforms smiling broadly, one of the boy's is holding a football.

As Adrian's attentions fall on the final photograph, he stands transfixed, mouth agape in horror. The photograph is of a man bearing a nonchalant expression. He is wearing a tan suit and has flaxen thinning hair. In every facet, he is identical to the man that has appeared nightly during Adrian's dreams, unmistakable as Charles Middleworth.

Turning in horror, Adrian runs from the garden. Attempting to hurdle the gate at the top of the path, he trips and falls to the ground, causing the Vincent & Ernst umbrella and pizza menus to fall from his grasp.

Not once during the flight down Newgate Road does he consider returning for the umbrella, despite the downpour that has just begun. His only desire is to escape from the house, the street and the city, that had been Middleworth's earthly domain.

The return train journey is spent fearful and confused, huddled in a seat at the back of carriage seven, in rain-saturated clothes. Departing the train at Worksop station, Adrian walks dejectedly out of the station and into the car park. The front passenger window of the Lexus LS 600h has been smashed and the Alpine stereo is missing. Unlocking the door, Adrian uses the car manual to sweep the pieces of glass from the leather seat. Driving home in the slow lane, twenty miles an hour below the speed limit, the fateful incidents from the day plague his mind, as wind and drizzle are driven against his exposed head.

On arriving at the house, Adrian proceeds directly to the cellar, where he grabs two bottles of red wine. These are not selected by vintage, grape or even nationality, but merely by their close proximity to the cellar entrance. Traipsing disconsolately upstairs to his bedroom, he slams the door behind him and locks it.

Collapsed on the Miracoil bed with spring system, Adrian cuts a morose figure, as he stares bleakly at the wall in front of him, whilst taking swigs of wine directly from the bottle. The bottle is finished in a matter of minutes. Shortly after reaching the midway point of the second bottle, Adrian's eyelids begin to flicker and within seconds he is unconscious.

Adrian is awakened by piercing screams. He sits bolt upright, squinting from the effects of the sunlight pervading the room through the open curtains. As a torrent of frenzied pounds rain down upon the bedroom door, panic engulfs his intoxicated beating brain, for he is fearful that the multitudes, along with Charles Middleworth have arrived and that his only defence lies in the fragile wooden structure now under assault.

A short while later he becomes aware that a hysterical female voice is screaming his name, over and over again. At the very moment the calling of his name degenerates into a tirade of Russian profanity, he realises that it belongs to Natalia. There is marginal relief that it is only his sister in-law. Assuming that the cause for her consternation must be the damage to the car, Adrian shouts at her to go away and then seeks refuge beneath his duvet. Several minutes later, Benedict approaches the bedroom door, bangs on it once with his clenched fist and then demands prompt payment for the replacement of the Lexus's window and stereo system. A silent Adrian slides his American Express gold card under the door, which seemingly has the effect of appeasing Benedict, who departs.

Now left to his own devices, Adrian is able to reflect upon yesterday's events, culminating in the photograph of Charles Middleworth. So acute is his anxiety over the otherworldly association with Middleworth that he notices neither the dull throb emanating from his head, courtesy of last night's wine nor the aching from his empty stomach, a result of having not eaten in over twenty hours. Collapsed upon the bed, exhausted, sullen and listless; his immense intellect, capable of the most detailed of scientific rumination, impractical for the current purpose of comprehending the incomprehensible. The only theory that occurs to Adrian, as to his unwilling association with the deceased Middleworth, is such a preposterously irrational, absurd and problematic notion that whenever it appears in his mind, he refuses steadfastly to deliberate upon it further.

Early that evening the Nokia beeps twice, signifying the arrival of a text message. Adrian looks at it glumly. It is from Benedict and reads, 'card outside door: rspnd ASAP.'

Adrian types 'THX' and presses send. He is surprised that Benedict had been so silent that he had not heard him approach the door, but is less so by the fact that despite being in the house he has chosen to text. Putting it down to the fact that it is typical of his brother to retreat to the solace of technology during personal trysts, Adrian approaches the bedroom door and opens it. The credit card is resting on top of a pizza box, a two litre bottle of Coca Cola by its side. Locking the door behind him, Adrian opens the box and is met by the sight of an eighteen inch pepperoni pizza. Recalling the image of the pepperoni pizza, masquerading as Mars, from the Planet Pizza menus the previous day; Adrian, in no mood to appreciate irony, closes the lid. He unscrews the top from the Coca Cola bottle and takes several large gulps. In his ravenous state however, he is unable to ignore the rich aroma of melted cheese and pepperoni for long and is soon opening the lid again. He devours the pizza in its entirety, advertised on the menu as being for four to five people.

Lying back on the bed, his head cushioned on the Microfibre pillow from ExtraComfort, the thought that had bothered him intermittently through the day appears before him. Now feeling marginally more lucid following the over indulgence that had been dinner, he allows for the first time the thought to linger, even though it continues to seem an utterly ridiculous and unscientific trail of thought. A short while later Adrian says 'reincarnated,' in a rather meek and hesitant fashion; a word that he is fairly certain he has never previously uttered in his life.

The more he dwells upon it, the more it seems that it is as if he, Adrian Raven was Charles Middleworth in a previous existence. A simple diagram appears in Adrian's mind, it looks like this:

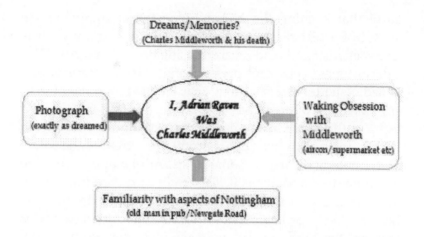

There is no sense of a sensational discovery of self, as often purported by individuals claiming to have been reincarnations of former selves. Quite the contrary, Adrian dearly wishes he had not reached this frightful conclusion and hopes that somewhere there is an algorithm that can refute this theory; one that is so entirely contrary to his own scientific world view.

Nine

It is mid-afternoon and the sky is an endless expanse of blue, broken only by a few small fluffy clouds of the cumulous variety. A sky lark is singing jubilantly above the trees, beating its wings frenetically as it does so. Chaffinches, robins and blue tits are energetically pecking at the nuts in the bird feeder that hangs from a wooden post at the edge of the lawn.

A large grey squirrel emerges and begins to climb up the wooden post, its nails scratching against the wood, as it scrambles upwards eyeing the nuts greedily with large dark eyes. The birds tweet loudly in alarm and scatter in all directions. On reaching the top of the post, the squirrel stretches out, clasps the feeder with its front paws and shakes it vigorously, attempting unsuccessfully to dislodge it from the pole. Despite witnessing this rather remarkable spectacle of nature from the teak bench on the veranda, Adrian does not appear the least bit interested. He sits despondently, a can of super-strength cider in one hand, his mind once more mulling over the recent events that culminated in the photograph of Charles Middleworth in Nottingham and his increasing obsession with the notion that he is, in fact, Charles Middleworth reincarnated.

One might assume that on such a fine day as this, the area's other residents would be revelling in their idyllic rural setting. However this is not the case, for at this very moment, merely five miles away, an irritable and ill-tempered Theodore is pacing in circles around the courtyard of Ramsbottam Hall. The nightmares, which continue to be the bane of Theodore's nocturnal hours, are one reason for his current disposition, but there are also others. Financial issues brought about in no small part by overspending, in addition to the potential threat of legal action over purported unethical business practices, in the construction of a condominium in southern Spain the previous year, are also cause for concern.

Clasped in Theodore's left hand is a loaded shotgun. The reason for the weapon's presence is the African collared doves that drift continuously between the adjoining meadows and Ramsbottam Hall's roof. Relations with the doves, which are owned by Theodore and Anastasia's neighbours, the McGlinstals, and are supposed to reside in and around their large corrugated roofed shed, had in the past always been cordial. In recent times however their numbers had increased exponentially, resulting in the hall's steeply pitched roof and decorative chimney pots being covered in droppings. Every few weeks Anastasia would inform Theodore that it was to be cleaned. At which time he would contact two minions from the local village, who would appear with an extending ladder and scrub it clean for a fee of forty pounds. As a cost cutting exercise, Theodore has made the decision to rectify the problem himself, permanently.

Looking upwards Theodore sees one of the delicate, pale greyish brown dove's drifting towards the roof to his left. Raising the gun he swings at the dove, fires and misses. He swears loudly. A second dove is approaching the roof, Theodore seeing it swings the gun again and fires. This time the pellets find their mark. The dove flaps desperately in the air, hits the wall of the house and falls dead at Theodore's feet. He punches the air triumphantly with his left hand and laughs aloud. Looking down at the dead bird, the decision is made that the cost cutting exercise will not extend to eating pigeons. Theodore places the shotgun on the white carrara marble topped courtyard table, bends down, picks up the dead dove with his right hand and hurls it with all his strength. It sails through the air and lands in the rhododendron bush at the top of the bank, nearly twenty metres away. The BlackBerry is vibrating in the pocket of Theodore's flannel trousers. Taking the phone out, he checks the screen for the identity of the caller, presses the accept button, raises it to his ear and says, 'afternoon Benedict.'

Having grown tired of staring sullenly out at the lawn, Adrian scrunches up the now empty can of cider and makes his way back into the house. Entering the study, he drops the can into the bin and collapses into Colin's chair. Benedict enters the room. He is conversing on his mobile telephone. 'Yeah sure I'll give it some thought,' says Benedict, who on noticing Adrian adds, 'let's catch up tomorrow or the next day, bye Theodore.' Benedict hangs up the phone and places it on the desk. Adrian, who has not set eyes on his brother since the incident with the car, apologises for the damage. Benedict reaches into the back pocket of his trousers and removes a small headed piece of paper. It is the quote from the local garage for the replacement of the window. He passes it to Adrian, who takes it and puts it in his pocket.

'Quest for Modernity?' suggests Benedict a short while later, breaking the awkward silence.

'Yes why not,' replies Adrian unenthusiastically. As they wait for the game to load, Adrian wonders if his brother has forgiven him or is merely keen to resume the saved two player campaign. He suspects the latter.

They proceed with making improvements to their realm in silence; irrigating, farming, hoarding supplies, ordering more weaponry from the blacksmith's and excavating a new quarry. They have been playing for a little over half an hour when Benedict exclaims, 'here they come.'

The very next moment, a horde of heavily armed Barbarians, some of whom are mounted on woolly mammoths and sabre tooth tigers, swarm out of the forest. Benedict watches in dismay as the horde surge unhindered through the non-existent defences on Adrian's side of the screen. He screams

'Counter attack,' but it is to no avail. As fields are trampled upon, dwellings set alight and the population massacred, Benedict notices that the defensive battalion Adrian was supposed to deploy is sitting idly in his toolbar. Within a minute the idyllic realm that had taken hours to painstakingly construct is returned to the Stone Age.

'Adrian you imbecile,' bellows a seething Benedict. 'What were you thinking?'

'I forgot,' replies Adrian abjectly.

'Did General Konev forget to counter attack at the Battle of Kursk,' rants Benedict. 'Or for that matter Ferdinand Foch. Did he forget about his counter offensive at The Second Battle of The Marne?' Adrian offers no reply. Benedict taking this as an invitation to continue says, 'what's the matter with you anyway? First the car and now hours of meticulous kingdom planning laid to waste.'

Adrian takes a can of super-strength cider from the side pocket of his beige safari jacket, opens it, takes a gulp and then looking pensively in his brother's direction says, 'well err it is difficult to explain.'

'Take your time Adrian,' replies Benedict in a sarcastic tone. 'I've got all day, it's not like I can go anywhere with no car.'

'If you'd phoned Auto Glass ...'

'Not now,' interrupts Benedict angrily. Pointing at the can in Adrian's hand he says, 'isn't that the drink of choice for homeless people?'

'I found it in the cellar,' replies Adrian defensively, looking uneasily around the room as he does so. Some seconds later he says, 'Benedict.'

'Yes.'

'I think err that there's a possibility...'

'A possibility of what?'

'That err, I might be.' Adrian pauses and then adds in a very quiet voice, 'reincarnated.'

'Excuse me,' replies Benedict, quite certain that he has heard his brother incorrectly.

'Reincarnated,' repeats Adrian in a slightly louder voice. Benedict, leaning forward in Colin's chair whilst at the same time looking angrily at Adrian says, 'this is no time for jokes.'

'It's not a joke,' replies Adrian, who then begins to explain why he is beginning to suspect that he is in fact reincarnated. Benedict staring at his brother bewilderedly is quite unable to respond, as he realises to his absolute horror that he is being serious. Coming to his senses at the moment Adrian has completed his description of the dreams, Benedict points accusingly at him with the index finger of his right hand and says, 'listen,' in a stern tone. 'Just because I attended some yoga classes, an activity that admittedly has elements of Eastern mysticism, does not mean that I am prepared to entertain retarded rhetoric of this nature.'

Standing up, Benedict grabs his mobile and wallet from the desk and then adds in a mocking manner, 'and dare I ask who you were in your previous life?'

'Charles Middleworth,' replies Adrian despondently.

Benedict shaking his head in dismay says, 'not the Charles Middleworth you asked me about in the car on the way to yoga?'

'Yes,' replies Adrian. 'I need to...'

'A word of advice,' interrupts Benedict. 'If you want to claim to be reincarnated, it is best that it's as an Indian slash Oriental saint or mystic type, not some gimp by the name of Charles Middleworth.'

Adrian is about to speak when Benedict says, 'I don't know why you are making this stuff up; I can only assume you find it amusing, but.' Benedict looks wrathfully at his brother before continuing. 'Do not under any circumstances mention this nonsense to father, he's back tomorrow morning.' Benedict is in the process of walking out of the room, when he turns and says, 'Theodore's about to be in touch.'

'Why?'

'The project you agreed to assist on.'

Adrian, who vaguely recollects agreeing to something in the car after yoga says, 'do I have to.'

'Yes, we need to talk about the details later.' Benedict, remembering why he had brought up the subject of Theodore says, 'I can't imagine that Theodore is shall we say the kind of person who umm is well disposed to reincarnation based conversations, so don't mention it.' Pointing at Adrian once more, he says, 'as for Natalia, please I implore you do not broach the subject. Though on second thoughts she'll probably think reincarnation is a perfume,' concludes Benedict, as he turns and departs the study, slamming the door behind him and storming off through the hall.

Recalling the fact that he was meant to update work on an estimated return date, Adrian reaches across the desk, takes the Panasonic KX-TG 8223 hands free phone from its stand and dials the number for Vincent & Ernst. The conversation with Ethel is an awkward one, in which he concedes that it is unlikely that he will be returning to the office anytime soon. No mention is made of reincarnation. Hanging up the phone, Adrian is surprised that he feels more distressed about Benedict's outburst than his disintegrating actuarial career.

That night for the most part Adrian sleeps remarkably well. Though there are a couple of times when his blissful slumber is infringed upon; first by the voluminous outpourings of the multitude, as he floats through a darkening sky immersed with storm clouds, accompanied by Charles Middleworth. Shortly before dawn images of the fire in the car appear before him, followed sequentially by Middleworth's home in Newgate Road, The King's Arms pub and an office with nondescript brown furniture and fading wallpaper of a similar shade. Papers bound in wide elastic bands are in piles upon its large wooden desk. Bent forward at the desk, analysing what appears to be a manual of some kind, is the unmistakable figure of Charles Middleworth.

Awakening the next morning, Adrian feels nauseous from the numerous super-strength ciders consumed the previous day. Recollecting on the image of the office from the dream, he considers that it resembles a memory. Yawning widely, he checks the time on the Casio Mudman G-9000 and is surprised to see it is 10:13.

Voices become audible, emanating from downstairs. Though they are faint, the sound of his father is instantly recognisable, calm yet authoritative. Adrian has not been looking forward to this moment, as there is no doubt in his mind that Benedict would inform him about his recent introverted behaviour, damage to the car, excessive drinking and the fact that he is taking extended leave from his actuarial duties. Concentrating his senses on the voices of his father and brother, he listens intently. The exact words are difficult to make out, but it is apparent from the tone that it is the usual pleasantries; how was your holiday and the like.

After a minute or so Benedict's voice becomes more earnest, his tone more harried and emotional. It is obvious to Adrian that Benedict is discussing his own recent behaviour. There is some consolation in the fact that he is confident Benedict will not cause his father undue distress by mentioning their reincarnation conversation. For Adrian is quite sure that any mention to his father about his suspicion that he is reincarnated would be most unwise; Colin is rigidly dogmatic in all issues relating to the spiritual.

Rising from the bed, he hurriedly dresses in yesterday's clothes and goes downstairs, passing a scowling Natalia coming the other way, who does not respond to the customary, 'good morning.'

'Good holiday father?' greets Adrian in as eager a tone as he can muster. 'How were the pyramids?'

'Very good indeed, marvellous time,' replies Colin, answering the questions in reverse order.

'Great,' replies Adrian.

'Good to be back,' continues Colin. 'I see the magnolias are out.'

'Indeed they are,' concurs Benedict. 'Let me take your bags upstairs.'

With this he gives Adrian a scowl that is almost as vindictive as Natalia's and then departs, struggling with both the large suitcase and a smaller though otherwise identical one from Samsonite's Cubelite range.

As Benedict disappears from view, Colin remarks sombrely, 'Benedict has informed me of some concerning developments, do you wish to elaborate?'

Adrian quite unsure as to how to elaborate remains silent.

'Unless I'm much mistaken you have been drinking,' continues Colin, looking with disdain at his son's bedraggled appearance, paying particular attention to the bright orange Quest for Modernity: The Beginning T-shirt, complete with several large and odorous super-strength cider stains across its front. 'In fact,' adds Colin, 'you look about as hygienic as a Cairo street urchin.'

'I had a few drinks,' replies Adrian apologetically.

'I trust this drinking is not connected to the damage to Benedict's Lexus.' Adrian assures his father that it is not. Colin proceeds to make enquiries about Benedict's assertions that Adrian has spent entire days in his room, in addition to his impromptu break from work, concluding with the comment, 'I must say this is most unlike you.'

'Sorry father, it has been err, a tumultuous time of late.'

'No need for an apology,' says Colin. 'We are concerned that's all.'

They retreat to the kitchen; Colin broaches the subject again uncertainly, emotional matters never having been his forte.

'Life is beset with unexpected issues, your dear mother departing us being a prime example.'

'Of course but all will be resolved,' responds Adrian unconvincingly.

'Evidently it would be beneficial for you to speak to someone external to the family about these matters,' continues Colin. 'Benedict and I are too close.' Colin stops at this juncture in obvious discomfort, before continuing hurriedly to get the necessary information relayed as quickly as possible. 'Mrs Higgins mentioned in passing a man the other day who lives locally and is quite eminent in his field, leave it with me.'

Adrian, unenthused about the prospect, moans audibly and looks down at the floor gloomily, quite unsure how to mount a protest against his father's proposition. Colin, changing the subject remarks, 'the pyramids were incredible. Take the Great Pyramid of Khufu for instance; it has a volume of approximately two point six million cubic metres and each block of stone weighs an average of two point five tonnes, truly remarkable. But I suppose you know all about the pyramids?'

Adrian does not respond and Colin is not even sure whether he has been listening. This he finds disturbing, as usually the subject would stimulate his son's interest immediately.

Colin breaking the silence says, 'tea?'

'Yes please,' replies Adrian.

It dawns on Colin as he walks through to the kitchen that he is very grateful for tea, as the offer of it can break even the most uncomfortable of situations.

Later that morning, Adrian now showered, shaved and wearing a freshly pressed white cotton shirt is sitting on the veranda, the Presario laptop on the teak bench in front of him. He is about to check his email inbox for the first time in nearly four days. This is the longest period he has gone without checking his email since opening his first email account, nearly seventeen years ago. For with the recent turmoil, checking emails, a habit that had been as routine as waking in the morning, had been forgotten.

There are fifty-three unread emails in the inbox. For the most part these consist of junk emails; adverts for Viagra, the promise of being able to add two inches to your manhood and the like; all of which are swiftly deleted. This leaves only two emails, one from Theodore and another from Franklin. Deciding to read the one from Franklin first; Adrian clicks on the message, it appears as follows:

....

Tues, April 31, 2011 at 9:07 AM, Franklin Meager <meagerfranklin@gmail.com> wrote:

Subject: Hiya

Hi mate,

How are you? Good seeing you the other day! I'm back in Hampshire, staying with Uncle Nestor for the foreseeable future. Remember him? That's right, the day we exploded those Leipzig condensers in his garage with that corrosive liquid. Ha ha thought you might! Late notice I know but there's a meeting about the meaning of life, hosted by the

Spiritual Science Foundation at Foley Meeting Hall (adjacent to church) next Thursday night, Start: 19:30, fancy it?

P.S. I've scraped together a few hundred quid to put towards the outstanding funeral bill. Maybe you can collect it at the event.
Love and Peace

Franklin
....

Adrian types a measured response.

....

Subject: Hiya
Dear Franklin,
I remember your uncle Nestor well and the incident. Though if I my memory does not deceive me, the condenser had an internal double spiral and therefore must have been a Dimroth, not a Leipzig.

See you at the event next Thursday.

Best regards

Adrian
....

Looking up from the screen, he considers the pivotal role Franklin has played in the Charles Middleworth saga, recognising that it was he who had supplied the information, which had led to the visit to Nottingham. Adrian wonders whether he might actually be better off if he had never contacted Franklin in the first place and concludes that he most probably would. After some minutes of pensive reflection, Adrian turns his attention back to the inbox and reluctantly opens the email from Theodore.

....

Wed, May 1, 2011 at 8:43 AM, Theodore Miller <millertheo@millerstranquiloestates.com> wrote:
Hi Adrian,
Benedict informs me you're keen to be involved in Tranquilo, that's great news, really looking forward to working with you. Here's some more info about this amazing opportunity, you're going to love it.
As you're aware I've got this incredibly successful property business based here and in Spain, you've probably come across us.

Miller Tranquilo Estates:

The overseas location of your dreams can be a reality today with Tranquilo Estates. The warm Mediterranean breeze, the lush green valleys of secluded Southern Spain conveniently located only fifty-seven minutes from Marbella airport. Choose from a wide selection of contemporary stylish properties from two bedroom apartments to five bedroom villas. First class facilities, including an eighteen-hole golf course in conjunction with Vince McGrath, (Tiger Classic winner 2009, European Super Cup runner up 2007), spa and a Michelin star restaurant. Become a part of the Tranquilo family today and relax with our professional service: Integritas, Caritas, Lucrum.
Tel: 0845 272 9999
(check out the attached photos and my website) - www.millerstranquiloestates.eu
Like the Latin motto? It was my idea! Let's meet soon.
Regards
Theodore Raven, B.A.
CEO & Founder Miller Estates

Moneygate Enterprise Magazine's Property Developer of the Year Award - 2007 & 2008
....

Adrian, rubbing his weary eyes with the palms of his hands, wishes he had not agreed to be of assistance on the project. He is also suspicious that this assistance is going to entail investing money. On signing out of the email account, Adrian forgets Theodore's correspondence immediately and is consumed once more with his ongoing obsession over Charles Middleworth.

Unanswered questions relating to the subject pester Adrian unrelentingly. He murmurs each one aloud as it comes to mind. 'What other possible explanation is there for my association with Charles Middleworth? Why is this happening now? When will everything return to normal? Are there other people out there, who suspect that they might be reincarnated?'

Holding his head in his hands, Adrian emits a doleful groan. He then stands up, goes inside and heads down to the cellar in search of a can of super-strength cider.

Ten

It is Tuesday afternoon. Adrian is cycling to Falgate, for an appointment with the expert Mrs Higgins had mentioned in passing to his father. Though apprehensive about the forthcoming appointment, Adrian is enjoying the journey. There is a freedom in the activity of cycling, which combined with the idyllic rural setting and fresh air of a fine, if rather blustery day, makes for an altogether agreeable experience. The bicycle is a Pashley Roadster Sovereign, a low maintenance bicycle with alloy hub brakes, front and rear. It belongs to Benedict, who much to Adrian's surprise had agreed to lend it to him.

In recent years Adrian has been vehemently opposed to road cycling, lecturing all those who cared to listen on the superiority of driving. The main thrust of the argument was always safety. Specifically cycling's unfavourable ratio of KSI (killed or seriously injured) when compared with driving. At this moment in time however the abundance of statistics he had memorised on the subject could not be further from his mind, for with his newfound fear of driving, cycling is proving an appealing alternative and at any rate he is wearing a cycling helmet, in addition to knee and elbow pads.

Shortly after passing Tatchin Junction, Adrian mounts the pavement, pulls to a halt and dismounts the bicycle. Checking the time on the G-9000 Casio Mudman, he is satisfied that the distance, speed and time calculation he had formulated prior to departure, has proven to be fairly accurate. At this juncture two distance, speed and time triangles appear in his mind.

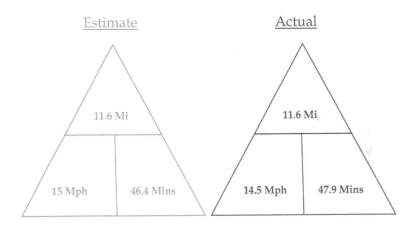

Five minutes and nine seconds later, Adrian is sitting on a Safco superior zero gravity chair, complete with lumbar, lower back supports and seat cushion. The chair is in fact virtually identical to his own, only it is bright green as opposed to black. In the middle of the room are two large couches of the same shade of green.

The door opens and a man enters. 'Adrian, wonderful to meet you, my name's Sri,' greets the man, as he approaches Adrian, clasps his hand with both of his and shakes it warmly. Sri is around fifty or so, approximately six foot tall, of slender build, with long grey hair, which hangs down in thin strands nearly to his waist. He is clad in loose fitting cotton garments, complete with a shirt depicting brightly coloured flowers.

'How do you do,' replies Adrian sombrely.

Sri appears to Adrian to be remarkably similar in appearance to the free loving, LSD consuming hippies of the nineteen-sixties he had seen on television. He wonders exactly what kind of 'expert' Sri is, for his appearance is in stark contrast to anyone he has ever previously come across in a professional capacity. Sitting down on one of the couches Sri asks, 'Adrian, what brings you here today?' in an enthusiastic manner. Adrian however is not listening and is instead pondering how Mrs Higgins, the very embodiment of conservative middle England, could have spoken so highly of this man, who appears to be so diametrically opposed to her own self.

'And what brings you here today, Adrian?' repeats Sri, without even a hint of annoyance at not being answered the first time.

Adrian considers the question momentarily and then replies,

'My father suggested it would be a good idea.'

'Would you like some tea Adrian?'

'Yes please,' responds Adrian, somewhat reassured by this familiar question. Reaching forward, Sri proceeds to pour tea from a small ceramic tea pot that is on the glass table between the two of them. Adrian's reassurance dissipates instantaneously on viewing the tea, as it is nothing like what he was expecting; the liquid a murky green that he assumes would not benefit from the addition of milk and/or sugar. Sri observing Adrian's surprise says, 'relax Adrian, you'll like it.'

Adrian considers it rather peculiar that Sri has stated his name every time that he has addressed him.

'What are your interests Adrian?' enquires Sri.

'I have multiple interests, including but not limited to, science, statistics, photography and classical architecture.'

Sri passing a small ceramic cup to Adrian asks, 'and do you use these interests in your working life Adrian?'

'I am an actuary.'

'A fascinating profession,' responds Sri.

Adrian taking a tentative sip from the cup is surprised that the tea is actually remarkably pleasant and concludes that despite the warmth of the liquid, it has a soothing quality.

The room is silent now and Adrian assumes that Sri is waiting for him to divulge his issues. Prior to departing the house for the meeting, Adrian had made the decision that his best approach lay in not disclosing any information relating to Charles Middleworth. Instead his plan had been to explain that his issues were of the typical work related stress slash middle age crisis variety. However Adrian now decides on a complete volte face, as there is a sudden and overwhelming compulsion to explain the actual unfortunate reality of the situation. He considers requesting a confidentiality form to sign but thinks better of it and begins to speak. 'It started with dreams, well, err, nightmares would be a more apt description. The nightmares commenced with me floating in the sky, when I became aware of this inane wailing sound,' explains Adrian. 'Below me, difficult to quantify exactly how far below, but I would estimate approximately nought point six to nought point eight miles was this mass of people. I appreciate this must sound ridiculous.'

'Far from it Adrian,' replies Sri. 'Dreams are an integral part of our existence.'

Adrian takes a sip of tea and then finishes the outlining of the dreams, omitting nothing. In chronological order he goes on to describe his increasing obsession with Charles Middleworth, the daytime auditory hallucinations, the information from the archives, the Alpha course, the fire, and finally Nottingham. This information relayed in a hurried, energetic manner, again not a single detail is emitted. Adrian is breathless on finishing and reclines back in the seat, surprised at the palpable sense of relief. Looking upwards, he notices a large Swatch wall clock that had previously escaped his attention. It is in the shape of a watch, only much larger; its dials are bright yellow and the numbers black.

'More tea?' asks Sri.

'Yes please.'

'You do like it then Adrian?'

'Yes. It has a rather peculiar yet pleasant taste; quite unlike any tea I have previously been acquainted with.'

'Fascinating Adrian,' says Sri. 'You are a remarkable person.'

'Why? Because of my opinion of the tea?'

Sri laughs and then says, 'Adrian, I mean the experiences you have been through recently.'

Adrian is quite surprised that he does not feel overly embarrassed about the information he has just relayed, perhaps he concludes it is because he can sense no malice or sarcasm in Sri, only kindness and understanding.

'And what is your explanation of these events Adrian?' asks Sri.

'Well, it is as if I am, well,' says Adrian, struggling to vocalise the word.

'Please Adrian, it's as if what?' asks Sri in a calm encouraging tone.

Adrian remains silent for several seconds and then blurts out, 'Reincarnated.'

Sri takes another sip from his tea, nods his head and says, 'I agree it does.'

'What do you mean you agree? Reincarnation is nothing more than a concept from the annals of history, that pre-scientific period, nothing more than irrational folly'. Adrian takes another sip from his cup and then adds, 'at least that's what I knew until ten days ago, now I have to confess that I am rather confused.'

'Adrian, today many people embrace the concept of reincarnation in some form or other,' continues Sri in a consoling voice. 'They believe that souls reincarnate again and again, a perpetual cycle of sorts, until a soul reaches perfection and returns to the source. Then...'

'Souls, source,' interrupts Adrian. 'You are not going to tell me you actually believe in this stuff?'

'This is not about me Adrian,' replies Sri, not the least bit defensively. 'It's all connected to karma you see. Are you familiar with the concept?'

'As in a lamb karma?' says Adrian in an attempt at humour. He is in fact vaguely familiar with the concept.

Sri smiles and takes another sip of tea. 'Many belief systems Adrian, acknowledge that there are heavens above and hells below.'

'How about purgatories?'

'What someone may perceive to be purgatory Adrian, to another may seem a level of hell or perhaps even heaven.'

'I doubt the latter,' responds Adrian miserably.

'I can understand you see it that way Adrian, though I've heard and read accounts of people's dreams and visions that you would probably think are far worse places than the one you've just described to me.'

'I see,' replies Adrian. 'So calling it purgatory is in fact a rather accurate description of the place, don't you think?'

'Many people,' continues Sri, 'believe that individual souls are allocated to these worlds, depending on their worldly deeds.'

'So are they suggesting it is a mortal existence in a parallel universe?'

'Yes just that. Once the karma is exhausted, it has been proposed that they return to the earth and the cycle begins once more and...'

Though previously relaxed in Sri's presence, Adrian, now becoming increasingly uncomfortable discussing such concepts with a stranger, decides that this is an opportune moment to leave. 'This is a quite ridiculous conversation,' says Adrian. 'What do I owe you for this, err, consultation?' He is in the process of reaching for his wallet when Sri explains how first time consultations are free of charge and that he would very much like it if Adrian were to stay for the remainder of the session.

After taking several sips of tea, Adrian is marginally calmer and agrees to stay. He apologises for his rudeness and confesses that he is still dearly hoping that somehow, there is a viable rational reason for his association with Charles Middleworth that does not involve reincarnation. Sri nods and says nothing.

'One question,' says Adrian. 'Why now? I mean suddenly this obsession with Charles Middleworth, so late in life?'

'This is for you and you alone to decide,' replies Sri serenely.

'Memories fade with age,' states Adrian. 'They do not gain clarity.'

'Relax and remain calm Adrian. Good times will come again I assure you.'

'I wish I shared your confidence,' responds Adrian drily.

'And Adrian, if I were to make one suggestion, it would be when you leave today, please consider doing some research and believe me you will be surprised that the things we are discussing are not as uncommon as you might think.'

'Really?' ask a surprised Adrian.

'Adrian you're not alone, believe me. I meet many people about a whole range of matters and reincarnation is a subject that has been brought to my attention by the most, umm, let's just say unlikely of people.'

'Are these people you have come across here or in the Hindu Kush?'

'Many right here in Falgate,' says Sri, smiling and pointing at the floor with the index fingers of both hands to further illustrate the point.

A little over fifteen minutes later the appointment draws to a close. As they leave the room, Sri places a reassuring hand on Adrian's shoulder and assures him all will be fine.

'It was special meeting you Adrian, let's meet again.'

'Thank you I will give it some thought.'

Sri hands Adrian an embossed business card, decorated with swirling colours. Adrian wonders whether the swirls represent the circle of life. The lettering on the card is in a font that Adrian is unsure is Calibri or Corbel. Momentarily he considers asking Sri but decides against it. Instead he bids farewell and exits the building. As Adrian retraces his steps to the bicycle, he considers that it was quite the most bizarre meeting stroke consultation he has ever attended; but concludes that he is both relieved and grateful for having been given this opportunity to discuss his problems.

Adrian is still in deep thought as he cycles out onto Tatchin Junction. The sound of a car's horn brings him to his senses and he brakes only just in time to avoid the oncoming vehicle. Returning hastily to the pavement, Adrian realises the lights are red and is relieved that he has avoided becoming another KPSI statistic; potentially one residing in purgatory, waiting for karma issues to be resolved. The thought causes him to shudder. Having successfully crossed Tatchin Junction after the lights had turned green; Adrian makes the decision to stop for a drink at The Tatchin Railroad Arms, convincing himself that the most dangerous part of the journey has been completed. Sitting deep in its darkened interior, Adrian takes gulps from a pint of Falgate Ale, whilst attempting to analyse the extraordinary discussion with Sri.

16:10 - Millonarios Resort, Costa Adeje, Tenerife - 'Jesus what's wrong with this bloody thing,' complains a sleep deprived, nocturnal vision- ridden Theodore under his breath, as he hits the enter button on the iMac keyboard for the fourth time in as many seconds. The browser fails to respond and the page remains blank. He is disgusted that a one thousand euro a night resort, in such close proximity to Western Europe does not have an adequate telecommunications network. Theodore's mood is further exasperated by a smiling uninvited staff member with sallow features and large protruding teeth sitting in the wicker chair next to him, seemingly there for no other reason than to annoy. Still the page does not load.

'You like England, it good place?' enquires the staff member.

'It's not bad,' says Theodore, who then adds, 'the internet, what is the problem with it? I assume it's the server.'

'It fine it come soon. I want visit England.'

'You wouldn't get past quarantine.'

'Qu-ran-tine, this where you from in England?' replies the staff member eagerly.

'Never mind, when will the internet be working?' asks Theodore, attempting to look directly into the staff member's eyes as he does so. The protruding teeth however force him to avert his gaze abruptly. He considers that they remind him awfully of a beaver he had come across on his gap year, in Yellowstone National Park.

'It come soon you like...'

'Vodka and tonic with ice,' interrupts Theodore.

The staff member leaves. Theodore sighs with relief. The page eventually opens, revealing his email. Theodore clicks on the inbox and miraculously the page is displayed almost instantaneously. He scrolls hurriedly down the list of emails looking for any items that need prompt attention. There is one from Vince McGrath; the professional golfer, who is providing the celebrity endorsement for Tranquilo Estates. Theodore clicks on it. As he waits for the page to load, his hands come together in a praying motion; such is his desperation for the message to contain good news. The email opens:

....

Tues, May 7, 2011 at 14:03 PM, Vince McGrath <VinceMcGrath@golfpro.co.uk> wrote:
Theo,
How are you. busy as hell with the volvic open next week wish me well tough field this year. Still up for tranquilo but can't do marketing video quite yet. sure you understand.
Vince

....

Theodore, acutely aware that a delay in filming the promotional video could have serious consequences, slams his fist with such ferocity on the desk that the keyboard jumps, resulting in his fellow internet beach hut guests looking up from their computers in alarm. To appreciate the potential consequences of Vince's email, it is necessary at this point to outline some of Theodore's contractual obligations.

Note: Two foreign investors have agreed in principle to provide the majority of the funding for the construction of The Tranquilo properties and golf course (Clause 3:i - loan to be repaid within three years, in addition to seventy percent of profits). This is however dependent on the following two conditions being met, prior to funds being made available. i). A top fifty World ranked golfer (as of Feb 18th 2011) to endorse the enterprise. Their role is to include presenting a promotional video, to be filmed onsite. (The investors' advisors had insisted this was necessary to bolster sales and gain competitive advantage, in this time of economic uncertainty). ii). There is a deadline of May 30th. Failure to comply will result in termination of the investors' involvement. (Theodore has attempted to negotiate on clause ii but had been informed that the date was not negotiable, due to complex new tax laws affecting liquid assets, which are being introduced in the investors' current country of domicile on June 4th. This allows five days for the investors to invest in one of two back up plans, should Tranquilo fail to adhere to the above terms).

As Theodore drains the contents of the vodka and tonic from his glass, he is worried that this leaves a very fine timeline. For any further delays brought about by Vince McGrath, logistical issues or bad weather could now prove disastrous. Theodore concludes that it is a shame Vince merely agreed informally to the venture and could not be coerced into signing a contract. However as no other golfer in the forty-nine positions above Vince in the World rankings (as of today Vince's ranking is fifty-seven) could be persuaded to be involved, there was not much that could be done.

Theodore rises and walks out of the internet hut, down the wooden steps and out onto the beach. The sunlight is glittering on the surface of the sea, small cumulus clouds pass slowly by overhead and gentle gusts of warm breeze cause the grains of sand to flutter along the beach. Looking up across the sand, his eyes fall on the rotund thatched hut that serves as the beach bar. Anastasia is leaning against the bar's wooden frame; even from this distance it is evident to Theodore that her recent glum demeanour has been replaced by one of delight. Theodore is about twenty metres from the hut when he notices the bartender draped over the bar whispering into Anastasia's ear. She giggles shrilly and passes one hand provocatively through her long golden tresses. 'Bitch,' snarls Theodore, breaking into a jog, placing one hand on his Panama hat as he does so, to prevent it being unceremoniously ejected from his head.

Eleven

On returning home that evening, Adrian follows Sri's advice and researches some of the concepts that had been discussed during the session. It transpires that Sri had been correct in his assumption that he would be surprised by what he discovers. For having typed 'reincarnation' into the Google search engine, he is astonished when the search yields sixteen point five million results.

The sense of surprise does not end here. That evening Adrian discovers that it is not only Sri openly discussing reincarnation in the local area. For on visiting the website of The Spiritual Science Foundation, the very organisation that Franklin had emailed him about, whose seminar they are to attend in Foley, two days hence; he discovers that they too embrace the notion. He is astounded that Foley, a traditional Conservative voting Church of England town that holds church fetes and jamborees, is also hosting meetings where such an alternative subject is to be discussed. Previously Adrian had been made aware of circulating rumours regarding secret heroin addictions and swinging parties in Hampshire's rural towns, villages and hamlets, but this he deems far more remarkable.

Through the evening and deep into the night, Adrian remains so immersed in his research that the Canon EOS Mark IV, the device that merely a few weeks earlier had heralded a new era, lies forgotten on the bedside table. And the update reminder for Adobe Illustrator, which pops up at regular intervals throughout the evening and needs merely a click of the mouse to download, is ignored.

In the early hours of the morning, Adrian is snoring contentedly on the Miracoil bed with spring system when he finds himself floating through an ominous sky, clustered with dark cumulonimbus storm clouds. As on previous nights, Charles Middleworth appears beside him and far below the multitude is visible, a vast expanse of piteous faces turned upwards towards the heavens, their lamentable wailing increasing audibly as the pair descends towards them.

As the descent continues, the individual faces become visible, uniformly irritable and distressed. As their wailing lament reaches its crescendo, both Middleworth and Adrian turn from them and proceed to soar upwards in unison through the air.

The storm clouds are clearing now and above them the sky is a vast expanse of blue, interspersed with small flocculent cumulous clouds. They ascend yet higher, driven by a light gentle breeze pressing them gently from beneath and are soon drifting effortlessly through a nebula world. On top of each of the clouds that are scattered liberally around them, rests a person, who without exception is in a state of harmonious repose; utterly content in their solitude, astride their downy carriage.

The following morning, Adrian propped up against the bed's headboard, ponders whether the people he had dreamt of on the clouds are souls residing in heaven, or at least a level of it. Reminiscing on the tranquillity of the setting, there is an overwhelming desire that when his current mortal existence reaches its conclusion, he too can join them, astride his own cloud, contentedly floating through the sky. At no point does he consider the laws that govern gravitational pull, even though a framed picture of

Sir Isaac Newton, the man who had first proposed the theory, is hanging on the wall above the bed.

During a break for sandwiches at lunch time, Adrian is in the process of rinsing two large leaves of lettuce under the cold tap in the kitchen when bullet points appear in his mind, outlining some of the reincarnation information that he has stored in his memory during the course of the morning. They look like this.

- In Hinduism the term Samsara refers to the cycle of birth, life, death and reincarnation.
- Theologian and church father Origen (184/5-253/4 A.D.) was officially condemned at The Second Council of Constantinople (553 A.D.), in part due to his teachings on the pre-existence of souls.

It occurs to Adrian as he is slicing the cheddar cheese for insertion in his sandwich that there could come a time in the not so distant future when he will possess as much knowledge about the particulars of reincarnation theory in Buddhism, Hinduism or even Scientology, as he currently has about each and every chemical element in The Periodic Table.

After lunch, Adrian returns to the computer, where he reads the findings of a recent poll on the subject of reincarnation belief in the Western world. The findings contain two pieces of data, which he considers to be particularly pertinent.

1). 28% of Americans express a belief in reincarnation.
2). 29% of Spanish Christians aged between twenty-one and fifty-five accept the premise that souls pre-exist.

Despite the security in finding that he is far from being alone in contemplating reincarnation, Adrian nevertheless is wary of the fact that large numbers, even majorities of people, are not always correct. He is aware of numerous examples of this, the best known perhaps being the popular belief in ancient times that the world was flat.

Later that afternoon, Adrian is snoozing on the veranda when images emerge in his semi-conscious mind, as if they were slides from a PowerPoint presentation. The first to appear is a picture of Newgate Road; the street lined with cars from a bygone era. This is followed by Middleworth's sitting room, a desk at one end and an old television with two large dials at the other. The cavalcade continues with the interior of The Kings Arms and then the office he had dreamt of, complete with filing cabinet. A picture of a girl, her hair in plaits appears in his mind. Even in his dormant state he is aware that she resembles the woman from the photograph with the dog he had seen through the window of five Newgate Road. Awakening, Adrian looks out at the lawn, contemplating that it is as if these are glimpses from a former life.

The Thomas Turner grandfather clock has just begun chiming for four o' clock. Adrian is in his bedroom sitting on his bed, the Compaq Presario laptop on the wooden Ikea laptop table in front of him. He is sifting through some of Google's sixteen point five million websites containing information pertaining to reincarnation when he discovers a bizarre online application, called The Reincarnation Portal. It works like this. The user is required to answer a series of multiple choice questions, all of which are moralistic in nature. On completing the questionnaire you are presented with the species of animal that you will be reincarnated as in your next life, should your present behavioural traits continue. Having not previously contemplated the possibility that people might be reincarnated as animals; he makes a mental note to discuss the theory with Sri.

Intrigued, Adrian surrenders to the frivolity of the exercise and proceeds to answer the questions, with the utmost honesty. He is fairly satisfied on being informed that his next life will be as a walrus, for this is very close to his animal of choice, a dolphin. He is at the point of completing the questionnaire again; this time planning to make small changes to his answers, in the hope of facilitating a dolphin when there is a knock at the door.

'Come in.'

The door opens. 'Afternoon,' greets Benedict, entering the room and hurriedly approaching Adrian, fidgeting impatiently with a pen in his left hand as he does so.

Benedict, who is now peering over Adrian's shoulder at the laptop screen says, 'tomorrow at one, we're um meeting T-h-e-o-d-o-r-e a-t t-h-.' His words petering out, as he begins to comprehend what it is that he is viewing on the laptop's screen. 'What is that?' he asks pointing at the screen accusingly with a trembling finger.

Adrian is at the point of opening his mouth to reply when Benedict holds out the palm of his right hand defensively and says, 'on second thoughts don't tell me.'

Clenching both fists, Benedict begins to pace animatedly in circles on the carpet, the jugular vein in his neck bulging menacingly. Somehow he manages to prevent an outburst and after completing his tenth circle is calm enough to recall the reason that he wished to speak to his brother.

'Tomorrow at one we're meeting Theodore at The Butchers Arms for a bite of lunch and to discuss what needs doing for Tranquilo.'

Adrian shakes his head in an apologetic fashion and says, 'I am quite busy, could we make it …'

'If you've time for that, you're not busy,' interrupts Benedict, pointing at the computer screen in disgust, animosity descending upon him once more.

Adrian enquires as to why both he and Theodore are so keen to have him involved, when he is not a property expert. He also mentions his suspicions about having to invest funds. Benedict explains how both Theodore and he believe that Adrian would be useful for financial forecasting, data presentation for the marketing collateral and advice on insurance related issues. 'It won't take much time,' concludes Benedict.

'So to clarify, I am not expected to provide any funding for the project,' replies Adrian, who for the first time in the conversation has granted Benedict his full attention.

'We need to talk about that.'

'Firstly, I have no intention of providing capital,' states Adrian authoritatively. 'Secondly at no point in time did I agree to do so. Thirdly and perhaps most pertinently, I cannot afford to, due in part to the fact I am currently on unpaid extended leave.'

Benedict taking a more consolatory tone says, 'maybe just a little from what mother left us.'

'Those funds are not intended for mindless speculation,' replies Adrian.

A fervent discussion ensues. By the time it has finished five minutes later, Benedict has persuaded Adrian to at least consider investing a percentage of these funds. Adrian is however unable to comprehend why what he believes must be a trivial sum of money in the context of such a large venture is relevant to the project, other than as an indicator of their enthusiasm to be involved. Benedict departs, leaving Adrian free to return to his reincarnation studies.

(Note: The Truth about the matter (of which Benedict is not aware): Theodore is desperate to get Benedict and Adrian to promise funds for Tranquilo. To understand why, it is necessary to gain a further understanding of the Tranquilo venture.

i). Theodore, as owner and CEO of Tranquilo Estates, is responsible for funding eighty percent of the preliminary project costs. The Tranquilo management team (consisting of two others) have agreed to divide the remaining twenty percent between them. These moneys are for costs incurred prior to the main investors' investment for the actual building work (as explained earlier). These expenses include the photo shoot in Spain, marketing collateral, professional fees, room hire for meetings & deposits for a number of specialised building materials. Theodore is uncertain whether he can fund the entirety of his share. Firstly his meagre share dividends, his only current source of revenue, are not adequate for the purpose. Secondly the investment arm of his private bank is reluctant to allow him to sell more than a small percentage of his remaining shares, unless the moneys are to be utilised to pay off his substantial and ever increasing overdraft.

Theodore has exhausted all other borrowing options on prior ventures (bank, friends, family, Colin, loan companies, remortgage of house and increasing car loan). His only hope in making up any shortfall is to either pawn items of value from his house or get funds from the Raven brothers and then pass them off as his own. He has decided on the latter.

Theodore has been made aware that with Benedict's own current debt problems, his only funds are those his mother had left him; which are co-owned by Adrian. Any investment in Tranquilo will therefore require Adrian's approval.

ii). Theodore is aware that Benedict's expertise in security technology and Adrian's knowledge, at least as purported by his brother in data presentation, financial forecasting and insurance matters, could both be useful and potentially save the Tranquilo team having to pay professionals for these services.

Two hours later, Adrian, still immersed in his research discovers the Dutch mathematical poet, Ed Schenk. Although uncomfortable with the terms mathematics and poetry being used together, he is intrigued by Schenk's work, particularly the formula he has devised for karma. Adrian reads it out aloud a number of times.

'karma = life (n + 1) − life (n)
where n=current life
life (n+1) = life (n) + karma
or
another life = this life + karma
or
this life = another life − karma'

That night, shortly before bed, Adrian is in the bathroom brushing his teeth with the Panasonic Dentacare electric toothbrush. Quite often whilst partaking in this activity, he would marvel at the specifications of this technological innovation in tooth care, such as the fact the electric motor gives twenty-six thousand vibrations per minute. Tonight however he has more pressing concerns, particularly over an issue that he is finding increasingly troubling relating to his connection to Middleworth. For he cannot comprehend why, if he is indeed Charles Middleworth reincarnated, it is only now in his middle age that he is being reminded of his former life. From his research, Adrian is under the impression that it is generally children aged three to five years old, who most commonly recollect on past lives. This he had concluded is unremarkable, as the memories are recent.

By the time the toothbrush has been returned to its recharger stand, Adrian is considering the frightful possibility that the intrusion of Middleworth on his life is some kind of warning, perhaps about an impending return to purgatory. Bending forward, he places both hands on the rim of the ceramic sink, his breathing coming in short agitated gasps as sweat forms on his brow.

That night as Adrian lies in bed waiting for the onset of sleep, the thought continues to trouble him. He speculates that perhaps his choice of the actuarial vocation is not a karma earner and that a new life strategy is required, in order to earn a place up amongst the clouds. The last thought that comes to mind prior to surrendering to a state of repose is that a karma meter would be an invaluable device. He assumes it would look rather like the tracking devices utilised for running, which collate data such as distance run, calories burnt and average speed. At the very moment the specifications for the latest device of this kind appear in his mind, Adrian falls asleep.

At times that night, he finds himself floating through the sky besides Middleworth, the multitude clamouring far below, as the pair descends towards them. As their lament reaches its crescendo they turn and surge upwards in unison through the sky towards the clouds with the contented souls astride of them. Shortly before dawn, Adrian's slumbers are interrupted by a vision of the car fire.

13:17 - The Next Day - Adrian is conducting reincarnation-related research on the internet. Only the location has changed, for with his father administering funerals that day, Adrian has exchanged his bedroom for Colin's office and it is here that he now sits behind the mahogany desk, reading reincarnation-related book reviews on Amazon's website.

The Nokia is vibrating on the desk beside him. Adrian picks it up and seeing that it is Benedict's number he presses the receive call button. Before Adrian has had time to say anything, Benedict screams, 'where the hell are you?'

'At home, why?'

'You're meant to be at The Butchers Arms, remember.' Only now does Adrian remember.

'I've tried to phone you three times, where've you been?' enquires Benedict angrily.

'In the garden.'

'Listen,' continues Benedict. 'I can't attend.'

'Why?'

'My client meeting in Portsmouth has been extended into the afternoon, can't get out of it, I've told Theodore.'

'So let's make it another time when we are both available,' suggests Adrian, reluctant to leave his reincarnation studies.

'Get over there now,' shouts Benedict. 'And I hope you're not playing that animal game.' He then hangs up.

Adrian considers being stubborn and staying where he is, as he does not take kindly to being ordered around by his younger brother. However he decides against this course of action, in part because he still feels guilty about the damage to the Lexus, but also because he acknowledges that it would be rude to inconvenience Theodore. Standing up, he puts the mobile in his pocket, walks out of the study, through the hall and out of the front door, locks it and heads off reluctantly on foot, towards The Butchers Arms.

<u>The Butchers arms 13:19:</u> Theodore takes a gulp from his glass of Chardonnay and glances at the gold Rolex watch that adorns his wrist. 'Jesus he's over eleven minutes late,' he mutters to himself. 'That cock sucker better not have forgotten.'

A few seconds later the BlackBerry beeps twice in his pocket, signifying an incoming text message. It is from Benedict.

....

Hi Theo,
A's on his way. V.sorry he's late.
Sender: Benedict Raven
Message Centre: +447802001331
Sent: 9 May-2011

....

'Impertinent prick and I'm the one doing him the favour,' remarks Theodore, slumping back in his chair and taking another gulp of wine. Theodore cuts a troubled figure, as he fidgets impatiently with a napkin on the table in front of him. For though having only arrived back from holiday that day, he is far from relaxed. The quality of his sleep remains dire and his other troubles are mounting. As he waits for Adrian's arrival, he mulls over his strategy for the forthcoming meeting.

Theodore is determined to instil in Adrian a passion for Tranquilo, in the hope that as and when he requires funds for the venture, Adrian will be as eager to provide them as his brother. He regards it as being most unfair that he is now essentially being forced to grovel for funding from the man who had informed Anastasia about the wallpaper retailer, Marquees. The thought of Marquees causes Theodore to curse under his breath and violently scrunch up the napkin in his hand.

By the time a dishevelled looking Adrian finally enters The Butchers Arms fifteen minutes later, Theodore's cheeks have reddened with rage and his pupils are brown pools of simmering hate. On seeing Adrian the enraged expression dissipates instantaneously. Smiling broadly, he rises to his feet and shouts out, 'Adrian, over here.'

Although relieved at Adrian's arrival, Theodore is somewhat concerned by his chaotic appearance, as he shuffles towards him, unshaven and clad in grey tracksuit bottoms and a yellow t-shirt with the words 'PC World' emblazoned across its front. Glancing nervously around the dining room, he is relieved that there are no acquaintances present; as he would have found it embarrassing to be seen associating with such an individual.

'Good to see you, how are things?' exclaims Theodore, in an enthusiastic tone that betrays none of his annoyance at Adrian's late arrival.

'Not bad,' replies Adrian unenthusiastically.

'Let's order,' says Theodore, thrusting a menu in Adrian's direction with his left hand whilst raising his right hand in the air and clicking his fingers to get the attention of the waitress.

Several minutes later Adrian is sipping on a pint of the local ale, Blue Abbot, while Theodore, glass of Chardonnay in hand, attempts to instil his passion for Tranquilo into Adrian.

'Tranquilo will revolutionise top-end foreign residential ownership in the Mediterranean, first in Southern Spain and within a few short years across The French Riviera and The Algarve,' states Theodore bringing his outstretched hands wider apart to further illustrate the grandeur of this proclamation. 'Imagine this,' continues Theodore taking on a hushed tone. 'Luxurious villas with marble interiors equipped with all the necessities for modern living sitting beside a truly world class eighteen- hole golf course of international tournament standard. Tranquilo is...' He pauses momentarily for added effect and then adds, 'going to change the world.'

Theodore would have continued speaking in hyperbolic terms about the Tranquilo project for quite a while longer, had he not noticed that Adrian appears completely inattentive to what he has been saying and is staring vacantly at the far wall. Falling silent, Theodore turns his head towards the direction in which Adrian is staring to see what momentous event can have caught his attention. However he can see only a wall and a mounted cuckoo clock.

The cuckoo clock appears somewhat familiar to Adrian, from the small wooden cuckoo house with the fading chipped red painted roof to the gold dials and the large circular maroon face. As he continues to analyse the clock, it dawns on him why it is so familiar. For this cuckoo clock is similar, if not identical to the clock he had seen in the sitting room of Charles Middleworth's former home.

'Hello earth calling Adrian,' says Theodore sarcastically.
Adrian does not respond.

'ADRIAN,' shouts a now livid Theodore.
Adrian returning to the proceedings turns his head away from the clock and says, 'yes,' in a rather bewildered and meek voice.

'You haven't been listening to a thing I've said, have you?'

'You were talking about your Spanish property venture; Tranuilo's.'

'T-r-a-n-q-u-i-l-o,' says Theodore very deliberately. 'May I continue?'

'By all means.'

Theodore continues to outline his vision of Tranquilo, explaining in great detail the 'guaranteed' profits that the project will reap. Adrian looking down disconsolately at his place mat pays little attention to what Theodore is saying, for his thoughts have turned once more to Middleworth.

Theodore is outlining the membership options for Tranquilo's golf course when the waitress approaches and places two bowls of steaming moules marinieres on the table. Pointing at his bowl, Theodore says, 'these mussels are quite exquisite.'

'I agree,' concurs Adrian several seconds later having tried one.

'I come here quite often, it's a real hidden gem,' says Theodore. 'Used to be a god-awful place under the previous ownership.'

'Last time I came here was err September, no October of ninety-nine,' remarks Adrian. 'I ordered gammon and chips, relatively simple to cook you would have thought, but it was abhorrent. The gammon was positively saline, as meat would have tasted in the years prior to refrigeration.'

'Quite, I had a similar experience with some lamb,' responds Theodore drily.

As they dine, Theodore continues the Tranquilo eulogy.

On finishing his bowl of moules marinieres, Adrian yawns and then checks the time on the Casio Mudman. He is anxious to return home, for he is keen to resume his reincarnation-related reading. Deciding that the best way to bring the meeting to its conclusion is to find out what contribution is expected of him, he asks, 'why do you want me involved in Tranuilo?'

Theodore clenches his fists so tightly beneath the table that his knuckles whiten; so angered is he that Adrian has mispronounced Tranquilo again, but remembering the importance of keeping Adrian onside, he does not correct him and instead smiles broadly, baring his ivory white teeth.

'Well Adrian I was just about to get to that bit.'

Adrian, now granting Theodore his full attention, listens attentively.

'What with your outstanding résumé and deep understanding of all matters financial, we felt you were the ideal person to present such a fantastic opportunity to.'

'Really,' replies Adrian, suspicious that Theodore is working up to asking him for money and uncertain whether he is aware that Benedict has already mentioned to him that he may be required to part with funds.

'We're family now Adrian, you and I,' continues Theodore, opening his arms in a welcoming gesture.

'Well if being related by internet marriage is family, I suppose we are.'

Theodore laughs aloud but his penetrating stare betrays the fact that he does not find the comment amusing.

'I must warn you that property is not my area of expertise; insurance is more my forte,' remarks Adrian a few seconds later.

'That reminds me,' replies Theodore, reaching into the leather briefcase at his feet and taking out a number of papers. 'I wanted to get your opinion on some insurance matters relating to a project I was involved in last year.'

Adrian looking down despondently at his mat realises that he will not be able to escape the meeting for quite some time. For the next half an hour, Adrian analyses an insurance policy document. Every so often he scribbles a note or offers a comment to Theodore about matters ranging from diversity of risks covered to instances of imprecise semantics. All the while he laments the fact that at this tumultuous time he is engaged once again in insurance related work, for it seems so mundane and inconsequential in the context of recent events.

On returning to the house later that afternoon, Adrian reaches out to grasp the brass door knob when the door opens and his aunt Gertrude appears in the doorway, a wide welcoming smile adorning her matronly face.

'Aunt Gertrude welcome; what a surprise,' exclaims Adrian.

'Is that alcohol I smell?' says Gertrude in a disapproving tone, as she leans forward and kisses Adrian on the cheek.

'Merely the result of a single drink at a business luncheon,' replies Adrian, who then adds, 'I never knew you were visiting; if I had known I would have made sure I was here.'

'I'm on my way back to Plymouth from Heathrow. I've been in Uganda on the annual Diocese mission.'

'How was it?'

'Wonderful. The children were fine, full of happiness and light,' replies Aunt Gertrude as they walk through the hallway and into the sitting room. Benedict from his seat on the sofa asks Adrian how the meeting with Theodore went. Adrian says it was fine and that he will tell him all about it later.

With the visit of Aunt Gertrude; the twin sister of Adrian's departed mother, the house is filled with a vibrancy that has been largely absent since his mother's death. The familiar aroma of homemade shortbread and scones waft out from the kitchen's Aga and the sound of laughter reverberates through the house. Over tea Gertrude holds court as she regales the family with tales from the mission. Colin, Benedict and Adrian listen attentively. Only Natalia appears disinterested. Her mouth is twisted in a malignant scowl every bit as spiteful as that her sister Anastasia had first developed during her cock-sucking period on the wastelands of Nizhny Novgorod. At intervals she yawns widely and glances at her white gold Chanel watch set in diamonds with a mother of pearl dial.

With each bite of the still warm shortbread, memories of his mother come flooding back. For all the exclusive cuisine he has eaten over recent months, Adrian cannot recollect any dish tasting so delicious. Not even the dinners at the TransGlobal in Athens or the moules marinieres at lunch, he concludes. Indeed the experience is so overwhelmingly pleasant as to fortify his very soul. As Adrian sips tea from the delicate porcelain cup and listens to his aunt, the similarity to his mother is evident. The extent of this amazes him, for though his aunt and mother had been twins, they were of the dizygotic variety and had non-identical chromosomes. At this juncture Adrian's mind wanders to the complexities of chromosomes. He abruptly halts this trail of thought, reminding himself that he should enjoy this rare instance of normality, in his now disjointed and fragmented life.

Ramsbottam Hall - That evening, over a dinner of spinach and ricotta ravioli, Theodore observes Anastasia across the Anderson Bradshaw mahogany dining table and is pleasantly surprised that she appears to be quite content, which is rather unusual of late. Her head is tilted slightly to the left and the corners of her mouth are curled upwards to form a smile, as she marvels at the depictions of temples and waterfalls on the Ming Dynasty wallpaper that had been hung the previous day.

Theodore smirks as he reminisces on the many occasions he has told a sullen sulking Anastasia, 'that a smile is free,' aware of the irony that this rare smile, far from being free, has cost over three hundred thousand pounds in wallpaper. Taking a sip from his glass of Cristal champagne, Theodore reclines back in the antique dining chair, confident that his recent financial problems and nightmare-riddled nights will soon be in the past.

That night, Theodore, mildly addled from the wine and champagne drunk that day, initially sleeps peacefully; a dark void filling his sedentary mind. During the early hours of the morning however he becomes restless and his breathing harried. Subconsciously he becomes aware that he is standing barefoot on cold slimy stone, as small droplets of foul smelling stagnant water splash on his uncovered head. A piercing scream fills the darkness, a sound more piteous than anything he has ever heard. Panicking, Theodore scrambles desperately across the slippery stone, attempting to escape the confines of this unholy place, when a single mosquito appears, darting menacingly above his head, buzzing irately; its tiny wings beating with a sinister ferocity. A moment later another mosquito joins the fray, soon followed by more. Within seconds a great swarm of the vile insects are forming a chaotic cloud of incessant, angry and persistent buzzing. Theodore awakens face downwards on the mattress clawing frantically at the bed sheets and mumbling incoherently. The light turns on. Theodore looking upwards sees Anastasia standing over him, bearing an expression of immense displeasure. There is not even the faintest hint of empathy as she points with an outstretched hand towards the darkness of the corridor and screeches, 'out, you sleep other room.' Clasping his pillow forlornly, Theodore leaves the room. Behind him Anastasia mutters obscenities in her native tongue.

Twelve

19:07 - The Next Day - Over the crest of the hill in the distance a cyclist appears, peddling furiously. He is wearing a helmet, in addition to fluorescent green knee and elbow pads. It is clear from the bicycle's alloy pedals, gold-lined mudguards and fold down wheel stand that it is a Pashley Roadster Sovereign. The cyclist is Adrian; he is on his way to The Spiritual Science Foundation Seminar in Foley.

A little over ten minutes later, having reached the centre of Foley, Adrian dismounts the bicycle, takes off his helmet and padlocks the frame to a set of railings. Removing the olive drab Maxpedition Pygmy backpack from his back, he unzips it, takes out a small hand towel, and wipes his face. He then returns the towel to the bag. Having taken several deep breaths to compose himself, with backpack in one hand and cycle helmet in the other Adrian crosses the road and approaches the hall.

The meeting hall is a cold, austere and unwelcoming building that adjoins Foley village church. It is constructed of red brick and terracotta tiles; quite typical of the period in which it was built. Adrian is apprehensive, fearful of what he might discover there. Tentatively he opens the wooden door and enters the hall.

The room is bathed in a luminous light that causes him to squint momentarily. As he surveys the bleached walls and orderly rows of chairs, the distinctive odour of disinfectant pervades his nostrils, giving him the impression that this sterile, sanitised environment resembles a laboratory.

'Hey Adrian, over here.' Franklin is standing by the far wall bearing a rather manic expression, all bulging eyes and agitation.

'Hello Franklin,' greets Adrian.

'We meet again,' says Franklin, gesturing with one hand towards an adolescent stood by his side. 'This is Tempest my nephew.'

'Good evening Tempest, nice to meet you.'

Tempest does not immediately respond. Adrian examines the diminutive youth warily, finding it most disturbing that his complexion is so pallid, as to be positively cadaverous, which contrasts alarmingly with the darkness of his hair and what appears to be mascara around his eyes. Tempest's clothing consists of a black cotton all-in-one outfit with the white outline of a skeleton printed both on the front and back. Even though familiar with a wide variety of apparel, Adrian has never previously come across an outfit of this ilk.

'Hi,' replies Tempest, before cowering behind Franklin, like some ghastly subterranean worm.

Sitting down to await the start of the meeting, Adrian notes that the chairs are of the durable polypropylene with a tubular steel frame variety, they remind him of school. The chemical formula for polypropylene $(C_3H_6)_x$ appears in his mind. As the hall begins to fill with people, their voices reach him as a cacophony of noise, harsh and unintelligible, reminiscent of the wailing multitude. Adrian begins to tremble as perspiration forms on his brow and his breathing accelerates. He wishes he were sitting in his own Safco chair at home, in the relative safety of his own solitude. In an attempt to compose his senses, Adrian closes his eyes and banishes all negative thoughts from his mind, instead focusing on the advice he had received from Sri the previous week that life is in perpetual motion and that better times will come once more. Even though his scientific mind is unable to fully comprehend the notion of life being a cycle, he begins to feel marginally calmer.

Several minutes later a tall woman with angular features and closely cropped hair makes her way to the podium at the front of the hall. Adrian notices that she has large earrings in the shape of stars. The woman now holding a microphone to her mouth says, 'good evening everyone and welcome to The Spiritual Science Foundation. My name is Cornelia and today I will be explaining the truth about life, the question that we all ask ourselves.'
Adrian sitting upright in his durable polypropylene chair listens attentively.

'The Spiritual Science Foundation was formed in nineteen-eighty-one by his Holiness Dr Vishwamber, a renowned clinical consultant hypnotherapist,' continues Cornelia, her thin lips forming a smile.
She then goes on to explain how 'his Holiness' had adopted a range of spiritual remedies that resulted in much improved rates of recovery amongst his patients. Tempest, two chairs to Adrian's right, yawns audibly. Adrian hopes that it will not be too long a wait before Cornelia starts discussing the afterlife, for he is eager to find out if there is anything that he might regard as relevant to his current predicament.

Cornelia proceeds to explain how the 'spiritual remedies' she had mentioned take a number of forms and then presses a button on the white remote control she is clasping in her left hand. A PowerPoint presentation opens on the projector screen behind her. The first slide has three bullet points.

Spiritual Remedies
- Performing certain religious rituals.
- Visiting sacred places.
- Spending time with spiritually enlightened individuals.

It occurs to Adrian that the slide would have had more impact had Cornelia chosen to utilise one of PowerPoint's Add Effect features, such as the entrance or emphasis effect.

It is a little over ten minutes later when Cornelia begins to discuss the concept of reincarnation. Adrian, who had been finding the seminar increasingly tedious and is slumped somewhat in his polypropylene chair, sits upright, granting Cornelia his full attention.

'This cycle of life continues until we either realise God or attain enlightenment or ...,' says Cornelia, pausing briefly before continuing. 'Or until dissolution'.

Some members of the audience gasp. Adrian looks across at Franklin in the adjoining seat, who appears to be immersed in Cornelia's words, his mouth agape. In the next seat down, Tempest stifles yet another yawn and looks at his watch.

Sometime later having outlined the Hindu concept of reincarnation and its place in The Spiritual Science Foundation's belief system, Cornelia presses a button on the remote control and a slide with the title, 'Wilful Action vs. Destiny' appears on the screen.

'How are we able to overcome destiny?' asks Cornelia.

'Well the answer depends on whether the destiny is mild, in which case moderate spiritual practice will suffice. If however the destiny is moderate, the spiritual practice will need to be intense and if severe, the destiny cannot be changed without the grace of a Guru.'

A ripple of discontent spreads through the audience. Tempest laughs aloud and a portly man a few rows behind shouts, 'nonsense.' Adrian though unable to fathom how destinies could be graded in terms of strength continues to listen intently. In spite of the mumblings from the audience, Cornelia continuing in the same authoritative manner says,

'Wilful action is sixty percent and destiny forty percent.' A pie chart appears on the screen to illustrate this.

'She's crazy,' whispers Tempest.

'This is really very confusing,' replies Franklin.

Adrian nods in agreement, for he is becoming increasingly incensed by the dictatorial dogma of Cornelia and The Spiritual Science Foundation.

Towards the end of the seminar Cornelia invites questions from the audience. A number of hands are immediately raised, some of which sway from side to side in an attempt to garner her attention.

The first to be chosen is a middle aged woman wearing tweed at the back of the hall. She asks, 'Jesus died for our sins, how do you Science Foundation people reconcile with this?'

'The Spiritual Science Foundation does not reconcile as you put it with Jesus dying for our sins, if this did indeed occur,' replies Cornelia.

'Absolutely outrageous,' replies the woman, her cheeks now flushed with anger. 'And what place does Jesus hold in your religion exactly?'

'We don't have a particular place for Jesus.'

'Outrageous,' replies the woman again, before getting up and abruptly leaving the hall. A few in attendance giggle nervously.

Next Cornelia points in the direction of a teenage girl. Adrian assumes that she is a Goth, as she is clothed in black.

'This is all too dictatorial, too dogmatic,' states the girl.

'What you should be doing is gently introducing people to these concepts. And this idea that people can't achieve things without the grace of a Guru is ridiculous and just wrong, individuals can achieve anything they want,' continues the girl, pointing her finger accusingly at Cornelia. A number of the audience clap including Adrian, for he agrees with her and considers that the prospect of the individual not being in control of their destiny, extremely concerning.

'What I said was that only in instances of severe destiny would this need to be the case,' replies Cornelia, before pointing to an elderly man towards the back of the hall.

'And you, yes you in the grey shirt.'

'Would I be correct in assuming that this Guru's grace is not free of charge,' says the man.

'Dr Vishwamber and his Gurus do an enormous amount of good free of charge and only collect money for the ongoing survival and growth of the organisation,' responds Cornelia.

'I'll take that as confirmation that it costs,' says the man.

'You can take it anyway you please,' replies Cornelia curtly.

Adrian puts his hand up. However Cornelia ignores him and pointing towards a lady a few rows behind him says in a gentler tone, as if to invite a kinder question, 'and what did you want to ask?'

'I have to say that reducing the mysticism of the divine to percentiles as your organisation has done is particularly unromantic and I might add not likely to bring in many new practitioners.'

'And the question?' asks Cornelia sarcastically.

'No question,' replies the lady.

'And how about you sir,' asks Cornelia pointing at Adrian.

'I am most intrigued to find out how your organisation came up with the sixty-forty ratios for wilful action and destiny.'

'Well what aspect would you like me to discuss?'

'The mathematical formula used.'

'Excuse me?' replies Cornelia now bearing a bemused expression.

'The formula please?' asks Adrian.

Cornelia does not respond and merely looks at Adrian blankly.

'Well can you please write it out for me?'

'I can't. It came from Dr Vishwamber and is therefore divine and does not need explanation.'

'Nonsense,' shouts Franklin.

'And was there anything else you wanted to criticise,' adds Cornelia defensively.

'I was not criticising merely seeking clarification,' replies Adrian. 'But now you mention it the PowerPoint presentation would have worked better had you used some of PowerPoint's enhanced features such as the emphasis and entry effect.'

Laughter erupts from various parts of the hall. Within seconds the meeting is descending into disarray, as Cornelia is harangued by members of the audience blurting out uninvited questions and accusations.

'Might be a good time to get out of here,' says Franklin, standing up and pulling his jacket from the back of his polypropylene chair. Franklin, Adrian and Tempest worm their way through the melée, out of the hall and across the road, in the direction of The Peacock Inn. As he walks, Adrian concludes that attending the seminar has been a counterproductive exercise. He is disappointed that The Spiritual Science Foundation expresses the same dictatorial, intolerant rhetoric that he had so often witnessed in mainstream religion. As he opens the door to the pub, Adrian decides that he will contact Sri tomorrow, for there are many questions that he wishes to ask him.

As the three of them approach the bar Franklin says, 'lest I forget Adrian here's two hundred and fifty quid towards my uncle's outstanding funeral bill.' Franklin hands over a tightly bound bunch of notes before adding, 'I'll get the rest soon, it's just taking me a while to sort out my finances.'

'Thank you,' replies Adrian. 'What is everyone drinking?'

As Adrian waits in the queue to be served, it occurs to him that he would very much like to discuss the Middleworth matter with Franklin, and he would have, had Tempest not been there.

Later that evening a number of Tempest's friends join them, including the Goth girl from the meeting. She congratulates Adrian on his sarcastic comment about the PowerPoint presentation, stating that this was the most amusing part of the evening. Adrian is about to correct her and explain that he had been serious in his suggestion, when he thinks better of it. Over the course of the evening numerous rounds of beer and Green Monk, a cocktail popular with Goths that consists of Benedictine, gin and black Curacao are consumed. At closing time, Adrian now somewhat inebriated is at the point of returning to the Pashley Sovereign when he makes the decision that it would be most unwise to cycle home in his current state; for he is aware that the probability of becoming another KPSI statistic has increased exponentially, both due to his intoxicated state and the fact it is now dark. Instead he makes the decision to collect the bicycle the next day and takes a mini cab.

On occasion as Adrian slept that night he became restless and clawed at his bedclothes, as the multitude clamoured intermittently. Waking, he struggled for breath in short agitated gasps, before wiping the sweat from his brow with the sleeve of his cotton M&S pyjama top. For the most part however he slept peacefully, as the small cumulous clouds with the souls sat astride them drifted past on a gentle breeze.

Shortly after dawn the next morning, Adrian is awakened by small shards of sunlight glinting through a gap in the curtains. Yawning widely, he stretches out to his full length and then lies blinking, his eyes struggling to become accustomed to the light. Recollections of the meeting and the dreams immerse his still barely-conscious mind. Believing that The Spiritual Science Foundation's rhetoric was too severe, it occurs to him, that just as Sri had done, he could introduce people to these concepts in a more relaxed, friendly and open fashion. However he is unsure how this can be achieved, especially as he is far from fully comprehending or even accepting notions such as life cycles and dissolution.

Attempting to rise from the bed, Adrian is defeated by a dull thudding pain emanating from his head, causing him to moan and fall backwards, clutching the source of the pain morosely with both hands. Recalling the large quantity of alcohol consumed the previous night, Adrian seeks solace beneath the eiderdown duvet. Two hours later he struggles out of bed, dons yesterday's clothes and heads downstairs. On entering the kitchen, Adrian is met by the sight of his father and Benedict in deep conversation and is immediately surprised by the earnest, energetic nature of the discussion; unusual for such an early time of the morning.

'It's unbelievable,' says Benedict on seeing his brother enter the room.

'You must have heard,' adds Colin, noticing Adrian's blank expression. Then their voices accost him simultaneously, the voluminous nature of which causes Adrian to step away supporting his head with one hand. With the other he grabs a glass of orange juice and then downs it instantly, as if it were a shot of Green Monk from last night.

'It's awful, such a shock,' says Colin.

'Unprecedented,' adds Benedict.

'What is unprecedented?' asks Adrian meekly.

'The stock market's crashed twenty-seven percent,' states Colin.

'I can't believe you haven't heard, it's a catastrophe,' adds Benedict.

Adrian collapsing onto one of the wooden kitchen chairs does not respond. Feebly he butters a piece of toast from the toast rack, as Benedict and Colin await his reaction; of which none is forthcoming. They stare at each other in disbelief, astounded by his disinterest, having expected a full analysis of the situation, possibly with the aid of graphs and charts. A few minutes later Colin announces he is off to the morgue.

The second he leaves the room, Benedict turning towards Adrian says, 'thanks for persuading me to transfer the stocks mum left us from UK equities. They came off the worse of the lot.'
Adrian takes a bite of toast and murmurs, 'you are welcome.' He then pours himself another glass of orange juice.

Five miles away in Ramsbottam Hall, Theodore had slept fitfully, tormented by nightmares and once more forced to sleep in the room at the end of the corridor by Anastasia. Despite this, he awakens that morning partially refreshed, courtesy of some hours of respite around dawn. Putting on his silk dressing gown, he goes downstairs and collects the morning newspaper from the letter box. Continuing through to the kitchen he greets Anastasia, who is preparing a vile green looking concoction in the blender. He then pours a cup of coffee. Opening the newspaper from the back, Theodore is surprised to see England have won the first Test Match against India in Mumbai. Seconds later his attentions turn to the front page. Theodore stares at the page for quite some time and then slamming his fists on the kitchen table, screams 'fuck' a number of times, his previously tanned face now an ashen white, he sits trembling and fearful.
'What now?' asks an annoyed Anastasia.
'The stock market's collapsed,' replies Theodore abjectly.
'And so?'
'And so we're hanging to the precipice by our fingernails,' responds Theodore, being uncharacteristically metaphorical in this moment of woe.
'We're still buying the Edwardian closet, aren't we?'
'No we're not.'
'But...'

'End of conversation Anastasia. Now go and do something useful like wash your hair,' exclaims Theodore struggling to contain his emotions.

Anastasia leaves the room, muttering angry 'niets' as she goes. Theodore walks through to the dining room, where he sits silently, mourning his loss bitterly and staring sombrely at the Ming Dynasty depictions on the wall of the temples, mountains and rice paddies. Surrounded by the wallpaper, it is to Theodore as if he is buried in a tomb; a final testament to his decadence.

Several minutes later, Theodore closes his eyes and begins to breathe deeply, allowing his lungs to expand to their full capacity, before exhaling gently. Gradually calmness diffuses through him, as his mind forces all negative thought from its confines. By the time the Lavezzi clock with the white aluminium relief begins chiming for ten o' clock, a resolve has replaced his sorrow and a plan is formulating in his mind. Looking upwards Theodore visualises Tranquilo being a success and the rewards it will bring; his destiny.

The door of the dining room opens slightly and Anastasia's slender arm emerges clasping the Bang and Olufsen BeoCom handset.

'Your bank manager Matthew Buckley's on the line.'

'Oh tell him to go fuck himself,' replies Theodore; his nearly restored calmness threatening to desert him at this intrusion.

'Matthew, Theodore says go…'

'No no not literally,' shouts Theodore, grabbing the phone aggressively from Anastasia's grasp and holding it to his ear. 'Hello Matt, how are you?' greets Theodore with as much enthusiasm as he can muster.

'Mr Miller I must get straight to the point, your portfolio,' replies Matthew Buckley.

'It's up shit creek without the proverbial paddle, c'est la vie.'

'It's near worthless. This really is bad timing.'

'Oh really,' replies Theodore sarcastically.

'We already had some serious concerns regarding your finances,' continues Buckley. 'Particularly your overdraft.'

'Do not concern yourselves,' states Theodore authoritatively.

'This paltry sum will be paid back in no time.'

'The sum is far from paltry Mr Miller. Your overdraft and credit card bill combined is....' Matthew Buckley falls silent as he calculates the amount and then exclaims, 'three hundred and ninety-one thousand three hundred and eighty-two pounds and seventy-three pence.'

'I'm aware of this,' says Theodore defensively.

'Mr Miller with no dividends, how exactly are you planning to repay us? Might I remind you that...'

Theodore interrupting him says, 'this is a temporary inconvenience that's all.'

'If you had only spread your portfolio as we advised and not put everything into those UK equities, the damage would have been manageable.'

'Yes thank you Matt,' replies Theodore.

The next few minutes are spent attempting to soothe the concerned Matthew Buckley with promises of redemption. During the course of the conversation Theodore negotiates another three months borrowing time. However the interest rate on the overdraft infuriates Theodore and to make matters worse his credit card is to be frozen with immediate effect. By the time the conversation is complete he has vowed to move to a different private bank, Southall's, reasoning that at Southall's they do not treat valued customers in such a disagreeable manner, host balls at Christmas and have those marvellous centennial umbrellas.

'The Edwardian closet?' interrupts an unseen Anastasia from the other side of the dining room door.

'NOT NOW!' screams Theodore, as the last semblance of calmness abandons him. Anastasia wisely falls silent. She had learnt at a young age on the wastelands of Nizhny

Novgorod that all men, regardless of how easily they might be manipulated, have a breaking point. This had been reached.

Theodore begins to circle the dining room angrily, setting an increasingly frenzied pace. Once more his attentions fall on the wallpaper and its beautiful depictions of seventeenth century Szechuan rural life, viewing with envy the freedom of the snow covered peaks, gushing rivers and temples, so far removed from the stressful constraints of his mortal existence. This unexpected metaphysical turn of thought he finds perturbing. Steadfastly he attempts to concentrate on the reality of his present predicament, as he continues to tread agitatedly in circles.

On each rotation of the room, Theodore's eye catches that of a man sat by the river. He has a long straggly beard and is wearing a decorative robe. Theodore attempts to ignore his constant scrutiny but this proves futile, as each time on passing the door he catches sight of him. It is as if the man from his seat by the river is watching him contemptuously and it serves to crumble his fickle concentration. Theodore notices a myriad of other characters, robed monks, peasants toiling in the fields and helmeted soldiers, each and every one of them with that same Confucian smugness. As his irritable attention flits from one visage to another, he suspects that they have silently yet smugly viewed many suffering individuals through their lives, always aware yet never interfering. A violent anger begins to stir in his suffering heart and on circling the room once more to be met by the arrogant man; he throws a wide-looping right punch at him. Theodore falls to the ground wincing in discomfort, pain resonating through his body; the courtesan's smugness remains unabated.

The pain has the effect of replacing Theodore's other woes and within minutes his breathing is more composed and clarity is clearing the angry mist from his mind. With this calmer condition comes an awareness that his only hope for redemption lies in the success of the forthcoming Tranquilo development. Theodore acknowledges that Tranquilo can now only become a reality if Adrian can be persuaded to provide what will now be the majority of the preliminary expenses for the venture. He finds it most distressing that his salvation now lies with the very man who had told Anastasia about the wallpaper shop Marquees, an incident that has led directly to his current precarious financial state. Lifting himself from the carpet, Theodore looks out through the large bay window and out onto the pebbled drive. A cock pheasant, its plumage iridescent in the morning sunlight is striding imperiously across the pebbles, head held high and clucking loudly.

Thirteen

Having finally recovered from his hangover around midday, Adrian returns to Foley by mini cab and collects the bicycle. After this he cycles the seven kilometres to Timmersham, purchases a bouquet of carnations from the florist on the high street and then makes his way to Timmersham parish church's graveyard, where his mother is buried. Arriving at the grave, Adrian unties the bouquet and arranges the carnations individually around the grave's granite kerb. The arrangement now complete, he takes out a white cotton handkerchief from his pocket and proceeds to polish the lettering on the granite headstone meticulously.

The gravestone's font is Perpetua, designed in the early twentieth century and based on the designs of early engravings; it is both formal and understated. As Adrian continues to polish the medieval style numbers, he acknowledges that his father's choice of Perpetua had been inspired. Adrian's preferred font for the headstone had been Mantinia, a more decorative style developed during the Renaissance. Yet not for the first time he admits to himself that the simplicity and elegant modesty of Perpetua better encapsulates his dear mother's humble and stoical nature.

Sometime later he walks around to the front of the graveyard and sits on the commemorative bench overlooking Timmersham Common. He briefly contemplates attempting to find the location of Charles Middleworth's grave and possibly visiting it, but concludes that this would be rather morbid. A small yellow butterfly flutters past. Adrian recognises it as being a Colias Croceus, and marvels at how it has attained a remarkable transformation from caterpillar to butterfly in such a short period of time. Feeling the Nokia vibrating in his pocket, he takes it out and answers it. 'Good afternoon, Adrian Raven.'

'Hi,' replies the voice. 'How are you?'

'Afternoon Sri, thank you for returning my call,' replies Adrian.

'I am marginally better, difficult to quantify the margin but if I were to, it would be as follows, wi = $α + β1uei + β2ue*i + …$,'

'Adrian please there's no need for this,' interrupts Sri. For the first time in the interactions between the two of them there is a hint of annoyance in his tone.

'All well with you Sri?' asks Adrian changing the subject.

'Fantastic thank you for asking, just off to The Ruhr Valley for a one week hiatus, can't wait.'

'Sounds interesting.'

'It will be fascinating,' replies Sri, who then adds, 'tell me something meaningful Adrian?'

Adrian falls silent for what seems to him like an inordinate amount of time, as he is quite unsure how to answer such an unspecific question. Eventually he responds. 'Yesterday I attended a Spiritual Science Foundation meeting with a friend.'

'That's great Adrian, good to see your getting out and about and engaging with the world,' replies Sri enthusiastically.

'What do you think of The Spiritual Science Foundation?'

'They are what they are Adrian.'

Adrian sitting upright on the bench says, 'Sri that is not an informative answer.'

Sri laughs aloud before responding, 'my role is not to judge Adrian.'

'Their teachings are dogmatic, their theology thoroughly confusing and ...'

Sri starts laughing again before Adrian is able to finish his synopsis.

'Why is that amusing?' asks Adrian.

'Please don't judge the Spiritual Science Foundation or any other organisation for that matter.'

'But....'

'Relax Adrian, they are what they are. You'll find your own way in your own time,' continues Sri in a soothing tone.

'I was thinking of introducing people to the concepts of reincarnation and life cycles in a gentler way, rather like you Sri.'

'That's fantastic Adrian, I congratulate you,' says Sri.

'Please think everything through prior to taking any action.'

'Of course.'

'Look forward to seeing you on my return Adrian. In the interim if you're interested that is, there's this wonderful lady I know called Patricia. I thought you might find it beneficial to speak to her informally on the phone.'

'Sure,' responds Adrian eagerly.

'I went to the liberty of giving her your phone number and she will be in contact. Let's just say she has faced a similar predicament to your dear self. You'll like her, she's very, umm, practical.'

'I will await her call.'

'Please remember it's confidential. Patricia has her everyday existence like everyone else.'

'Of course,' responds Adrian.

'Good luck Adrian, let's catch up when I return,' says Sri, before hanging up.

Later that afternoon on returning to the house, Adrian on opening the front door is met by the sight of the reincarnation-related books, ordered from Amazon days earlier. He hastily removes the packaging, tosses it in the brown leather bin and walks through the hall towards the stairs. Noticing Benedict through the open door of the sitting room, Adrian enters the room. So intently is Benedict studying the papers in his hand that he does not notice his brother. Natalia is slumped in Colin's favourite arm chair painting her nails. She ignores him.

Benedict looks up and seeing Adrian says, 'afternoon Adrian, where have you been?'

'Visiting mother's grave.'

'Have they got round to mowing the grass yet?' enquires Benedict.

'They have indeed,' says Adrian.

Benedict looking at his brother with a focused intensity says, 'We need to talk.'

Natalia stands up, casts a malevolent glance in Adrian's direction and departs the room. Benedict motioning towards the sofa says, 'take a seat.'

'Can we do this later,' says Adrian, keen to delve into his newly-acquired reincarnation-related literature.

'It's urgent,' replies Benedict.

Adrian sighs and sits down on the sofa.

'It's about Tranquilo,' states Benedict.

Adrian sighs again and checks the time on the Casio Mudman.

'To cut a long story short, Theodore's in a bit of a predicament,' says Benedict. 'The stock market collapse has left him without adequate funds for Tranquilo's provisional start up costs...'

'What exactly has this got to do with me?' interrupts Adrian.

Benedict does not reply. Instead he stares wide-eyed at the three books in his brother's hand. His face is now etched with tension, as his cheeks begin to redden. Several seconds later he looks away from the books and returning to the proceedings says, 'I need your permission to invest the funds mother left us.'

Adrian now granting Benedict his full attention says, 'No.' A fervent conversation ensues. Adrian argues that to invest in such a high risk venture would be most unwise. He does though reluctantly agree to attend a Tranquilo meeting with Theodore and the investors in London the following week.

At the conclusion of the conversation Adrian leaves the room and heads upstairs clasping the books in one hand and the remainder of the shortbread that Aunt Gertrude had made in the other. In the solitude of his room Adrian begins to read his new books. The first of which was written by the parents of a boy, who they claim is a World War II pilot reincarnated. Having read the back of the book and the first few pages, Adrian is suspicious about the book's assertions. In part this is due to the potential financial motivations of the parents for inventing such a story and also because they might have implanted these 'memories' in their young son, who has now rather conveniently forgotten them. Nevertheless Adrian reads at a feverish pace, so desperate is he to find any correlations with his own experiences. A short time later he becomes aware that his father is calling him in a harried and impatient tone.

'Adrian, Adrian.'

'I am in my bedroom,' shouts Adrian.

Colin, who is slightly hard of hearing due to a childhood propensity for clay pigeon shooting without ear protectors, does not hear him.

Getting up from the bed and walking out to the corridor, Adrian shouts, 'upstairs father.'

Seconds later Colin appears breathlessly carrying the hands free phone and announces, 'Theodore's on the line.'

'Great,' says Adrian sarcastically, annoyed by Theodore's interruption. He takes the phone from Colin and placing it to his ear says, 'good evening Theodore.'

The Next Day

Lady Pinky and The Trinkets

Anastasia is weaving her way down the lane in the Aston Martin V8 at a leisurely pace. She is travelling to Lady Pinkerton's with some of Theodore's family jewellery. Lady Pinky, as her friends refer to her, runs an antique jewellery business and when Anastasia had phoned her the previous day, she had stated that she might possibly be interested in purchasing some pieces. Theodore was keen to press on Anastasia that under no account was she to appear desperate when she met with Lady Pinky. Anastasia wondered how else she could possibly appear, selling off family heirlooms the day after a stock market collapse.

As the Aston Martin weaves effortlessly down the lane, the image of the Edwardian closet she had been so tantalisingly close to obtaining appears in her mind, in all its finery. The laid rosewood exterior, the exquisite floral inlaid design and the large bevelled mirror, would have reflected Anastasia in all her glory. A ripple of conceited anger radiates through her slender frame, as the image evaporates. Seeing a baby rabbit emerging from the long spring grass and scampering unaware onto the far side of the road, Anastasia turns the V8's vinyl steering wheel abruptly to the right, squashing it flat beneath its wheels. Immediately she feels better and smiles, basking in her reflection in the car mirror.

As she continues the journey, her mind wanders to her childhood, as it often does during solitary moments. She recollects on her meteoric rise from her adolescence spent sucking cocks on the wastelands of Nizhny Novgorod, to the wife of a millionaire socialite. She recalls the dilapidated apartment in the grey stone Soviet era monolith overlooking the industrial wasteland, with the communal bathroom for seventy. Personal space was at a premium in the three roomed flat with five brothers, a sister and an emaciated dancing bear chained to the sink as company. Sometimes in her sleep the images come racing back, the sodden tattered socks are drying on the clothes line draped across the kitchen, the flickering of the black and white television, the framed picture of Lenin, the stainless steel mugs and cutlery rattling loudly as the factory train passed by. Father always drunk and ruddy faced, laughing haughtily at a comedy on the television or berating mother or her siblings with his belt. The distressed bear, its bells decorated in red ribbons, pawing feebly at the door.

Turning right at the stone gargoyles, Anastasia puts the Vantage into first gear and creeps down Templeton Hall's drive very slowly. Aware of the financial benefits the meeting could yield, a steely resolve consumes her. Lady Pinky views Anastasia suspiciously when she explains about no longer needing the jewellery. Being scrutinised by Lady Pinky's piercing eyes, it is to Anastasia as if she is once more bereft of her designer clothes and clad in the garish red and blue shell suit from her youth, worn at the knees from the amount of time spent performing fellatio on the wastelands of Nizhny Novgorod. Half an hour and two cups of Lapsang Souchong tea later; Anastasia is departing the hall, four thousand pounds in cash richer.

The Vulture and the Chablis

Whilst Anastasia is conducting her business with Lady Pinky, Theodore is travelling to the residence of the Vulture in his Range Rover Sport 5 V8, with forty boxes of Chablis from his cellar. An associate from the local golf club, the Vulture, real name Frank Spitz, had acquired his alias in part due to his resemblance to the bird bearing that name. He possesses a thin beak-like nose that protrudes a quite surprising distance from his face, in addition to small dark beady eyes. However the primary reason was because of Spitz's skill at achieving financial success through others' misfortune.

Theodore is apprehensive on arriving at the Vulture's residence. Spitz had given no indication on the telephone that he would necessarily purchase the wine and had merely suggested that Theodore should come over in person to discuss the matter. It is evident to Theodore that he is in a very weak bargaining position and quite at the Vulture's mercy, for both knew there was no one else in the proximity who would take the wine for cash on short notice. All the major companies either gave credit or sent out cheques weeks later. Theodore had already explored these avenues.

The Vulture is waiting outside his residence, already somehow aware of Theodore's imminent arrival.

'Hi Ed good to see you,' greets Theodore cheerfully as he clambers out of the Range Rover.

'Ninety-nine you said it was didn't you,' replies the Vulture, never one for formalities.

'Indeed yes, splendid stuff it is too.'

'Damn shame it's not the eighty-six, as that vintage is currently much in demand,' remarks the Vulture.

'The ninety-nine is savoury and light bodied, fantastic in fact, you've tried it right?'

'No. My palate prefers something more refined,' responds the Vulture drily.

It seems to Theodore that Spitz has never quite so resembled a vulture as he gazes forlornly into his eyes, black pools of nothingness, devoid of even the faintest hint of human emotion. The Vulture does not invite Theodore into the house, preferring to conduct his business outside in the elements.

'Surprising time to sell I must say Theodore.'

Theodore is unsure whether this is a question or a statement. Before he can answer the Vulture continues. 'What with the stock market collapse and all.'

'Just wanted to free up some space in the cellar.'

The Vulture examines him suspiciously. At that moment Spitz junior, a child of three or so, arrives peddling a toy tractor and begins to silently circle Theodore.

'A speculator like you would of course have envisaged the collapse anyhow. After all it was rather obvious wasn't it?'

'Oh yes for sure,' says Theodore.

The Vulture does not reply. Theodore attempts to appear as a bastion of good health as he stands erect, whilst exposing his ivory white teeth. Spitz junior continues to circle Theodore, round and round relentlessly on his little tractor. Theodore views with concern Spitz junior's same bill-like nose and dark, soulless eyes. Adamantly he refuses to portray any weakness as the seconds pass like an eternity.

'Seventy pounds a box cash. That's a total of two thousand eight hundred pounds,' says the Vulture eventually.

'You're not being serious.'

'Deadly.'

'But I was hoping for about one hundred pounds a box.'

'Hope, Theodore, is inconsequential.'

Theodore considers arguing further but is aware that it would be to no avail. Several minutes later he has finished unloading the boxes from the vehicle, all the while watched silently by the two vultures. Throwing the bundle of cash in the glove box he leaves angered, without a customary goodbye. It occurs to him as he pulls out onto the A11 that whilst observing others' ruination at the hands of the Vulture is a most amusing thing, it really is no fun when it is you.

'Seventy pounds a box, it is daylight robbery,' exclaims Theodore to his thoroughly disinterested wife on entering the house. 'How did you get on at Pinky's?'

Anastasia feels only disdain as she hears the desperation in Theodore's voice and she does not answer immediately, taking a peculiar pleasure in her husband's discomfort, as he stands pleading like a dog for good news at the door.

'Well?' asks Theodore again several seconds later.

'Three thousand pounds,' replies Anastasia coldly.

'Good old Pinky.'

'Don't you mean good me?'

'Oh yes, good old Anastasia.'

'Not old just good.'

Theodore is not sure how to respond.

'Again,' demands Anastasia some seconds later.

'Good Anastasia,' replies Theodore obediently.

Anastasia turns abruptly, passes through the hall and up the spiral stairs, disgusted at the frailty now evident in her husband. Frailty is a trait she disgusts above all others. As she ascends the stairs her mind's eye wanders back to her youth and her first memories of the weakness of men. Ageing ragged railway workers on the wastelands, fumbling through frayed pockets in a futile attempt to gather enough change for sexual services.

The relief at receiving this money is short-lived. Theodore remains desperate for news that Benedict will persuade Adrian to provide funds for the Tranquilo project's provisional expenses; the first costs of which are due in a matter of days. Adrian had given no such promises during their telephone conversation the previous day and Theodore had been left infuriated once again by his palpable lack of enthusiasm in the project.

Theodore is in the garden, consumed by an unremitting despondency, punctuated by sporadic violent outbursts. At these times he would drive golf balls with his seven iron from the perfectly manicured lawn, oblivious to the damage it might cause the turf, and take aim at birds' nests, ducks on the stream and squirrels, as they nibbled on nuts high in the garden's trees. It is only after striking a duckling on the stream that some semblance of normality is restored, as if he had somehow transferred his own misery to the now deceased bird.

Sometime later he returns to his desk, his mind a turbulent mass of malignant energy, as he works unrelentingly on the presentation for the Tranquilo meeting in London the following week. Unshaven and wearing a tracksuit, Theodore cuts a very different figure from his usual suave self, as he works frenziedly, steadfastly ignoring the fatigue, courtesy of the nightmare-plagued nights. And so the pattern continues for the next few days. Chaotic nights and days spent organising the forthcoming Tranquilo project; his existence one of lucid disarray.

Fourteen

Over the next few days Adrian remains immersed in his reincarnation studies. At regular intervals he leaves the house and enjoys the serenity of the surrounding countryside; the green hedgerows, the Friesian cows chomping on the lush succulent grass, the immaculate thatched dwellings and the warblers, robins and thrushes, whose song hangs in the air like colour shimmering.

Intermittently during his sleeping hours Adrian finds himself floating through the sky beside Middleworth, as the multitudes become visible far below, their unremitting wailing as voluminous as ever. He would then awaken, his breathing coming in fitful gasps, his heart rate accelerated. At other times a myriad of visions fill his dormant mind; the drab office, the house in Newgate Road and the fire in the car. As dawn approached however Adrian's sleep would become a tranquil dormancy and small cumulous clouds would appear before him. Contented, he would watch them float by, with the souls sat atop of them, relaxed and benign.

Each morning on awaking there was a deep longing to be able to float unheeded through the air atop of one of these clouds. Not once did he reflect on the impossibility of being supported by water vapour. As he lay in bed, Adrian would speculate on how once this life has reached its conclusion, he can avoid the multitudes and achieve attainment amongst the clouds.

It is early evening and Adrian is in the sitting room, immersed in a book by Sathya Sai Baba, the Indian mystic who claimed to be the reincarnation of the revered saint, Sai Baba of Shirdi, when Benedict, having just returned from a day's work in Portsmouth enters the room. For the fifth time in the last two days Benedict accosts his brother with an impassioned plea for him to agree to invest the moneys their mother had left them in the Tranquilo venture. Adrian gets up and leaves the room, heads upstairs to his bedroom, locks the door behind him and continues reading.

An hour later, Adrian is still sitting on his Safco chair reading the book, when the Nokia begins vibrating on the bedside table.

Adrian picks up the phone and answers. 'Good evening, Adrian Raven.'

'It's Patricia Ayew here, I'm Sri's friend.'

'Thank you for phoning,' replies Adrian, who had been eagerly awaiting the call since Sri had first mentioned it.

'Happy to have a chat with you,' says Patricia. 'But please, this is confidential. I've got my everyday life, job etc, and need to keep the two separate. Sure you understand.'

'Yes of course,' replies Adrian. Unsure as to what to say next, he asks, 'what is it that you do?'

'I own a cable company. We supply a range of electrical cables for construction, power transmission, telecoms, that kind of thing.'

Sensing that it would be quite inappropriate to start discussing reincarnation-related matters with someone he has only ever uttered twenty words to, Adrian asks hesitantly, 'I would be err very interested to hear your opinion on the new LSZH flexible cables?'

'I haven't phoned you to talk about cables,' responds Patricia curtly, who then adds, 'look it's obvious you're uncomfortable with this. I'll tell you about what I've been through and you listen, then we can discuss.'

'Sounds good,' replies Adrian, much relieved.

'It began when I was a child with dreams,' says Patricia.

'Really full on ones. They were of what I could only describe as some kind of hell. Huge numbers of people in a small space, all really miserable. It was quite, well really scary actually, not your everyday kind of bad dream.'

'I have also been having dreams,' interjects Adrian.

'Anyway to cut a long story short,' continues Patricia. 'I kept having this feeling I was someone else from the past.'

'Who?'

'A market trader from Ghana.'

'What?'

'A market trader from Ghana,' repeats Patricia.

'That's extraordinary; I have been through a rather similar set of circumstances.'

'These things are apparently not that extraordinary Adrian, though when the whole thing started it seemed it was.'

Adrian is about to speak when Patricia says, 'listen, these experiences are going on all over the world every day. Might well be a fairly small minority of people but the numbers are large believe me, I've come across a fair few the last few years.'

'I just can't rationalise, you know scientifically explain, what has happened.'

'Don't think I could either,' replies Patricia. 'Anyway how you plan to deal with it is your business. The important thing is to know you're not alone and not insane, at least not necessarily.'

'That's good to hear, a couple of weeks ago I believed I might be.'

'I know its early days for you but how have you been coping with these umm, changes in your life?'

'There is the mental degradation, oh yes and I am resigning from my job. In addition there's the confusion, depression, the struggling to find an understanding and a scientific world view left in tatters. Well I could go on all day.'

'I remember only too well,' says Patricia in an empathetic tone. 'Things will gradually improve trust me.'

'Sri said that very same thing.'

'So he did to me, didn't believe him at the time.'

'I have been marginally better the last week,' replies Adrian, deciding against trying to quantify the amount. 'But under no illusions that this is the end of it.'

'Sounds like you're not doing too badly. I ended up in a mental institution and if I hadn't met Sri, I would probably still be there, dribbling in a strait jacket.'

'That must have been horrendous.'

'My advice would be to try and relax and get back to normal life. Time is a fantastic healer, trust me,' advises Patricia.

'But I must avoid dissolution and I cannot return to that place to await a new life,' replies Adrian in a panicked tone.

'I'm not an expert on these things but if you're trying in life, chances are you're not going to be dissolved. As for the other I really don't know.'

'What is your avoidance strategy?' asks Adrian.

Patricia ponders the question briefly and then says, 'I've thought about these things Adrian, but it's not all about me. I've got two children. Regardless of if I'm reincarnated or not or what my destiny holds, I have bills to pay and responsibilities to be met.'

'Of course it is...'

Patricia interrupts again. 'Think externally and get back to the everyday, the world doesn't just stop for you. Working with cables certainly helped me with that believe me.'

'What do I do now?'

'I don't have the answer to that. Things will work themselves out, don't try and solve everything today,' replies Patricia. 'Support is a good thing; talk to Sri once in a while. He has seminars and events from time to time, he'll invite you along.'

'I look forward to them,' replies Adrian.

'As you begin to appreciate you're not alone in this, it just gets easier.'

'Of course, it has just all been very disturbing, as you are obviously able to appreciate.'

The conversation is entering its sixth minute when Patricia says, 'I have to go, is there anything else you want to ask?'

Adrian considers the question and then replies, 'yes going back to the LSZH flexible cables ...'

'You've got to be kidding me Adrian,' interrupts Patricia.

'I don't know what to say.'

'Well in your professional opinion do you believe that LSZH cables are the most effective cables for interference free data and signal transmission ...?'

Before Adrian is able to finish the question, Patricia says 'goodbye' and hangs up the phone.

As Adrian leans back in the Safco chair he feels both invigorated by the discussion and most grateful for the opportunity to have spoken to someone claiming to have been through a similar experience to his own. The practicality of Patricia and the seemingly banal everyday existence of her former self impresses Adrian, for it is far removed from the glamour of the celebrities, mystics and heroes most people evidently claim to have been in their former lives. Not for the first time however Adrian is troubled as to why he is only having these recollections of a former existence now, so late in life. There is a lingering concern that the reason for this is some dire warning from beyond the grave that a return to the multitudes in purgatory could be imminent.

With Colin attending a two day conference on morgue health and safety in Penrith and Benedict and Natalia dining out at the Chinese in Foley, Adrian eats alone that night. After dinner he makes his way to the veranda and sits on the teak bench. Reaching into one of the inside pockets of his beige safari jacket, he takes out a lighter and a half empty packet of cigarettes, left over from the recent night out. Lighting a cigarette, he looks out pensively into the fading light. Several inhalations later it strikes Adrian that the decision to smoke is a bad one, as it seems to him unwise to be indulging in potentially harmful activities when his fate is not yet sealed. Abruptly he stubs the cigarette out on the paving at his feet. As he does so, two bullet points appear in his mind.

- Cigarette smoke contains 200 chemical compounds which have been proven to be poisonous.
- 60 of these chemicals are carcinogens.

To Adrian, smoking's potential risks have now been multiplied with the threat of a smoking-related death leading directly to a stint in purgatory, another layer of hell or possibly being reincarnated as an organism with a lowly standing in the food chain. He vows never to smoke again but decides that renouncing alcohol will have to wait. At the moment a stream of data relating to the effects of alcohol on the health is about to present itself, Benedict appears through the door of the veranda. 'Evening,' greets Benedict.
'Fancy a fortune cookie?'
Adrian takes the cookie from Benedict's hand and says,
'Please tell me it is not going to say invest in Tranquilo.'
Benedict does not respond. Adrian un-wraps it, bites off one of its corners, extracts the message and reads it aloud. The message says, 'perilous times lie ahead, tread with caution.'

Adrian scrunching it up remarks, 'I was under the impression fortune cookies were meant to give positive messages. Did you not pay the bill?'

Benedict laughs and then sitting down on the bench beside his brother, removes his spectacles and says, 'Tranquilo.' Adrian emits a doleful moan, dismayed that this venture, so irrelevant to his current predicament, is becoming such a nuisance. This time however he remains seated, as Benedict begins his rehearsed monologue about the profits their involvement could yield and about how they should support Theodore, 'a member of our family.' Half an hour later, Adrian surrenders to the inevitable and agrees to sign off the funds, rationalising that in the long run this will be easier than being continually harassed by Benedict. However he has one condition. The investment is to be in the form of a loan, the rationale being that should the venture fail, their funds are still secured.

That night, five miles away in Ramsbottam Hall, in the room at the end of the corridor, Theodore sleeps fitfully, once again tormented by nightmares. During the early hours of the morning he finds himself floating in the cool water of a small river. Tree branches hang over the river, from whose branches partially clad damsels with long golden locks reach out with offerings. The offerings consist of Theodore's favourite hors d'oeuvres; eel zakuska, piroshky and cabrales cheese with smoked duck. Other damsels reach down with glasses of Burgundy and lines of cocaine on silver trays that sparkle in the sunlight. An unremitting lust consumes Theodore and he reaches out greedily to grab these sumptuous delights. This however proves in vain, as they remain just out of reach. Burning with a desire to consume these, his favourite of all consumables, Theodore kicks his legs frantically in the water, forcing his weight upwards. As previously his efforts are met only with frustration and the items remain tantalisingly just beyond the reach of his arms and he is left languishing in the stream, nearing exhaustion and failure.

Refusing to be defeated, he forces his body up from the water one final time, his eyes monstrous and blood shot, a squall forming in the water around him from his kicking. Propelled upwards, he paws determinedly at the plates, shrieking maniacally as he flounders once more at the last. This time on his descent he clutches onto one of the damsel's golden locks, hanging to the silky tress with a grim resolve, as he attempts to pull her down into the river. The girl giggles provocatively as the tress slips from Theodore's grasp and he is left flailing in the water, screaming obscenities. From the banks of the river comes laughter, an unremitting mirth that continues unabated as Theodore is forced downstream by the current and away from the objects of his desire.

Theodore awakens still kicking out furiously, as if he were still fighting the dreadful current. Becoming aware that he is in the bedroom, he lies panting, weary limbs hanging limply by his side. As time elapses Theodore resolutely strives to remain awake, so fearful is he of the consequences of sleep. Gradually however an overpowering lethargy envelops him and sleep finds him once more. For several hours he lies peacefully, his mind dormant in his exhausted state.

Shortly before dawn he finds himself in the bowels of the earth, struggling in the darkness across cold slimy stones in a futile attempt to escape this frightful dungeon. The mosquitoes come upon Theodore in a cloud, a swirling mass of unremitting biting and buzzing. Clambering across the stone in his efforts to escape these loathsome insects, he slips and falls to the ground, where he remains, futilely attempting to brush the mosquitoes off with flailing arms. He is still clawing at the air feverishly even after awakening and it is quite some time before he comes to his senses.

Somewhat bewildered the following morning, Theodore sits in the courtyard, so as to avoid the smugness of the

Ming Dynasty characters that adorn every inch of the house's walls, with the exception of the cellar and attic. In one hand he claps an espresso cup, in the other a loaded shotgun. His mind wanders back to the Classical Civilisation classes of his youth and a vague recollection of Sisyphus and Tantalus's suffering in Tartarus. Though he is unable to remember their names or the finer details of their torment, having never been the most attentive of students, he is shocked at the similarity to his own dreams and deeply concerned about his declining mental state.

Three double espressos and two African collared doves later, the BlackBerry begins beeping in his pocket. Taking it out, he checks the identity of the caller and answers.

'Benedict what's the news.'

'Good news, Adrian's agreed,' replies Benedict.

Theodore shouts 'Yes' very loudly. When the call ends Theodore lets off a victory salute in the form of several volleys of shotgun fire, and then jumps up and down triumphantly. Not even the fact that he was informed that Adrian is insisting that the funds will not be an investment but rather a personal loan can dampen his joy.

At this very point in time, in the Raven household, Adrian is preparing the loan forms in Colin's study. Bending over the desk, assiduously analysing several person-to-person loan templates downloaded earlier that morning, it is almost as if he is back sitting in his Safco chair with seat cushion in Vincent & Ernst, absorbed in his actuarial duties. Over the next hour, Adrian works meticulously on the loan agreement. As the Thomas Turner grandfather clock completes its final chime for eleven o' clock, the document is complete. Adrian reads it through, checking the repayment schedule, each of the detailed clauses, the interest due and the additional percentage of profits, should Tranquilo prove a success. He emails a copy to Benedict, who is on a contract in Portsmouth and then awaits his permission to forward the agreement to Colin's lawyer in Tatchin to look over prior to forwarding it to Theodore.

This is the longest period of time in several weeks that Adrian has not thought about Middleworth and his now-altered existence, so engrossed has he been in the document. As he gathers his papers and leaves the study, he is forced to admit to himself that perhaps Sri and Patricia had indeed been correct in their advice that he should get back to everyday tasks.

That evening Adrian and Benedict conduct a conference call with Theodore to discuss the work expected of them. Benedict's responsibility is integrating the sophisticated internet and security systems for the soon to be built Tranquilo Estate. The expectations of Adrian are really rather minimal to his palpable relief. He is to attend the meeting the following week in London and give a short overview on estimated profits, as the investors wish to see professional endorsement of the project. No mention would be made of Theodore's relationship to the Raven family. In addition he is to manage the presentation of data in the sales and marketing brochures. Adrian agrees, convinced that the work will take no more than two days of his time. As soon as the conversation ends, Adrian returns to his bedroom to finish reading the Sai Baba book.

Fifteen

10:30 - The Day of the Meeting – Adrian and Benedict are sitting in the Lexus LS. Natalia, still wearing her nightgown and bearing her customary scowl, bids them farewell. Pointing a finger threateningly in Adrian's direction she says, 'He no drive.'

'As if, after last time,' replies Benedict.

Adrian is once again incensed by Natalia, though more by her inability to construct grammatically correct sentences than by her insolence.

   The journey passes without incident until they reach the M3, some twenty minutes later. Adrian recalling Charles Middleworth's fate is nervous on entering the motorway. This concern is exacerbated by Benedict's insistence in putting the Lexus's superior acceleration to the test at every opportunity. They are passing the turning for the A303 when Adrian becomes convinced that the odour of gasoline is permeating through the vehicle, becoming increasingly more noxious. The rattling sound emitted from somewhere in the back of the car begins soon after, very faint at first but amplifying with time. Adrian wishes he had checked the boot prior to departure for any loose objects.

   Benedict, inattentive to Adrian's woes, turns on the CD player. The sound of the Nirvana track, Territorial Pissings from their Nevermind album fills the car. The frenetic drumming only serves to intensify his increasing fear. Panicking as images of Middleworth's demise envelop his tortured mind, he is at the point of surrendering to his fears and ordering Benedict to slow down when they converge upon traffic around Basingstoke.

With a new speed of twenty-five miles per hour and Benedict having turned the music off, comes a degree of solace for the suffering Adrian. Attempting to hasten their journey, Benedict proceeds to weave in and out of the traffic, including using the emergency lane for the purpose. This proves futile however, the effort only incurring the chagrin of the other drivers, who sound their horns in annoyance. Surrendering to the inevitable, Benedict settles despondently in the middle lane. For the first time during the journey he speaks. 'You fully prepared for the meeting right?'

'Yes,' replies Adrian unenthusiastically.

'This is important,' says Benedict. 'I could do with your support on this.'

'I am here, am I not?'

'In body yes, but in spirit I'm not so sure.'

Adrian does not reply. Benedict taking this as an invitation to continue says, 'this meeting is just what you need to get you back into circulation.'

'If you say so.'

'You can't spend the rest of your days moping around the house and surfing the net for porn.'

'I do not surf the net for porn. Do not judge me by your own depraved standards.'

'Whatever Adrian,' replies Benedict, before articulating for the umpteenth time, how the Tranquilo project will prove to be very lucrative and how fortunate they are for Theodore giving them this opportunity.

A little over an hour later they arrive in Canary Wharf, where the meeting is to take place, on the eighty-second floor of a giant glass monolith. Adrian is apprehensive on entering the external glass lift that proceeds to ascend the building rapidly. Peering down to the ground below, he sees swathes of office workers emerging for their lunch breaks. The mass of people remind him of the multitude, as viewed from high above during his dreams. He grips the lift rail resolutely with both hands.

Benedict sensing his brother's discomfort says, 'relax, we're going up for a meeting not a bungee jump.'

The meeting room is narrow and has a long oval shaped table, not dissimilar to Vincent & Ernst's. The external wall is glass, allowing for spectacular views of the surrounding area. An internal door opens at the far end of the room and Theodore emerges with his secretary in tow.

'Afternoon boys, good to see you, how are you both?' greets Theodore, as he walks up to Benedict and Adrian and slaps them on the back.

'Good thank you,' reply Adrian and Benedict in unison.

'You took the stairs Adrian, you know there's a lift,' exclaims Theodore, noticing Adrian's clammy appearance.

'There's a washroom at the end of the corridor, we'll turn the aircon on.'

Adrian departs the room, welcoming this opportunity to restore his composure.

'Which way do the poles go in again?' asks Theodore's secretary Carin, struggling to assemble the projector screen.

'Carin's as dumb as a post but she makes up for it in other ways,' whispers Theodore to Benedict, nodding in the direction of Carin's pert posterior which is raised upwards, as she tries in vain to assemble the apparatus.

On returning from the washroom several minutes later, Adrian finds the meeting room a bustling mass of humanity. Rolling down the sleeve of his M & S shirt, he checks the time on the Casio Mudman, counting down the seconds until twelve-forty when the meeting is due to commence. He is relieved when Theodore instructs everyone to their seats and the confusion of the last few minutes is replaced by order. It is evident to Adrian that it will probably be quite some time, the exact amount of which it is presently impossible to quantify, before he will be comfortable in large groups of people.

Theodore introduces the investors one by one, starting with Anatoly Sarkissian, a corpulent Armenian with decidedly porcine features and numerous chins. A George Smith, who will be assisting with the managing of the project and a Cornelius Brewer, whom Theodore mentions has been involved in some of his previous projects. Adrian pays scant attention, as his eyes are drawn to the view through the glass wall of a sky filling with nefarious storm clouds. Simultaneously his auditory senses are drawn to the dull hum of the Daikin air-conditioner that seems to be murmuring the name Charles Middleworth continuously, as at his final meeting at Vincent & Ernst.

Adrian is further alarmed on Theodore's introduction of Sasha Kornilenko, the primary investor, who had until this point escaped his notice. Kornilenko is wearing a beige suit. He has thinning flaxen hair and a slender physique. Small metallic-rimmed designer spectacles are perched precariously at the end of an unremarkable nose. The similarity to Charles Middleworth startles Adrian and he stares transfixed at Kornilenko. Kornilenko, becoming aware of this peculiar attention removes his spectacles very deliberately and focuses on Adrian with pale blue eyes that bear a sinister ferocity. Adrian turns away from Kornilenko's demonic glare and looks down at the table, at the same time gripping the armrests of his executive leather chair. Fear consumes his wretched being at the thought that while he, Adrian Raven, is Middleworth's soul reincarnated; this man Kornilenko is some diabolical reincarnation of Middleworth's body. Adrian does not even register when Theodore, introducing him, uses a different surname. The attendees observe Adrian's troubled appearance with concern. Although he has a sudden urge to flee the building, somehow he remains seated.

On completing the introductions, Theodore speaks of Tranquilo, using hyperbole liberally, as is the custom of skilled sales persons. With the exception of Adrian, he has the other attendees' full attention as he regales them with his charisma. He cuts a suave figure in his hand tailored Savile row suit, his manner professional and meticulous, each movement of his lithe body expressive and perfectly executed. Theodore is the very embodiment of persuasive confidence, thriving in this, his environment. There is not even the slightest hint at the tumultuous events of recent weeks, neither the stock market collapse nor the fearful chaotic nights. 'Welcome to Tranquilo, the dawn of a new era,' declares Theodore, stretching his arms upwards and outwards to magnify this proclamation, in a manner that he imagines Moses would have done when presenting the Ten Commandments to the Israelites. Carin meanwhile hands out copies of the promotional brochure.

As the attendees turn their attentions from Theodore to the glossy front page of the brochure in front of them, they are met by the embodiment of his promise; a utopian computer-generated image of the completed project. The elegant curves of the lush, green and perfectly manicured grass of the golf course slope gracefully down to Tranquilo's majestic lake; rays of luminescence from a resplendent Mediterranean sun sparkling on its translucent surface. The villas in all their grandeur provide the backdrop; shimmering white palatial structures, complete with Ionic columned colonnades and inner peristyles, teeming with exotic plants and statues.

Theodore waits for precisely fifteen seconds, while the attendees marvel at the image. Even Kornilenko and Sarskissian appear impressed. This Theodore takes as proof of the quality of the image. As he had previously noted it was no easy feat to impress them; they for whom a diet of lobsters and private yachts were typical fare.

'Impressive isn't it? We must thank Benedict for this; the company that did the design are associates of his,' exclaims Theodore. Applause fills the room. Benedict looks exceedingly pleased with himself, oblivious to his brother huddled and suffering in the chair beside him.

'How many of you have seen Jurassic Park?' asks Theodore. This is followed by a number of 'Yeses' and raised hands.

'Well this lot make the effects in that seem amateurish,' continues Theodore. 'I'm sure you would agree.' He pauses briefly for added effect and then states in a euphoric tone.

'And the good news is they're flying out to Spain with us to do the promotional video.' More applause follows.

'And a big thank to Sasha for his use of the private jet,' continues Theodore. Sasha Kornilenko nods in acknowledgement. Adrian looking up views Kornilenko's humourless features and cold inhuman eyes despairingly.

'We meet today at the dawn of a new era,' continues Theodore. 'When unrivalled Mediterranean residential exclusivity becomes a reality. It is we that have had the courage to embrace the future and to us that the rewards will be yielded.'

Once more the audience applauses. Theodore waits for silence to prevail before continuing. 'This is the most ambitious project Southern Spain has seen in decades.' Theodore presses the button on the remote control he is holding in his left hand. A PowerPoint presentation appears on the projector screen, at the same time the room's lights dim. Adrian is relieved that Sasha Kornilenko is now barely visible.

'The Tranquilo project will see the construction of thirty bespoke villas and fifty apartments,' says Theodore.

Bullet points appear on the screen with this information.

'The raison d'être of the project is the eighteen-hole PGA standard golf course, in collaboration with Vince McGrath, one of the world's premier golfers.'

Theodore spends the next few minutes explaining how the golf course will allow for spectacular profits, due to the large membership fees proposed for non-residents. This is demonstrated with the aid of a large multi- coloured graph, complete with steep gradient. Adrian, still traumatised, does not analyse it, instead he stares upwards at the ceiling.

At the moment Theodore finishes the presentation, Carin and a male assistant appear with trays and hurriedly begin to hand out glasses of Cristal champagne.

'I propose a toast. Integritas, caritas, lucrum,' says Theodore raising his glass.

'Integritas, caritas, lucrum,' reply the attendees eagerly, with the exception of Adrian who does so in a meek voice, clasping his champagne flute in a trembling hand.

'This motto translates as integrity, charity and gain. It reflects our ideology,' states Theodore. 'Integrity, as we are to be true to ourselves with our impeccable standards of workmanship and customer service. Charity as we are to promote the area we serve. As for the gain bit, you can probably figure that one out for yourselves.' The attendees laugh aloud with the exception of Adrian. Theodore smiles widely exposing his overly white teeth.

'I understand gain as well as any,' interrupts Anatoly Sarkissian, his numerous chins quivering as he speaks. Theodore murmurs, 'yeah, weight gain' under his breath.

'Only it has come to my attention that some believe that you ignored both integrity and charity in your previous Spanish project; Timeshare Dreams,' continues Sarkissian in his impeccable English.

George Smith and Cornelius Brewer squirm uncomfortably in their seats, for they too had been involved in this unscrupulous venture. Theodore however does not emit any outward sign of discomfort and merely smiles.

'There has been one individual that has been complaining.' Theodore holding out the small finger of his left hand to further emphasise the point then adds. 'A single trouble-seeker out of hundreds of contented customers.'

'Yes indeed this is the case,' interjects George Smith. 'Our lawyers are currently in the process of prosecuting her for libel.'

'Exactly right,' continues Theodore. 'We tried to help this woman, who was on shall we say a limited budget, achieve her dreams and this is the thanks we get.'

Sarkissian nods in acknowledgment and the meeting continues. Infuriated at the interruption Theodore vows that he will ring Rebecca Daltry's neck if he ever sees her again. The finale to the meeting is a number of the attendees voicing their expertise. Theodore had planned this to further increase Sarkissian and Kornilenko's trust in the project. George Smith talks about the legal aspect, primarily the imagined successful negotiations with Marbella City Council over obtaining planning permission and the correct licenses; in reality these are still ongoing. He pauses constantly to allow Kornilenko's interpreter to translate.

Benedict discusses at some length the details for the integrated bespoke wireless security system, computerised golf course irrigation system and custom made networking solutions. Adrian, who is the next to speak, breathes deeply and attempts to relax as he waits. However the dark storm clouds on his left and Kornilenko only seats away, are causes for grave concern.

'To summarise, this integrated based system allows us to monitor and administer to all of Tranquilo's technological needs without external assistance,' states Benedict. 'This, ladies and gentlemen, gives us control of our destiny,' concludes Benedict in Theodore-like fashion. He then sits down and looks across at Adrian.

As Adrian stands up, his gaze unwittingly falls on Kornilenko. Kornilenko glares back at him with demonic eyes that to Adrian seem to be boring into his soul. He stands mesmerised, unable to speak. Some seconds later

Benedict kicks Adrian's ankle exceedingly hard. Abruptly he returns to the proceedings, takes a large breath, looks away from Kornilenko's frightful glare and begins to speak.
'My expertise as Theodore mentioned is actuarial science. Actuarial science as I am sure you are all aware is the application of statistical and mathematical methods for the assessment of risk,' states Adrian, pausing to allow Kornilenko's interpreter to translate. Steadfastly he refuses to look in Kornilenko's direction.

'Traditionally for the most part this work has been conducted in the finance and insurance industries. Typical tasks include benchmarking studies, due diligence for merger and acquisitions, statements of actuarial opinion, cash flow projections, reserve valuations and pricing and loss forecasting,' says Adrian. 'This explains what we do, but why property and why Tranquilo? Actuarial science has previously been sceptical of bricks and mortar. Why you ask? Quite simply we actuaries argued this was due primarily to property's unpredictable performance and poor liquidity.' Adrian pauses again to build the suspense as advised by Benedict. 'Ladies and gentlemen this has been changing in recent years and with the recent stock market collapse, funds will continue to increasingly turn to property. Property is now viewed as a bond which offers medium to long-term income flow.' He pauses again for several seconds while Kornilenko's interpreter translates.

Adrian breathes slowly in an attempt to remain as calm as possible. 'Why Tranquilo? Quite simply the Tranquilo Valley promises outstanding profits.' Adrian looks across at Theodore, who presses a button on the projector controller. A complex table appears on the screen.

'Before we look at the data, let me explain the fundamentals of the non- linear dual stochastic process model and its relevance to residential property prices.' Several minutes' later Adrian having completed his talk sits down, relieved that it is over and that somehow in defiance of the terror inducing circumstances, he has achieved what was expected of him. To regale the investors with analysis so complex that they will be quite unable to understand it, therefore question it and will hopefully simply accept it as fact. Looking out through the glass wall to his left, Adrian sees a beam of sunlight penetrating through a gap in the storm clouds. The meeting draws to a close soon after. Theodore departs first with the investors for a luncheon at The Connaught Hotel. He whispers, 'good job boys, see you soon,' as he walks past Benedict and Adrian towards the door. There is reprieve for Adrian as Sasha Kornilenko departs the room with Theodore and the other investors, before descending in the lift.

Taking the next lift, Adrian is relieved that the descent is not the tribulation it had been on the ascent. As Adrian and Benedict exit the building, the area is remarkably quiet; the majority of workers having returned from their lunch break. A stout elderly man, wearing a fluorescent yellow and pink anorak is wandering around shouting into a microphone. As he passes close to them, Adrian hears his words.

'I am he that liveth, and was dead; and, behold, I am alive for evermore, Amen; and have the keys of hell and of death.' Adrian recognises the words as being from Revelations 1, though he cannot remember which verse. It occurs to him that perhaps he too armed with a microphone could preach as he wanders around the city. He hopes that this could be achieved in a more charismatic manner than this rather peculiar specimen now before him. Turning to Benedict he asks, 'am I in anyway charismatic?'

'Yes, in the way that a chair is. Up for a pint?'

'A pint, are you not driving?'

'Yes, hence why I suggested a pint not pints.'

'How about lunch?'

'Sure, it's on me. Where did you have in mind?' asks Benedict.

'Henry's Oyster Bar.'

'No thought for your poor brother's wallet then.'
They walk in silence. A short time later Adrian turning to his brother says, 'Benedict.'
'Yes Adrian.'
'Have you ever given any thought to reincarnation and/or karma?'
'What a random question,' replies Benedict incredulously.
'Well have you?'
'I haven't given it much thought, it's all bollocks anyway. You know that as well as me or at least you did.'
'Don't be so dismissive.'
'You're not actually considering this crap again, are you?' exclaims Benedict now somewhat annoyed.
'Well what do you believe?'
Benedict considers the question and then replies, 'basically accumulate wealth and if you can get laid along the way all the better.'
Adrian wonders what he would think of Benedict, if he were not in fact his brother. Some seconds later Adrian says, 'life, Benedict, is a continual cycle, well at least until…'
'Adrian shut up that is unless you want to swap lunch at Henry's for McDonald's,' interrupts Benedict.
'I only wanted to explain…'
'One religious fanatic is more than enough for today,' interrupts Benedict, gesturing back in the direction of the microphone-wielding anorak clad man. Not wanting to put his free lunch at Henry's in jeopardy, Adrian remains quiet and the two brothers advance in silence. As they walk, Adrian reflects on the meeting. Now removed from the harrowing ordeal, he realises that perhaps he had been somewhat irrational in the comparison between Kornilenko and his former self, Charles Middleworth. After all there must be numerous people out there possessing slender physiques, flaxen thinning hair and spectacles.

After lunch at Henry's, Benedict departs for Hampshire and Adrian returns to his house. On unlocking the door, he is unable to force it open. The frightful thought occurs to him that squatters have invaded the property and bolted it from the inside. However after pushing it with all his strength, it finally opens just enough to squeeze his frame through. A large pile of post in the hallway reveals itself as the culprit. Walking through to the sitting room, Adrian stands aghast at the entrance. The interior lies forgotten and forlorn; its confines stale and stagnant, a thin film of dust covering every surface. To Adrian surveying the sitting room it appears to represent the ruination and decay of his former life. Forcing these negative thoughts from his mind, he spends the next few hours hoovering, dusting and polishing at a feverish pace, vowing to never neglect the house again.

The cleaning now completed, Adrian collapses exhausted on the Burlington leather sofa and lies there taking gulps from a can of Stella Artois. He considers whether the now immaculate house symbolises his own rise from the abyss and a return to some pretence of order and stability. Seconds later he banishes the consideration from the confines of his mind, concluding that there is nothing that can be drawn from the cleaning. Merely that the house was dirty and is now clean. The fact so obvious, an equation is not needed to prove it.

Despite his fatigued condition, a myriad of other thoughts begin to circle his increasingly convoluted mind. As each thought reveals itself, he attempts to rationally evaluate it and then file it, before examining the next. Once more wondering vaguely what he is to do, the question so vast and undefined, he ignores it and moves on. The statistic of how one in three Americans believe in reincarnation appears before him, so vividly that he recognises it as being in a bold type, with a Times New Roman font, point size twenty. Adrian wonders that if the same ratio were valid for the

United Kingdom, how many people in the United Kingdom believe in reincarnation. He begins to talk aloud. 'Thirty percent of the mid two thousand and ten estimate of sixty-one million, three hundred and ninety- eight thousand people is.' Adrian quickly calculates the amount, which takes merely a few seconds and then says, 'eighteen million, four hundred and nineteen thousand, four hundred people.'

Sometime later Adrian realises that the fifty inch Panasonic television screen is still covered in a canvas of dust and that in his haste he had forgotten to wipe it. Sighing in annoyance, he considers rising to his feet to clean the offending item but cannot muster the energy and remains beached on the sofa. As the yoga practitioners had in the former Methodist chapel in Falgate, Adrian begins to focus his breathing. After several minutes of concerted effort, he is aware of a ripple of relaxation transmitting through his body, gradually becoming a swell. The significance of the day's proceedings are now only too evident to him; the terror of the motorway and the frightful ordeal of the meeting. Now removed from these events, he is satisfied that despite the tribulations of the day he has survived. Through perseverance he has avoided defeat and, having overcome these obstacles is better equipped for tomorrow. This thought is enlightening to him and the mild frustration caused by the dust on the television is instantly forgotten.

Remembering the man in Canary Wharf with the microphone quoting from Revelations, Adrian begins to ponder the possibility of introducing people to the concept of reincarnation using the same method. Not in a dictatorial dogmatic manner but in an open inviting way, with the aim of providing encouragement to people potentially suffering from reincarnation-related issues, like himself, who not so long ago had seemed so alone in his predicament.

Later that evening, he watches one of Sri's seminars that had been uploaded onto YouTube, marvelling at Sri's graceful ease, charismatic nature and relaxed yet forthright manner. That night while lying in bed, head cushioned on the Microfibre pillow from ExtraComfort, he looks across at the Canon EOS on the bedside table. There is an obvious irony in the purchase of the camera that had previously escaped him. Notably that arrival of the EOS Mark IV, which was meant to bring a fresh clarity to the world through its stunning image resolution and Sigma 50-500mm f/4-6.3 lens, has instead coincided with the world appearing more undefined to him than at any time previously.

Awakening early the next morning, the first thought that comes to mind is that he should address the general public, as the man yesterday in the anorak had. Any lingering self-doubt disappears on peering out from under the blind at the day outside. The sky is a radiant blue, with small clouds of the cumulous variety interspersed across it, appearing as small balls of wool; identical in fact to those from the dreams of the previous night with the souls astride of them. There is a desire to reach out and touch these clouds, to clasp their promise of salvation.

Two hours later Adrian is ready to depart, the plan of engagement having been decided upon. Standing in front of the mirror for a final check, there is satisfaction that his choice of attire is appropriate for the purpose; loose-fitting flannel trousers and a pressed shirt, the top button of which is undone to give a casual, welcoming and warm impression to the general public. He decides against bringing an anorak, even though the weather forecast warns of light rain in the afternoon.

Now on board the train, which is mercifully only half full, Adrian outlines the plan of engagement once more. There is an awareness that he must be stringent and under no circumstances allow his delivery to become overly convoluted with complex logic, especially of the algorithmic variety. From observing Sri, Adrian has noted that it is of vital importance to engage with the audience using a simple and coherent message. For this purpose he has decided on the words, 'You're not alone,' to begin his address. This will be followed by a straightforward explanation of how reincarnation issues may be manifesting themselves in peoples' lives, using his own experiences as a point of reference. Stage three will entail the utilisation of some simple statistics. Concepts such as linear regression have been deemed too complex for the purpose. Two of the statistics appear in his mind, as bullet points.

- 1 in 4 Americans believe in reincarnation.
- This equates to approximately 78,230,000 people.

As the train progresses towards central London, there is apprehension. Adrian is acutely aware that he is unfamiliar with activities of the nature he is about to indulge in. Breathing deeply he imagines the clouds from his dreams with the souls atop of them. There is an appreciation that his former self, Middleworth, has allowed him a glimpse of salvation and that it is now his duty to assist others.

Adrian disembarks the train at Tottenham Court Road station, several stops from his final destination, as there is the pressing issue of purchasing a microphone. He has chosen to avoid his usual haunt, Premier Electrical Goods, due to the prospect of being embarrassed by potential questions from Asad regarding the intended purpose of the microphone. Instead he has chosen the Electronics For You store and it is here that matters become complicated. For as he peruses the shelves that contain the microphones, he is quite unsure which model best suits his purpose.

There is a choice of seven but he discounts four of them, as being either unsuitable or due to their oppressive price tag. The three models competing for his affections are the Shure PGX2/PG58, the Sennheiser SKM 100-835 G3 and the Beyerdynamic Opus 89. Reading the labels and analysing the features, he is impressed with the Sennheiser's effective output of two point one dbm, though considers it slightly heavy at four hundred and fifty point eight grams. The Beyerdynamic is appealing as it is the least expensive of the three and has an impressive frequency response. Turning his attentions to the Shure microphone, he remembers what he had told himself earlier about the significance of simplicity today. There is disappointment that the activity has not yet begun and he has already failed. Adrian approaches one of the shop's staff and asks them to make an informed decision for him. Predictably the shop assistant chooses the Sennheiser, the most expensive of the three.

Thirty minutes later, Adrian is finally in position outside the Nike Town store, opposite Oxford Circus tube station. The pavement is packed with shoppers and workers, who scurry past in both directions. There is trepidation, due in part to the crowd of people and also an uncertainty about how exactly to progress. Looking up at the sky above, he focuses on the small cumulous clouds, imagining the souls atop of them and their promise of redemption. The possibility of salvation that they offer gives him the courage to begin and he takes a deep breath, allowing the air to fill his lungs gradually. 'Life is a cycle,' begins Adrian, only to realise that the sound of his voice is barely audible. Noticing that he has forgotten to turn the microphone on, he does so and resumes. 'Life is a cycle.' He pauses for precisely three seconds for affect and then continues. 'Every one of us is in a perpetual cycle, this will continue until dissolution or attainment amongst the clouds. Attainment, I hear you ask?'

The majority of the pedestrians alter their path to allow for additional space between themselves and Adrian. Adrian is contemplating mentioning the reincarnation statistics, when he becomes aware that someone is tapping him on the shoulder. Turning around he is astonished to see it is the man from yesterday in Canary Wharf, wearing the same yellow and pink anorak. The man appears to Adrian to be very old. He looks up at Adrian, bearing a pernicious expression, the lines across his forehead forming deep furrows and the hair on either side of his bald palate sticking out animatedly in tufts.

'Hello,' says Adrian.

'This is my spot, move on,' says the man.

'This is public property and at any rate I was under the impression your spot is in Canary Wharf,' responds Adrian, placing his hands on his hips in a defensive gesture.

'You're spreading lies and corruption,' continues the man, shaking the microphone he is holding at waist level maniacally. It appears to Adrian from the design to be the Beyerdynamic Opus 89 but it is impossible to be certain, from the angle with which it is being held.

'The Apocalypse is coming when you unbelievers face annihilation,' adds the man a moment later.

'Have to say it is the first I have heard of it.'

'Revelations 1:18,' states the man. 'I am he that liveth, and was dead; and, behold, I am alive for evermore, Amen; and have the keys of hell and of death.'

'Matthew 11:14, concerning the identity of John the Baptist,' replies Adrian. 'And if you are willing to accept it, he is the Elijah who was to come.'

'Isaiah 51:11,' responds the man. 'Therefore the redeemed of the Lord shall return…'

Adrian, deciding that this is an opportune moment to find a new spot, ambles off down Oxford Street, towards Bond Street station.

Even with the change of location, the results are no more encouraging. A disinterested public continue to hurry past, punctuated with sporadic looks of derision in his direction. Adrian reminds himself that this is a pious act and the rewards may not be tangible. He is hopeful that even if his words bring even one person to the realisation that they are not alone in their suspicion that they are reincarnated, then the ordeal can be deemed worthwhile.

Later that morning Adrian is outlining the reincarnation statistics again, unaware that a man is watching him through a shop window, whilst his wife scours items of clothing on a shelf. The man is Cornelius Brewer from the meeting yesterday. Reaching into his pocket, he takes out his mobile phone and selects Theodore's number from the phone book. After the second ring Theodore picks up.

'Morning Cornelius.'

'Theodore hi, I'm on Oxford Street looking at a strange man with a microphone telling people about the end of the world or something. I can't really hear from in here.'

'I'm confused,' replies Theodore. 'What's this got to do with me?'

'I'm pretty damn sure it's that actuary from yesterday's meeting.'

'I very much doubt it; Adrian's living down this way now.'

'Well it certainly looks just like him,' responds Cornelius, scrutinising Adrian through the glass.

'Those train spotter types all look alike,' remarks Theodore.

'Well its concerning if it transpires to be him when he is involved in Tranquilo,' replies Cornelius.

Theodore says, 'don't worry he's not involved, he was there shall we say for window dressing purposes.'

They proceed to talk about the plans for Tranquilo.

The sky is overcast now and it begins to drizzle, dampening Adrian's increasingly frayed spirits yet further. Over the course of the morning it has gradually dawned on him that there is nothing charismatic about his address and that he is merely appearing as a lunatic. In the three hours he has been orating so far, the only words that have been uttered to him have been offensive ones and it is beginning to affect his confidence.

Determined not to surrender quite yet, he takes a deep breath and says, 'life is a cycle. Every one of us is in a perpetual cycle, this will continue until dissolution or attainment amongst the clouds.'

A short while later the sound of ringing bells and chants becomes audible, even above the sound of his voice, amplified by the Sennheiser microphone. Looking up he sees the distinctive bright orange of the Hare Krishnas approaching, their demeanour as always one of absurd jollity. As they approach him they stop, the bells fall silent, shaven heads turn towards him, etched in concentration. Adrian delighted to have attention at last, begins to speak to them directly. Aware that they are already familiar with the concept of reincarnation due to their supposed Hindu origins, he decides not to patronise them by reiterating that life is a cycle. Instead he starts with the statistics. 'Did you know that an estimated one in every four Americans believe in reincarnation.'

He stops for precisely three seconds and then continues.

'Taking the population estimate of Two thousand and ten, this equates to a staggering seventy-eight million two hundred and thirty thousand people.'

There is no response from the group. The lead Hare Krishna points accusingly at him, shaking his head as he does so, which results in the rat tail on the back of his head flapping from side to side. They begin to complain bitterly amongst each other as Adrian watches silently, unsure how to respond. The volume increases, reaching a crescendo moments later, their voices accosting him as a cacophony of hate. He makes the decision to depart hastily and begins to walk briskly down Oxford Street, aware of bells ringing close behind him, growing louder, more persistent and threatening with each passing moment. Adrian increases his pace. Two minutes later and he is outside the main entrance to Selfridges. Putting the microphone in his inside pocket, he enters the shop through the revolving doors. Turning back he sees the Hare Krishnas entering the revolving doors, one after another. Out of nowhere several security guards appear, refusing them entry with outstretched arms.

Returning home that night on the train, Adrian considers the often intolerant nature of organised religion towards others. Specifically how the self-righteousness of its believers is often deemed acceptable due to the fact it is occurring within a group. This is a phenomenon he is aware has occurred throughout human history and is now prevailing more upon his own life, with his new found spiritual exploration.

Later that evening sitting despondently in front of the Panasonic television, Sri's advice to not be too hasty and to think things through prior to acting come to mind. It is now obvious, with the advantage of hindsight that he has failed to adhere to this. It is also apparent to Adrian that he is not exactly cut out for charismatic activities of this ilk and decides for the time being at least to leave these matters to the experts. However despite the tumultuous events of the day, the humiliation and embarrassment, these emotions are dulled somewhat in the context of the recent discovery that he is likely Charles Middleworth reincarnated, who has been residing in purgatory. Remembering the meeting that is to take place at Ramsbottam Hall tomorrow, Adrian reluctantly turns his attentions to the creation of the Tranquilo charts. In a little under an hour, he has designed three bespoke charts that he determines are ideal for the presentation of data in the Tranquilo sales brochure.

Adrian, close to exhaustion, yawns widely and is at the point of turning off the laptop when for no apparent reason he recalls the name Sarkissian had mentioned in the meeting, Timeshare Dreams, one of Theodore's former projects. In his fraught state during the meeting Adrian had thought nothing of it, but is now intrigued. He types the name into Google. Thirteen results are returned. The second entry catches his attention, he clicks on the link; www.timesharedreams/fraud.com.

The website is amateurish. To Adrian's expert eye it is immediately apparent that the site has been put together in WordArt. The HTML is poorly coded and the embedded photographs so large that they take an eternity to load. The website is devoted to attacking the Timeshare Dreams project as a travesty. Adrian is shocked to find a deluge of criticism from a host of Timeshare Dream apartment owners.

The photographs tell their own tale of misery. A grim faced Timeshare Dream apartment owner, Rebecca Daltry, stands in the shabby dimly lit corridor of the Timeshare Dream apartment block, holding a sodden dead rat aloft by its tail. Another image shows the view from the apartment block, of a rain-swept industrial wasteland, littered with piping and piles of bricks. In the background a grey and unforgiving sea is visible. The photograph is in stark contrast to the image inserted next to it, from Timeshare Dreams marketing collateral, showing a luscious lawn and immaculate flower beds leading down to a brilliant blue sea. Adrian holds his hands to his head, traumatised at the prospect that Benedict and he may have got themselves involved in an unscrupulous venture. The decision is made to broach the subject at the meeting tomorrow.

As he lies awaiting the onset of sleep, he is consumed with pity for the elderly Timeshare Dream owners he imagines have probably scrimped and saved their entire working lives for a tranquil retirement that now lies in tatters. Unfortunates denied a short window of harmony before a stint in purgatory that will cast a shadow upon their afterlives. This distressing thought is still with him, even as the oppressive wailing of the multitude becomes audible, their lament reaching him as waves of despondency.

Sixteen

07:00 - The Next Morning - Adrian is sleeping peacefully. The voluminous outpourings of the multitude have long since ceased and the small cumulous clouds now float by; the celestial souls astride of them. A loud and persistent beeping interrupts the idyllic scene. Adrian awakens abruptly.

08:00 – Adrian is standing in the sitting room, clutching the Samsonite overnight bag under one arm. Walking through to the hallway, he grabs the Renault Twingo Gordini RS car keys from the wooden key holder and walks assuredly out of the front door. Striding down the front garden path, he unlatches the gate, turns right and walks calmly up to the garage entrance, unlocks the padlock before opening the heavy duty exterior steel doors and entering the garage. Two further steps bring him alongside the Renault Twingo Gordini. He unlocks the car door, clambers into the interior, places the overnight case on the passenger seat, checks the mirrors, adjusts the seat, places the key in the ignition and turns it, at the same time as placing his left foot on the clutch.

The engine starts instantaneously; the sound of which so startles Adrian that he jumps in the seat, hitting his head on the car's roof, at the same time his foot comes off the clutch, stalling the vehicle. Clutching his sore head with one hand,

Adrian abruptly turns off the ignition and gets out of the car, vowing to never be behind the wheel of a car again, for he dare not risk meeting his demise for a second time in the same fashion. The decision is made to place an advert for it in Auto Trader magazine that very day. There is not even a hint of sadness at the prospect of the Twingo being sold, the car that emits less than one hundred and forty g/km of carbon dioxide and contains both renewable materials and recycled plastic.

09:25 – Adrian boards the 09:27 Southern train service to Falgate.

10:20 – Winding down the country lanes in an ABC taxi, mercifully at a slower speed than last time, he views the rural scenery through the window. Friesian cows and rabbits chew the succulent grass in the sun baked fields, as skylarks soar overhead. Thrushes dart in and out of the hedgerows, clicking in alarm.

Turning the corner at the end of Fordingham Lane, the newly built supermarket becomes visible. The size of the building shocks Adrian, the monolithic structure casting an Orwellian gloom on its surroundings. Fifty metres further down the lane, a building site surrounded by an enormous placard promising idyllic rural living comes into view. The pictures that adorn the placard are of glass and concrete residences, modernistic structures that are in stark contrast to the surrounding traditional homes. The commotion of the mechanical diggers and heavy drill are in operation, drowning out the rural sounds. Examining the offending site, Adrian wonders whether this obtrusion is courtesy of Theodore.

As the taxi continues onwards, he considers the unwelcome changes in the valley where his family have lived for centuries, encroachments on a traditional country life that has reigned here for millennia. Recognising that so obsessed has he been with the tumultuous events in his own life that he has not noticed the changing rural world. A new world that will compartmentalise rural existences, suppress individuality and force unwanted standardisation on all around. This thought reminds him of the multitude languishing in purgatory, and he shudders.

On arriving at Ramsbottam Hall, Adrian is met by the sight of Anastasia clad in a pink Velour tracksuit, performing stretches on the front steps.

'Good morning Anastasia,' greets Adrian.

'Morning,' replies Anastasia coldly.

He considers continuing the conversation but on observing Anastasia's contemptuous expression thinks better of it and instead stands silently, awaiting her invitation to enter the house.

'Theodore and Benedict are inside,' adds Anastasia several seconds later. Adrian pushes the hall's gargoyle door knob. On entering the hall he gazes transfixed at the interior. A majestic neo-Baroque crystal chandelier serves as the hall's centrepiece, its array of shimmering crystal lights bathe the room in a flattering low-level luminescence. Beneath the chandelier is a Georgian Chippendale mahogany dining table of grandiose proportions, the curvaceous contours of which are further enhanced by the rays of flickering light that dance invitingly on its polished surface. Decorative jewel encrusted mirrors in a variety of sizes adorn the walls that Adrian considers would not have looked out of place in the Palace of Versailles. At the very moment his attention turns to the Chinese panoramique wallpaper, Theodore's voice, an unwelcome intrusion, calls out from another room.

'We're in the study.'

Unable to locate the exact direction of Theodore's voice, Adrian is about to enquire which of the numerous doors leads to the study when Theodore calls out again.

'Door directly opposite the front door, down the corridor first left.'

Walking across the Persian carpeted corridor, Adrian wonders why if Theodore was aware of his arrival has he not performed the basic courtesy of coming out to greet him. This along with the growing animosity towards his business practices angers Adrian and he enters the study indignantly, regretting the decision both to attend and agreeing to lend Theodore money.

'Morning, all good in London?' greets Benedict from his seat on one of the room's exquisitely upholstered chairs, festooned with depictions of pheasants in a variety of poses.

'Yes it was fine,' replies Adrian.

'Take a seat,' instructs Theodore from his position perched precariously on the corner of an identical armchair, as he leans forward wide-eyed whilst feverishly typing on the latest iMac that sits on the glass table in front of him. Viewing Theodore's agitated appearance; Adrian wonders how many coffees he has consumed that morning.

Adrian slumps into another identical chair, places the Samsonite overnight case on the floor beside him and surveys the spacious interior of the study. The rich aroma of recently brewed coffee permeates the room causing Adrian to eye the now nearly emptied ceramic cups on the coffee table in front of him lustfully.

'Presenting figures in the sales brochure,' remarks Theodore suddenly.

'Yes Adrian what have you come up with, any ideas,' continues Benedict, looking invitingly in his brother's direction.

Theodore turns adroitly, facing Adrian for the first time.

'We're nearly there with the promotional stuff, just some stats and of course the photos and video we'll be doing on site next week.'

'Great,' replies Adrian, unsure what else to say.

'Sure is, Vince is coming over later this morning to discuss plans for next week,' continues Theodore.

'So we might get to meet a celebrity Adrian,' exclaims Benedict.

Adrian merely shrugs his shoulders and does not respond.

'Anything you'd like to share with us regarding the design of the data presentation?' continues Theodore.

Adrian's focus lingers on the empty porcelain coffee cups and he does not reply immediately, in the hope of facilitating an offer of coffee.

'Well?' asks Theodore again impatiently several seconds later.

'I propose embedding three statistical charts within the sales brochure,' states Adrian authoritatively. To Adrian's consternation, Theodore continues typing on the iMac in front of him.

'Namely the bar chart, line chart and the frequency polygon,' continues Adrian.

'Interesting choices,' remarks Benedict.

'Ok' says Theodore. 'Why and what will they look like?'

'These three are personal favourites of mine when dealing with lay people, where the primary objective is eye catching display as opposed to necessarily detailed quantitative analysis,' states Adrian with a new-found enthusiasm.

'Agreed, they can be really useful,' says Benedict.

'I concur,' responds Theodore, still facing the iMac.

'The bar chart and line graph allow one to captivate an audience…,' continues Adrian.

'Yes yes sure we get the picture, show us some examples?' interrupts Theodore, glancing in Adrian's direction.

Adrian clenching his teeth in annoyance at Theodore's interruption determines not to surrender to his demands, at least not immediately.

'Yes I am in possession of a number of templates,' replies Adrian.

'Let's see em,' orders Theodore.

'Yes get them out,' adds Benedict, rubbing his hands together in anticipation.

Adrian begins to rummage through the contents of the Samsonite overnight case at his feet. The intention is to only emerge with the SanDisk memory stick that contains the templates after some considerable amount of time; the exact amount as of yet undecided. As Adrian rummages he continues to talk. 'These are not your average run-of-the-mill Excel charts. Each template is bespoke and has been created using Adobe Illustrator.'

Theodore makes eye contact with Benedict on the other side of the room, and then holds out his right hand, bringing the tips of his thumb and index finger together, before moving his hand up and down in a masturbating gesture. Benedict sighs and looks at the ground. Adrian oblivious continues.

'The significance of this is that it allows for a level of aesthetic subtlety that is not catered for by Excel.' He stops pretending to search through the bag and then adds, 'oh yes by the way I would strongly recommend using Oracle Data Mining for all analysis.'

'Really,' says Benedict.

'Yes really. For ODM contains algorithms for regression, prediction, classification, anomaly detection ...'

'Have you found it yet,' snaps Theodore irritably, cutting off Adrian mid- sentence.

'Oh yes that's where I put it,' says Adrian, holding the memory stick aloft with his right hand.

'About time,' adds Benedict.

'There's the computer, get to work,' says Theodore turning the iMac towards him.

Within seconds Adrian has located the charts on the memory stick. In spite of not being particularly keen on Macs, preferring the practical simplicity of the PC, Adrian gasps in wonder as the frequency polygon appears on the screen in all its splendour; courtesy of the NVIDIA GeForce 320M graphics card.

Benedict approaching the screen remarks, 'Looks good.'

'Cool,' exclaims Theodore as he peers over scrutinising the images. 'Do we just replace the data in that table thing at the bottom and it then updates the chart.'

'Exactly, same for all three, you click between them using these tabs,' instructs Adrian pointing at the screen.

'Good stuff that's that sorted then, just have to come up with some numbers to put in them.'

'Come up with,' stammers Adrian incredulously.

'You don't really expect us to be using our valuable time running around in anoraks collecting data do you?' replies Theodore.

Adrian sighs abjectly and leans back in the upholstered chair. Some seconds later Adrian announces, 'time for a coffee.' He then looks expectantly in Theodore's direction.

'Could do with some more myself,' says Theodore. 'First door on right as you enter the hall then go through the dining hall, the kitchen is straight ahead, machine by the sink coffee is ready, cups in cabinet directly above, bring the beaker with you.'

Discontent engulfs Adrian as he walks through to the kitchen. He is disgusted at how the proprietor of such fine furniture could be so uncivil as to not even offer a guest coffee, a guest who has travelled from London to assist him with his work. Perhaps if he were aware of Theodore's fearful nights and tortured visions there might possibly be a modicum of empathy, but he is not.

Now standing in the kitchen, Adrian admires the elegant simplicity of the Alessi coffee maker. Through the kitchen's window he sees Anastasia standing on the pebbled drive screeching into her mobile phone, seemingly oblivious to the beautiful day. As he watches her the full extent of his regret over the encroachment of the Miller family upon his own is evident to him. Realising that so engrossed has he been over Middleworth-related issues as to ignore this other blight; Theodore, Anastasia and most pertinently Natalia. Adrian, helping himself to a plum from the fruit bowl by the sink, is unable to fathom why Theodore is being so overly obnoxious this morning, even by his own standards. For he is unaware of Theodore's growing animosity towards him. This is due largely to the wallpaper and the fact that the Tranquilo investment has been in the form of a loan, not an investment. In addition Theodore despite his initial relief at receiving the funds had been infuriated over the number of clauses and conditions that Adrian had inserted into the documentation. This he considered extremely rude. The final reason for his consternation is that during the post-meeting lunch with the investors in London, Sasha Kornilenko's interpreter had mentioned to him in passing about what she described as the 'bad vibes' Kornilenko had got from, 'that actuary.'

Returning to the study with the beaker, Adrian decides to bring up the subject of Timeshare Dreams at the first opportunity. Now back in the study, Theodore pours the coffees, at the same time he converses with Benedict.

'Can appreciate it's a bit of a predicament,' states Theodore.

'Needless to say this hasn't gone down well with Natalia, she was expecting an indoor swimming pool and underground parking,' responds Benedict.

'Just like her sister then,' replies Theodore, his hand trembling as he grips the handle of his porcelain coffee cup.

'We just need to do the basics and move in,' says Benedict.

'Of course move in yes,' replies Theodore looking anguished for no apparent reason, as he stares at the Szechuan wallpaper.

Theodore is about to change the subject of the conversation back to Tranquilo when Adrian, leaning forward pensively in his chair addresses him. 'Theodore.'

'What?'

Adrian looking directly at him says, 'I have come across some, err, disturbing information regarding one of your previous projects, Timeshare Dreams.'

Theodore frowns and turning to Adrian says, 'is that so.'
'And what might that be?' asks Benedict jokingly.
'Please tell us what you've found that's so disturbing?' asks Theodore, smiling widely and turning his palms upwards in an open gesture, determined not to portray any displeasure at having this project mentioned yet again.

'This is not about me, it's about them,' remarks Adrian.

'Them and who might they be?' asks Theodore accusingly. Adrian notices that the porcelain cup in Theodore's right hand is trembling incessantly. Looking directly at Theodore, Adrian says, 'Rebecca Daltry amongst others.'

'Don't ever mention that name in this house again,' bellows Theodore, shaking the coffee cup in his right hand menacingly inches from Adrian's face.

Adrian falls silent. The two brothers look in shock at each other across the room. Theodore regretting being uncharacteristically overwhelmed with bitter acrimony adds in a calmer tone, 'listen, I only made some small alterations to the properties. I was forced to by their meagre budgets.'

'An admittance of guilt,' says Adrian.

'Tranquilo is different,' continues Theodore.

'Really?' asks a confused Benedict.

'Absolutely,' says Theodore.

'No defence of your alleged unscrupulous activities then?' enquires Adrian.

'Let's stay calm,' exclaims Benedict rising to his feet and holding his outstretched palms towards them, desperate to avoid another outburst from Theodore.

'I don't answer to you,' states Theodore calmly, pointing at Adrian as he does so. 'But let me explain something for your benefit.'

'Please do.' says Adrian.

'Whilst you, loser number crunching geek that you are, have spent your entire life in oblivion…'

'You can't speak to my brother like that, what's got into you?' interjects Benedict.

Theodore, ignoring him, continues. 'I've been building a legacy that is changing the very world in which we live.'

'Not the spouting hyperbole act again,' remarks Adrian.

'Whatever,' responds Theodore nonchalantly.

'That's enough both of you, please,' pleads Benedict.

'If this legacy as you describe is taking advantage of people, it is certainly nothing to be proud of,' continues Adrian.

'Jerk off, that's business I wouldn't expect you to understand,' says Theodore.

'And there was me thinking business is the economic system whereby goods/services are exchanged for ...'

'Trust you to come up with the bloody dictionary definition,' says Theodore interrupting Adrian mid-sentence yet again.

'It is the Investor Words definition actually,' responds Adrian.

'Whatever you want to think is fine with me,' remarks Theodore.

'There's no need for this, let's all calm down,' implores Benedict.

Adrian looking across at his brother says, 'I fear we have been most unwise in not scrutinising the legal contracts, detailed plans and planning permission documents for this project, prior to providing the loan.'

'Whatever Adrian,' says Theodore.

'Clause 3:i, the loaner reserves the right to recall the loan at any point in time,' replies Adrian.

Benedict, who appears to be in deep thought, the fingers of each hand touching the other in a steepling gesture, says,

'Wait a second; you've got planning permission right?'

'We will do yeah,' replies Theodore.

'Will do,' shout Adrian and Benedict in unison.

'Yes we're sorting it out,' replies Theodore, already deeply regretting that in his fraught state he had made the mistake of mentioning it.

'Sorting it out,' remarks Adrian. 'I was under the impression that building work is due to commence ...'

'And so it shall, have you never heard of retrospective planning permission,' interrupts Theodore.

'Oh no Jesus Christ,' says Benedict in alarm before covering his face with his hands. 'This is bad. Really bad.'

'This is terrible karma,' remarks Adrian.

'Don't start on that again,' says Benedict looking up.

'It's all under control,' replies Theodore in as calm a voice as he can muster, smiling broadly as he does so; his tense body language however suggesting otherwise. Theodore is about to continue when out of the corner of his eye he notices something. Swivelling his head ninety degrees, he is met by the sight of Vince McGrath standing in the doorway.

'Vince!' exclaims Theodore his complexion paling instantaneously. 'Good morning. I didn't see you there. Take a seat.'

'I knocked on the front door a number of times but no one answered,' replies Vince McGrath, running his hands nervously through his long swept back blond hair as he speaks.

Theodore stares at Vince in alarm for a second and then says, 'coffee?'

Vince ignoring Theodore's question looks at Benedict and Adrian in turn and says, 'hi I'm Vince by the way.'

'How do you do,' greet Benedict and Adrian in unison.

'They were just on their way out,' says Theodore now bearing a wide maniacal smile. 'Let me just see them out'.

'But Theodore, we are yet to receive an adequate response about the planning permission,' remarks Adrian.

Adrian barely has time to grab his Samsonite overnight case before Theodore is ushering his brother and he out of the room and marching them down the corridor towards the hallway, pushing them rudely from behind as he does so.

'That's the celebrity endorsement you fucking imbecile,' snarls Theodore as they reach the front door. 'Benedict how could you have recommended this fool, he could fuck up a cup of coffee.'

'It strikes me Theodore that you are the imbecile,' remarks Adrian.

'Oh really, is that so.'

'For it was you who put yourself in the position of allowing the celebrity endorsement to overhear information he was not supposed to be privy to,' continues Adrian.

'My wife was meant to inform me on his arrival, ok.'

'Let's go. See you Theodore,' says Benedict wishing to terminate the conversation with immediate effect.

'Any problems with Vince I'm holding you personally responsible do you understand. You too Benedict,' warns Theodore, prodding Adrian in the chest with his index finger as he does so.

'Would have thought it being your business venture, you would be responsible,' responds Adrian, pushing Theodore forcefully with both hands. Theodore collides with the Chippendale table behind him and falls unceremoniously to the ground.

'Get out of my house,' screams Theodore as he struggles to his knees.

A shocked Benedict considers apologising on his brother's behalf but seeing Theodore's frenzied expression thinks better of it. The two brothers leave the property hurriedly. As they run towards the Lexus LS, Benedict scolds his brother. 'You're out of your mind assaulting him like that.'

'I lost my temper, sorry.'

'Jesus, he only prodded you,' exclaims Benedict breathlessly as he clambers into the car. 'And have you forgotten we've got money in this venture?'

Adrian, securing his seat belt, replies, 'I know, but he deserved it.'

'All I know is he's completely lost it, he's normally so calm. It's as if he's like, I don't know, possessed or something.' replies Benedict, before reversing rapidly, spinning the

Lexus ninety degrees and speeding up the drive, past the columns with the black marble balls atop of them and out onto the main road.

The five mile drive from Ramsbottam Hall back to the Raven household is spent in fervent discussion about the events of the day. Benedict is incensed as to why Adrian had mentioned the planning permission issue after Vince McGrath's arrival. By the time they are turning into the driveway of the house, Adrian has concluded that this is the first time he has been forced to face everyday reality for such a prolonged period of time in quite a while, though this current predicament is not exactly a welcome interruption from his other woes.

Back at Ramsbottam Hall, Theodore having clambered up from the hall's floor is in the kitchen getting a coffee cup for Vince, feverishly imploring himself to form a coherent plan for his return to the study and wondering where the hell Anastasia is.

'How's the golf?' enquires Theodore eagerly on returning to the study.

'Theodore what was all that about?'

'Minor disagreement, Adrian's quite an aggressive character at times,' replies Theodore whilst pouring the coffee.

'What was all that stuff I heard about planning permission?' continues Vince uneasily, unaccustomed with such awkward situations.

'No need to worry,' responds Theodore. 'Getting back to next week's shoot in Spain...'

'Theodore.'

'Yes.'

'What was all that talk about planning permission?'

'That was something entirely different,' says Theodore.

'That conversation was about the barn. Yes the barn, the one we're umm planning to erect just over there,' he continues, pointing out of the study's window to a field on the other side of the river.

'Theodore please, this is pretty embarrassing, we both know that's not the case.'

Theodore spends the next ten minutes in a desperate but futile attempt to persuade Vince to set a date for next week for the video shoot in Spain, assuring him all is fine and insisting the planning permission has been granted. However Vince's suspicions have been raised and he insists that he will make no guarantee with regards to his involvement in the project, without first discussing matters over with his manager. Despite further pleading, flattery and as a last resort the promise of further riches, it proves futile.

Seventeen

On entering the house, Benedict notices Natalia lying on the sofa in the sitting room playing on her Nintendo DS. He turns to Adrian and says, 'see you in a minute.'

'I will put the kettle on,' replies Adrian.

Over the angry hissing of the kettle Adrian can hear Benedict's voice emanating from the sitting room. This is followed by a tirade from Natalia, a disorderly mix of colloquial English and Russian, followed a few seconds later by the sound of the front door slamming shut. Adrian is carefully measuring the half a tea spoon of sugar Benedict takes in his tea when he enters the room dejectedly.

'She's gone to see her sister,' he announces.

'Good, here is your tea,' replies Adrian handing Benedict the cup.

'What a day,' remarks Benedict before adding, 'you don't like her do you.'

'No I do not,' replies Adrian without hesitation. Even though having previously feared this question arising, he feels no regret at the forthright answer.

Benedict contemplates asking why but on further consideration can think of a host of reasons. Instead the brothers return to their discussion on Tranquilo. Adrian, distressed at the prospect that they have loaned money to an unscrupulous venture, warns Benedict about the potential

karma ramifications. Benedict shakes his head in dismay at the word karma being mentioned again but admits to his concern over the lack of planning permission. Both brothers are aware that should Theodore refuse to repay the loan, it would take a considerable effort to redeem it. They stand drinking their tea in silence. Adrian looking out of the window at the blue sky interspersed with small flocculent clouds feels that he is further away from achieving salvation than ever. Sometime later Benedict says, 'well father's not back for hours, how about some Quest for Modernity IV?' Adrian considers the question for a second and then replies,
   'Why not.'

Back at Ramsbottom Hall, after Vince leaves the house, a distraught Theodore is phoning George Smith, the assistant manager on the project. George Smith is an acquaintance of Vince's manager and it was he who had arranged Vince McGrath's participation in the first place. Theodore stands pleading for George Smith to answer the phone, after several rings he does.
   'Hi Theodore,' greets George.
   'Bad news, there's a problem with Vince.'
   'What problem has he ...'
Theodore not allowing George to finish continues. 'He's suspicious we haven't secured planning permission yet.'
   'What, are you sure? Why would he suspect that?' asks a confused sounding George.
   'He overheard a conversation.'
   'A conversation with who? where?'
   'With Benedict Raven and that loser of a brother of his at my house earlier,' responds Theodore, refusing to vocalise Adrian's name.
   'Surely not about issues with the planning permission,' replies George, becoming increasingly concerned.
   'Afraid so.'
   'While Vince was there?'

'I didn't know he was, ok,' responds Theodore defensively.

'Didn't know!' shouts George.

'I guess I fucked up.'

George exhales sharply and replies, 'you could say that.'

'Contact his manager and tell him that Vince is mistaken,' orders Theodore.

'Wait a second, does Vince actually know we don't yet have planning permission and …'

'I've denied everything but he's suspicious,' interjects Theodore. 'Find out what we've got to do to reassure him its ok.'

'How?'

'Reassure him or something,' responds Theodore. 'I don't know suck his dick.'

'Very helpful,' replies George drily. 'If he's suspicious we've got problems…'

'That much I know already,' says Theodore, interrupting George yet again.

'Listen,' states George. 'Frank, Vince's manager agreed to get Vince involved on the understanding that this was all above board.'

'Yes yes of course,' replies Theodore hurriedly.

'You know as well as anyone there've been some high profile unscrupulous property ventures in Southern Spain in recent years,' continues George.

'I've denied everything alright,' responds Theodore 'Find out what we need to do to sort it out.'

'I'll call him and try and convince him all is ok, but you owe me an explanation about exactly what occurred,' responds George curtly.

'No celebrity endorsement, no project,' warns Theodore.

'Call you back once I've spoken to him.'

'I'm counting on you.'

'You've got some explaining to do putting our necks on the line like this,' remarks George before hanging up.

Theodore proceeds to pace around the house relentlessly, his heart pounding incessantly, aware that the reckless incident both instigated and further aggravated by Adrian threatens him with destitution. Without Vince McGrath there is no project and without the project he has no way out of his precarious financial state. To compound matters the investors' deadline is fast approaching.

It culminates in the dressing room with Theodore kicking out at one of the Georgian antique wooden wardrobes with such ferocity that his foot goes clear through its pine front. Collapsing to the ground, he lies pounding his fists on the Persian carpet, consumed by an unremitting anguish and desperately pleading for George to rectify the situation. The very moment his mobile screen illuminates, Theodore snatches at it frantically.

'Please tell me what I want to hear,' pleads Theodore.

'If it's that your delivery is ready for collection then I've got good news,' replies the woman at the other end of the line.

'What delivery who is this?'

'The curtain rings you ordered from Rural Homes Direct.'

'Not now,' screeches Theodore before hanging up.

Several fraught minutes later the mobile's screen illuminates again.

'Tell me good news,' demands Theodore on answering the phone.

'I told Frank there's been a misunderstanding and that all's fine,' states George. 'He's already spoken to McGrath and the two have decided that...'

'That?' exclaims Theodore, unable to wait.

'They're demanding to see Marbella City Council's correspondence verifying that planning consent has been granted,' continues George.

'I see,' replies Theodore, unsure whether this news is good or bad.

'There's no way round it,' adds George solemnly. 'I don't know what you were thinking getting us into this mess.'

'Let's reconvene later,' responds Theodore, abruptly terminating the conversation.

Theodore hurriedly locates the number for his contact at Marbella City Council, Antonio Manuelos, an unscrupulous employee from the Land Registration department. The call goes unanswered and Theodore much to his annoyance is left with no alternative but to leave a message on his voicemail. To his immense relief Manuelos phones back a few minutes later. Sensing the desperation in Theodore's voice, he agrees to email a fraudulent letter, in exchange for a one thousand Euro fee. During the conversation Manuelos repeats his previous assurances to Theodore that when his uncle wins the delayed mayoral election later that year, as everyone knows he will, planning permission will be granted. With the possibility of redemption instantaneously restored, Theodore punches the air triumphantly and then jumps up and down in jubilation. Returning to the study to wire the money from his online bank account, the frightful thought occurs to him that he does not have the one thousand Euros to send. However his luck is turning and the loan from the Raven brothers is finally showing in the account.

Later that afternoon finds Theodore in the Aston Martin, weaving his way down the country lanes to the bank in Foley. With one hand he grips the vinyl steering wheel, whilst with the other the initial building material deposit list for Tranquilo, his attentions alternating between the list and the road. The plan is to locate the building materials for which a deposit is required and where the costs can be reduced and the difference pocketed. Theodore reasons that with the dire state of his personal finances, he is left with no alternative. By the time Theodore is entering the bank, he has concluded that adhesives promise the best hope of success. Due to the fact there is a high probability that this minor alteration would go unnoticed by the surveyors hired by the investors to scrutinise the finished properties.

Theodore approaches the teller and asks for three thousand pounds in cash; he would be back for more. On the return journey home, his harried mind ponders the finer logistical points of the plan. Only too aware that all receipts must add up to the monies provided by the investors, the decision is made that he will purchase the premium adhesives, as initially set out in the plans. However using the seven day money back guarantee offered by Costa Building Solutions in Marbella, he will simply cancel the order in the allotted time frame and order a lower quality adhesive. This will allow him to pocket the difference in cost whilst keeping the receipt from the transaction for the more expensive adhesive for the company records. He assures himself that no one will ever cross reference the receipts against the individual items on the bank statement, they never do.

On entering Ramsbottom Hall, something of Theodore's customary arrogance is returning once more and is evident in his gait as he swaggers through the hall. He is met by the sight of Anastasia and Natalia in the sitting room giggling shrilly as they engage in a Mario Kart battle on their Nintendo DSes. Both sisters sway continually from side to side, as if this action will aid them in the turning of the corners on their respective screens' racetrack.

'Afternoon children, glad to see someone's having fun,' greets Theodore.

The sisters continuing with the game ignore him.

'Need a word Anastasia,' states Theodore sternly.

Anastasia frowns, presses the pause button and mutters an instruction to her sister in Russian. Natalia departs the room haughtily.

'What?' asks Anastasia.

'We agreed, did we not, that you'd let me know when Vince McGrath arrived.'

'I forgot,' responds Anastasia, not sounding the least bit apologetic.

'No shit you forgot,' continues Theodore. 'Where the hell were you?'

'Jogging by the river.'

'Having left the front door open and unattended.'

Anastasia offers no response and merely shrugs her shoulders.

'Vince wandered in of his own accord to hear some information he was not supposed to.' continues Theodore.

'This nearly caused a catastrophe.'

'What's a ca-ta-st-ro-phe?'

'It's a really bad thing.'

Anastasia finding the conversation increasingly tedious looks sullenly at the floor.

'Well fortunately it's going to be ok, no thanks to you,' continues Theodore reaching into the inside pocket of his blazer. 'Darling.'

'What now?' says Anastasia looking up to be met by a tightly bound wad of fifty pound notes flying towards her. She snatches the bundle from the air greedily, her previous acrimonious expression replaced by one of glee.

'There's five hundred quid there,' says Theodore.

Anastasia skips gaily towards the door to go and tell her sister the good news.

'Not so fast,' exclaims Theodore, beckoning for her to approach with his outstretched hand, before pointing at his lap. Frowning, Anastasia walks up to Theodore and lowers herself to her knees. As she unzips his trousers the thought occurs to her that some things in life never seem to change.

Eighteen

Adrian and Colin, whisky tumblers in hand, are in the sitting room playing chess. Adrian struggles to maintain his concentration on the game, as his thoughts fluctuate from the events of the day, to Middleworth, purgatory, and hopes of redemption. Within the hour the game has been lost and his father is chastising him for his feeble performance, for which Adrian offers no defence. Both father and son drain the remnants of their tumblers and call it a night.

Lying in the Miracoil bed with spring system awaiting the onset of sleep, Adrian is once again deeply concerned that the recent emergence of his former self Charles Middleworth in his life is some form of premonition and that his fate is soon to be sealed. That the floating through the sky between the multitudes in purgatory below and the celestial souls in heaven above, somehow represent how his fate is as yet undecided. So prevailing is this sense that he does not dwell on the tumultuous events of recent days, neither the preaching in London or the visit to Ramsbottam Hall.

Five miles away in Ramsbottam Hall, Theodore is lying in bed in the room at the end of the corridor, having been ordered there by his wife. Anastasia's good humour having dissipated beneath a disorderly tirade of Russian profanity and piteous wails on witnessing the damage to her beloved Georgian antique wooden wardrobe. Theodore remains deeply troubled, for despite the avoidance of the calamity that Vince terminating his involvement with Tranquilo would have caused, matters remain uncertain. Lying on his back staring up at the ceiling so as to avoid the sight of the Ming Dynasty wallpaper, Theodore recollects on how only weeks ago, Adrian was merely an irrelevancy in his life. So much so that he was not even sure to whom Colin was referring to when he had mentioned his name, during the telephone conversation that day at the graveyard. This in spite of the fact he had met Adrian on a number of occasions.

Theodore laments the fact that in the short time since, Adrian has become the bane of his waking existence and through his words and actions threatens him with oblivion. In his uncharacteristically pensive mood, the events that have led to this conclusion occur to him sequentially. Firstly Adrian's mention of Marquee's to Anastasia at the least opportune time, weeks before the stock market collapse. This event leading directly to his dependency on the Raven brothers' loan for the Tranquilo project set-up costs, followed by the tortuous amount of time Adrian had forced him to wait before finally agreeing to the proposition. Only for Adrian to threaten this prospect of deliverance by bringing up the subject of the planning permission in Vince's presence and then irrationally, against his very own vested interests remarking on it again.

Theodore is confounded as to how Adrian, previously nothing more than a tedious and instantly forgettable actuary, now wields a power to control his destiny, as if he is some form of deity. Theodore makes the decision that he will stay well away from Adrian from this point in time onwards and vows that in the end, it will be he, Theodore Miller, who will reign triumphant.

On turning off the bedside light, darkness engulfs the room and Theodore's lingering fear of the night returns. So engrossed has he been with other matters that the perils of the night, forgotten temporarily, now weigh heavily upon him. Steadfastly with a concerted effort Theodore banishes all negative thoughts from his mind. Instead he focuses his concentration on the image from the front cover of the Tranquilo sales brochure. After a prolonged effort, the valley in all its splendour forms in his mind's eye. The rays of a hot Mediterranean sun shimmering on the surface of the lake's crystal waters, as the immaculately manicured lush green grass of the golf course sway in the gentle breeze, the villas looming majestically in the background. The image of the Tranquilo Valley is extinguished the very moment sleep descends upon him and once more he finds himself frantic and fearful, in the dark confines of a netherworld. Only the light of dawn the next morning impinging on the darkness from underneath the velvet curtains brings some respite from his woes. Within seconds of waking, his focus returns to the Tranquilo project, his rabid being clinging to this hope of redemption.

Half an hour and two double espressos later, an irritable Theodore is in the study typing frenetically on the iMac, when an email from Vince McGrath's manager arrives in his inbox. The email states that Vince is delaying the photo shoot by a further two days. The excuse being that as he feared there was no planning permission, he had booked a day's training at Sandwich golf course and when the email had arrived from Marbella City Council, it was too late to cancel. Theodore screams 'ADRIAN,' very loudly, furious that he is still being affected by the ramifications of his actions. Remembering that Kornilenko's private jet is booked for the trip in two days' time, Theodore screams, 'ADRIAN,' even louder than the first time and bangs his fist on the arm of his chair. Grabbing the Bang & Olufsen telephone from its holder, he hurriedly dials the number of Kornilenko's office.

Having explained the need to rebook the use of the private jet, Kornilenko's English-speaking personal assistant Ana informs him that the following Monday is the only day it is not booked between now and the May thirtieth deadline set by the investors. In defiance of Theodore's insistence on the use of the plane for two days, Ana remains adamant that this will not be possible. Theodore demands to speak to Kornilenko directly. Ten minutes later Kornilenko is finally located by Ana. An impassioned speech ensues, in which Theodore explains the importance of a two-day booking for the photo shoot, in case of logistical or weather related issues; all of which is translated by Ana. At the conclusion of his appeal, Theodore waits impatiently as Ana finishes her translation. The remainder of the conversation consists of a single 'niet.'

To compound matters having contacted Guildford Corporate Video Solutions to reschedule the team and equipment for the following Monday, Theodore is informed that due to it being less than ten days' notice, he has to pay a penalty.

At the completion of the call, Theodore tugs at the curls of hair on the back of his head, exasperated that the consequences of Adrian's actions are still manifesting themselves as multiple inconveniences at every turn. He is perturbed that there is to be only one day for the photo shoot, aware that it is absolutely essential that next Monday is a sunny day. Though appreciating that the odds of this occurring on a late spring slash early summer day in Southern Spain are stacked in his favour, Theodore is unable to relax. Closing his eyes, he attempts to evoke the image of Tranquilo from the sales brochure, as he had done the previous night. This time however, despite a concerted effort, he is unable to do so. For in his fraught state his irritable mind is quite unable to focus. Not only is this due to the events of that morning but also the nocturnal ordeal of the previous night.

Sometime later Theodore opens his eyes and downs the remainder of his double espresso, stands up and heads down to the cellar. After unlocking the gun cabinet, he runs his fingers along the barrels of his collection of exquisite hand-crafted English and Spanish shotguns. Instead of selecting one of his favourites, Theodore takes out the crudest and cheapest of the weapons, the factory produced four-shot Russian Saiga pump action. A gun that he would never be seen with socially, but due to its multi-shot capability, he surmises that it is the most effective for his current purpose; mindless solitary destruction. Grabbing a handful of cartridges from the box on the floor, he heads upstairs and out into the courtyard. The familiar cooing of the African collared doves no longer resounds here and all is silent, for the birds are avoiding Ramsbottam Hall, a result of the fate of their companions. Theodore makes the decision to pursue them in the meadow.

Back in the Raven household, Adrian having only recently awakened is taking sips from a mug of Twinings English Breakfast Tea. The previous night had been a particularly torrid experience. On numerous occasions he had found himself alongside Middleworth, as the two of them flailed helplessly in a sky filling with sinister storm clouds that surged ominously past all around them. The clamouring of the huddled masses far below was louder and yet more intimidating than ever, as they descended towards them. As their wretched features became discernible, gusts of wind would propel the pair upwards, away from the universal lament and towards the small cumulous clouds with the souls astride of them far above. Soaring higher, Middleworth and he in unison their arms outstretched, laughing in joyous harmony. Only for the wind to change direction and they would descend, desperately clawing at the air in a futile effort to avoid the inevitable wailing, more voluminous with each insufferable second.

So repeatedly did this occur that Adrian would awaken dizzy and nauseous. After fumbling for the bedside light, Adrian sat propped up against the headboard beneath the picture of Isaac Newton taking gulps of water from a bottle of Evian and attempting to compose himself before sleep would find him once more.

Adrian takes another gulp of tea and looks aimlessly out of the window, distressed at the frantic nature of these dreams and the fear that matters are escalating once more. This he deems most unfair, for having gradually come to embrace concepts that had until so recently been alien to him, such as reincarnation and life cycles, he has now reached another ceiling and is unable to comprehend the illogical and unexplainable fear that the end time is impending when his destiny will be decided. Desperate to achieve attainment amongst the clouds with the celestial souls yet unaware how to achieve this, Adrian bangs his fist against the wooden kitchen table in frustration. His complex, logical, scientific mind is once again deemed useless in the face of these unexplainable forces. Sometime later Adrian becomes aware of his brother's voice emanating from outside. Through the widow he sees Benedict pacing irritably in circles on the front lawn whilst talking on his mobile.

Adrian is on the verge of completing the buttering of a piece of toast. There now being butter of approximately three millimetres thickness covering virtually its entire surface area when Benedict enters the room with Natalia in tow.

'Morning,' greets Adrian.

'Just had Theodore on the line,' says Benedict. 'He's still really mad at you about yesterday.'

Natalia hands on hips stares at Adrian wrathfully and adds,

'Very,' in a dramatic and forceful fashion.

'New word Natalia,' says Adrian before taking a bite from the piece of toast. Natalia does not respond.

'Apparently Vince McGrath is still on board,' continues Benedict. 'However the photo shoot in Spain's been delayed for some reason.'

'Really,' replies Adrian, wishing he had not spent so long buttering the piece of toast, as it is now not as hot as he would have liked.

'So no photo shoot until next Monday,' continues Benedict.

Colin enters the room and says, 'morning all.' He then grabs the car keys from beside the kettle.

'Nice top Natalia,' remarks Colin. 'Cashmere?'

'Pashmina,' replies Natalia eagerly, enthused that the topic of conversation has turned to her.

'Is it new?' asks Colin.

'Yes,' replies Natalia.

'Another new word,' exclaims Adrian.

Natalia scowls and then pulls the Nintendo DS from the garment's large front pocket and departs the room abruptly. Benedict looks in annoyance at his brother. Colin stifles a laugh and then he too leaves the room. Benedict sits down, pours himself a mug of tea and says, 'have to confess I'm not looking forward to going to Spain.'

Adrian drops the remnants of the piece of toast in his hand; it falls to the plate, scattering crumbs. 'You're not still going,' says Adrian. 'After it has transpired that Theodore is a lunatic and doesn't have planning permission.'

Benedict explains how Theodore has now got documentation to suggest otherwise.

Benedict's continuing involvement in the Tranquilo project upsets Adrian considerably and his mood is a self-deprecating one. He had been hoping that Benedict would insist on recalling the loan and he does not believe Theodore's assertion that planning permission has now suddenly been granted, less than twenty-four hours after he had admitted that he didn't have it. Adrian is distressed by his inability to persuade his brother to abandon the project and angered by how Natalia and Theodore are leading to a contamination of his family's values. Above all he misses his mother and wishes she were here to rectify these matters; he dearly hopes that she is not languishing in purgatory. Moments later he banishes this awful thought from his mind, realising it is a futile one and recognising that even in this worst-case scenario, there will come a time when another mortal existence will be granted her.

Later that morning Adrian wanders through the garden taking photographs of the daffodils with the Canon EOS, zooming in and out using the TS-E 24 mm f/3.5L II lens. Adrian quickly tires of this activity and is soon slumped on the veranda's teak bench, the camera ignored on the table in front of him. Adrian's attentions turn to some of the countless unanswered questions that have been tormenting him; from how to attain the necessary karma to achieve attainment and avoid purgatory, to his concern that the end time is approaching and his fear that he and Benedict have loaned their mother's inheritance to an unethical business venture. That afternoon there is reprieve in the form of an email from Sri in his inbox:

....

Mon, May 20, 2011 at 14:24 AM, Sri Kuhn <srikuhn@worldpeacecorps.org> wrote:

Hello Adrian,
Just back from The Ruhr, it was a wonderful trip, look forward to telling you all about it. Are you around next Monday? Hosting a charity event (Kerala mud slide appeal). Sorry about the late notice, things are bit chaotic right now with Meredith (my secretary) on holiday. I'm pretty much useless without her.

Venue is Somersham Gardens (4 miles on from Ramsbottam on the A19) from 2p.m. Please bring friend/s, more the merrier, £30 donation per person (cash only please). Short talk, drinks and some activities, will be good fun. Hope to see you there.

Sri
(p.s. let's meet one on one soon)
…………………………………………………………………………..

Adrian replies in the affirmative.

Nineteen

Sunday Evening - The satellite image of Southern Spain appears on the iMac's twenty-seven inch screen. Theodore presses print and fidgets impatiently whilst he waits for the image to be ejected by the Epson laser printer; snatching the sheet of paper from the printer's in-tray, the second it is emitted. He places it on the desk next to the satellite image of the same area from four hours' previous, takes a ruler from the desk's drawer and measures the distance between the thin band of cloud casting an arc over the Andalucía region and the Tranquilo Valley to the south. In both images the distance is precisely seven point five millimetres, which equates to forty kilometres.

There is a modicum of relief that the band of cloud has not encroached further. Theodore slumps into the leather chair and runs his hands through his hair, before reaching across the desk and grabbing the Bang and Olufsen handset from its stand and pressing redial. He taps the fingers of his right hand on the glass desk top irritably while he waits for the call to Instant International Weather Information to be answered. The hold music is the song Keep Holding On by Avril Lavigne. It was two days' previous during the first of his twenty-seven calls that Theodore had concluded it was an entirely inappropriate choice of music. Due in part to the fact that invariably a considerable amount of time was spent waiting for the call to be answered. At first he had disliked Lavigne's whining tone and the song's sentimental lyrics; over time this had festered into hatred. Seven minutes and twenty seconds later a voice comes on the line, it is a male with a distinctive Indian accent. 'Good evening International ...'

'Need an update for the Marbella region tomorrow,' demands Theodore interrupting the call centre agent in customary fashion.

Balraj the call centre agent, recognising Theodore's voice, sighs despondently and then says, 'Mr Miller no change since last time we spoke, forecast is sunny, small risk of...'

'No not forecasts, not after twenty-seven calls,' says Theodore. 'I need certainties and I need them now.'

'Mr Miller we can only report on...'

'I demand to speak to the manager at once.'

'But if you would...'

'Now,' bellows Theodore.

'Good evening Mr Miller,' greets the manager fully two minutes later.

'I need to know exactly what the weather will be like in the Malaga region tomorrow,' instructs Theodore, in as calm a fashion as he can muster.

'Mr Miller we provide forecasts, not certainties,' replies the manager.

'Might I remind you I'm paying sixty pence a minute for this service.'

'There is no correlation between costs of service and forecast probabilities sir,' states the manager, somewhat annoyed to be relaying this information for the umpteenth time.

'No you listen here it's only twelve hours or so away, I'm not asking you to be Nostradamus, just tell me in layman's terms is the weather going to hold?'

'Mr Miller ...'

Theodore cuts her off again. 'Listen I can forgive a few of the little clouds, what do you call them.'

'Cumulous clouds Mr Miller.'

'Yeah them they're fine, it's the rain fuckers,' continues Theodore.

'Nimbus clouds Mr Miller and might I remind you again about our swearing policy.'

'Tell me what's going to happen?' implores Theodore.

The manager considers the question and then replies, 'if I was putting money on it I would say it will be a sunny day.'

'Go on,' says Theodore.

The manager proceeds to explain in great detail the processes that lead to the formation of nimbus clouds and the resulting precipitation. On hanging up the phone Theodore leans back in his chair once more, relieved that the odds for a fine day for the photo shoot are high. As he sits staring at the ceiling, he wonders if clouds are affecting anyone as much as he in the entire world, quite unaware of Adrian's predicament, merely five miles away.

Meanwhile Anastasia is in the sitting room humming the theme tune to Tchaikovsky's The Nutcracker; the harmony wistful and enchanting. Despite the current turmoil within the household, her demeanour remains indifferent and unresponsive, for she had become accustomed to upheaval from an early age. The collapse of the Soviet Union during her childhood had altered the fabric of an entire society. It was during this turbulent time that Anastasia first ventured from the apartment block to the surrounding industrial wasteland. The first inclinations towards capitalism stirring in a heart, that would soon be as cold and uncompromising as the rocks and twisted metal that littered it.

05:45 - The Following Morning - Theodore awakens abruptly, sitting bolt upright in bed, his face gleaming with beads of perspiration. The previous night Theodore had once again been subjected to a torrent of the chaotic and unexplainable. On pulling open the Dupioni silk window curtains, the grey light from the gloomy morning outside pervades the room. Theodore takes several deep breaths, his eyes focusing with a steely resolve, aware that the day of judgement has arrived and determined that it will be a success. Walking through to the bathroom, he washes his face in cold water before putting on a pressed white dress shirt and linen beige travel suit.

06:15 – Having hastily consumed a bowl of Alpen cereal, he makes a final visit to SatelliteWeatherUpdater.com. The satellite image shows a fine dawn with a few interspersed clouds of the cumulous variety that appear on the image as if they were small plumes of smoke. The band of cloud to the north in the Andalucía region appears fairly harmless and at any rate has moved only marginally south over the course of the night. Theodore punches the air triumphantly and shouts 'Yes'.

07:00 – Theodore is sitting behind the vinyl steering wheel of the Aston Martin V8 convertible considering whether to return to the house to bid farewell to Anastasia, who has not yet awoken. He concludes that it would be wise not to disturb her and turns the key in the ignition. By the time he is turning out of the drive onto the main road, he is adamant that his fortunes are changing for the better.

07:50 – Theodore is parked in the car park of Recton airfield awaiting the arrival of the others. A flock of rooks are circling the field adjoining the airstrip, kaahing continuously as they do so.

08:25 – Mark and Louis the film crew from Guildford Corporate Video Solutions are unpacking the filming equipment from the back of their Land Rover Defender.

08:43 – Vince has now arrived and is in animated conversation with Mark and Louis about the draw for the forthcoming Abu Dhabi Golf Championship the following week. Theodore checking the time on his Rolex watch wonders where Benedict has got to.

09:13 - A tiny beacon of luminescence appears in the grey mist, growing persistently brighter. Within a minute a Gulfstream G650 jet becomes visible. Benedict has still not arrived. Theodore tries his mobile without success.

09:28 - Kornilenko watches expressionless from the comfort of his on-board leather armchair, as the team load the airplane. A surly Armenian of gargantuan proportions, who serves as his security stands beside the chair with arms crossed. A petite cabin attendant in a pleated skirt pours espressos into two ceramic cups. Theodore entering the jet is concerned that Kornilenko has attended in person, as this brings considerable extra pressure.

'Hi Sasha, good to see you,' greets Theodore warmly. Kornilenko does not reply and merely nods in acknowledgement.

'Let me introduce the man himself,' continues Theodore putting an arm around Vince's shoulder. 'The golf champion extraordinaire, Vince McGrath.' Once again there is no response from Kornilenko.

'And this here is Mark and Louis from Guilford Corporate Video Solutions, continues Theodore, as Mark and Louis enter the aircraft, weighed down with camera equipment. Kornilenko however has already returned his attentions to NTV news, which is showing on the cabin's flat screen television. Theodore glances at his Rolex again, infuriated by Benedict's late arrival and now worried that he is not coming. This is a concern to him, for with so many people present including Kornilenko; he is keen to have someone with a vested interest in the project to assist in managing everyone. As Theodore waits impatiently, he blames Adrian.

09:31 - The tyres of Benedict's Lexus grate against the gravel of the car park.

'Where the hell have you been?' asks Theodore as Benedict enters the jet.

'Sorry was talking with Adrian,' replies Benedict. Theodore clenches his fists and grits his teeth at the mention of Adrian's name but says nothing. Benedict stands in awe as he surveys the opulent interior of the aircraft and then texts Adrian with an update.

09:36 – The roar of the Rolls-Royce BR725 engine reaches its apex and the jet leaves the runway and begins to ascend effortlessly into the sky.

Fifteen minutes later the passengers' faces are pressed against the cabin windows, as they view The English Channel's busy shipping lanes far beneath them. The mist has cleared somewhat and the sky is a greyish blue, interspersed with large cumulous clouds that tower upwards majestically from their flat bases, as mounds of undulating white.

Vince's complexion is now a greenish hue. He holds a paper bag to his mouth whilst resting his head against the cabin window.

'Vince are you feeling ok?' enquires Theodore noticing his suffering. Vince shakes his head miserably but does not mouth a reply. Theodore observes his celebrity endorsement anxiously, but concludes that he will be fine once they are back on land.

A little over an hour later The Pyrenees in all their grandeur appear far below them, the sun glinting on the remnants of snow that cling stubbornly to their jagged peaks.

10:28 - Benedict, Mark and Louis are sitting around the jet's conference table for an impromptu meeting. Vince, unable to attend, stays in his seat with the now permanent feature of the paper bag attached to his mouth. Kornilenko and the large Armenian remain in their leather chairs watching a Russian basketball league highlights show. Theodore standing to the side of the table rolls down the sleeve of his shirt to check the time, before announcing. 'Gentlemen in forty-six minutes we will be on the ground.' Pointing at the

map on the iMac which is positioned on the conference table with his pen he adds, 'we will be landing right here, approximately five kilometres from the Tranquilo Valley.'
Unexpected turbulence rocks the jet, causing Theodore to grip the chair in front of him resolutely to prevent himself being unceremoniously knocked to the ground. Vince wretches loudly much to the chagrin of Kornilenko, who stares at him with eyes that bear a savage malignity. The turbulence passes as quickly as it begun and Theodore continues.

'Two vehicles will meet us at the landing strip and take us to our location.' Theodore goes on to explain the itinerary for the day before concluding some minutes later with the words, 'Integritas, caritas, lucrum.'

10:57 – The splendour of rural Andalucia appears beneath the plane. A myriad of hills and vineyards interspersed with rural dwellings. Theodore his nose pressed up against the cabin window screen peruses the horizon, his eyes flitting from side to side as he does so. After a minute or so he jogs to the other side of the aircraft and repeats the vigil. Having repeated the exercise several times he is satisfied that the pristine blue sky is not threatened by ominous weather conditions lurking on the horizon. He smiles widely, content that by the time the day is out his woes will be behind him.

11:20 – The drone of the Rolls-Royce BR725 engine grows steadily more subdued as the jet gradually comes to a halt on the bumpy sun-baked airstrip. Through the cabin window Theodore viewing the fine day wonders what he was so worried about. Even Vince is looking healthier now, the brownish glow from hours spent on sun-strewn golf courses returning to his cheeks once more.

11:38 – Theodore, Benedict, Mark and Louis are sitting exposed to the elements in the back of a two wheel drive Nissan Titan, their hair being ruffled by the wind.

Kornilenko, the Armenian and Vince McGrath follow behind in a Range Rover Sport.

'Listen guys,' shouts Theodore, in order that his voice is heard over the noise of the engine and the wind. 'Don't let the Russian or Vince anywhere near the lake.'

'Why can't they swim,' replies Benedict.

'No you idiot,' says Theodore. 'The water's pretty stagnant and apparently doesn't smell so good.'

'In the marketing brochure it looked as clear as crystal,' remarks Louis as he grips the side of the vehicle with one hand and the camera tripod with the other.

'And so it shall,' states Theodore with characteristic certainty. 'Once there's been some rain, we're going to divert a stream to flush it through.' Pointing with his index finger at Benedict, Mark and Louis in turn he adds, 'but for today we'll keep the shoot at least thirty metres up from the valley floor, ok.'

'Ok,' respond Mark and Louis in unison.

'Sure,' says Louis brushing the long locks of blond hair away from his face.

'We've got lenses that'll make it feel like we're right by it anyway, even at thirty metres,' remarks Louis.

The vehicles continue to bump along the track and are soon passing through a gap in the hills and entering the Tranquilo Valley. Surrounded by the rugged rock-strewn hills, the valley appears as a utopian enclave, closed off from the rest of the world. The gentle slopes are a vast expanse of grass, though rather browner than in the brochure that rolls down to the shimmering lake below. Benedict, Mark and Louis gape in wonder at the spectacular scenery.

'Didn't I tell you?' says Theodore to Benedict, feeling immensely proud of himself.

'This place really is quite something,' exclaims Benedict, holding his glasses to his head with one hand to stop them being blown away.

Theodore proceeds to point out the flat area at the far end of the lake where the villas will be situated, followed by the proposed location of each of the golf course's eighteen holes. All the while they drive on into the heart of the valley, as a hot dry wind swirls around it, kicking up dust from the track.

Several minutes later an animated Theodore pointing ahead exclaims, 'That's the spot.' The vehicle comes to a halt and the passengers clamber out clutching the filming equipment. The wind is brisker now and the blades of long browned grass sway in unison.

'It's getting pretty windy,' says Louis.

'Sure is, let's a get move on,' adds Mark shielding his eyes with one hand from the hot sun.

'Let's go,' orders Theodore clapping his hands. Vince gets out of the other vehicle and joins them. Kornilenko and the Armenian watch the proceedings with their driver, from the confines of the Land Rover.

Mark and Louis hastily assemble the tripod, unpack the camera and attach the thirty-five mm lens. Theodore, notebook in hand, runs through a dress rehearsal with Vince.

Mark says, 'we'll use the sun screener as a wind-break.'

Benedict pulls it from the back of the truck and drags it behind him through the grass. He walks about ten metres and then asks, 'How about here?'

'Another five,' instructs Louis.

'How about here,' shouts Benedict again a few seconds later.

Louis says, 'That's great. Pin it down with the strings at the bottom,' as he notices the wind gaining momentum.

Five minutes later Mark shouts, 'We're ready.'

'We'll start with the panoramic of the valley,' says Louis swivelling the Sony XDCAM camera on its tripod as he speaks.

As the camera swivels from left to right, Theodore feels a surge of relief. Basking triumphantly under the

Mediterranean sun, he views the vast expanse of grass and the lake below with pride; with one hand he holds down his panama hat, to prevent it being blown away by the wind. Looking down into the valley he imagines the completed villas and carefully-manicured grass of the golf course.

A few minutes later Theodore shouts out to Mark and Louis about ten metres to his left and slightly behind him.

'Ok guys you done.' There is no response so he calls out again. 'Vince are you ready.' Again no reply is forthcoming. Turning around he sees the three of them stood with their heads turned to the heavens, mouths agape. Bewildered he follows the direction of their gaze and is met by an arc of the darkest, most ominous storm clouds he has ever had the displeasure to witness, pouring angrily over the ragged tops of the hills towards them. He too stands aghast, unable to react to the impending doom. The noise of the driver slamming the Nissan's door shut behind him brings him to his senses and he cries out, 'FILM.'

'Yes,' replies Vince meekly, continuing to stare in shock at the sky.

'Stand there,' shouts Theodore pointing towards the wind screener. 'Mark Louis roll.'

Louis swivels the camera on the tripod towards Vince, who has run over to his allotted position, to the left of the wind screener.

'Roll roll,' shouts Theodore again, his face contorted with terror.

A startled Vince begins to repeat the lines he has rehearsed.

'Welcome to Tranquilo, a utobian paradise.'

The camera stops. Louis looks in Theodore's direction.

'Utopian not Utobian you imbecile,' berates Theodore before shouting, 'Roll roll roll,' as he jumps up and down gesturing a rolling motion with both arms. Vince starts again but doesn't get any further than 'welcome' when a roll of thunder announces the beginning of an unremitting deluge.

'To the vehicle!' shouts Benedict, struggling through the rain towards the Nissan Titan; the others follow. His first thought as he drags his sodden carcass aboard, is the realisation of the absurdity of his instruction to return to the van, as with no roof, it offers no respite from the downpour. This is followed by another, that the choice of a roofless vehicle seems an act of hubris now.

'It will pass,' screams Theodore. 'Get Vince inside the other vehicle he must be kept dry for when we reconvene.'
Vince and Theodore clamber out of the truck and across the ground, a myriad of tiny muddy streams, to the Land Rover. Theodore pulls at the near side passenger door handle. The door is locked and he slips backwards in the mud. Pulling himself upright Theodore attempts to open the other doors. They too are locked. He begins to bang on the window with his fists, yelling at the incumbents to allow Vince inside. Through the rain-streaked glass Kornilenko stares out at him with blue soulless eyes and mouths 'niet', for he does not wish to cause himself discomfort by getting the interior of the vehicle wet. Theodore pleads at the window, his hands forming a praying gesture. Kornilenko remains unmoved. Theodore huddles behind the vehicle screaming obscenities and shaking his fists at the heavens in desperation, fear and derision in equal measure, as the torrent drives down mercilessly upon their wretched beings. Benedict appears beside them shivering in his saturated shirt yelling, 'We've got to get out of here,' a number of times.

'No no it will pass,' dismisses Theodore from his position crouched down behind the Land Rover.

'The driver says it's too slippery for the truck on this gradient, we've got to get down to flatter ground.'
Theodore is about to argue when the sound of the truck's engine reaches them. Dragging themselves out from behind the vehicle they cross the terrain slipping and sliding, before clambering aboard the truck. The journey is a slow wretched ordeal, as the vehicle slides downwards,

struggling to gain purchase in the mud, the sodden passengers cowering miserably inside. The Land Rover Discovery follows behind in a steady, more dignified fashion. Its three litre V6 turbo charged engine and Pirelli Scorpion Zero tyres perfectly adapted for these adverse conditions.

As they approach the lagoon the ground levels somewhat. The reprieve however is a temporary one. Vast swathes of mosquitoes and midges are emerging from the lagoon's fetid waters, a consequence of the deluge and darkened sky. Buzzing vociferously, the insects envelop the vehicle as a veil of malignity. The sharp pain of innumerable proboscises being driven into their flesh causes the passengers to wail deliriously. Coughing and spluttering the driver forces the vehicle onwards, whilst he swipes at the insects with one hand.

'Faster,' screams Theodore, waving his panama hat in front of him in a vain attempt to stave off the remorseless attack.

'Faster,' shrieks Benedict, his shirt now pulled over his head as the insects encroach into his nostrils and ears. Vince, who up to this point had been screaming lamentably and rolling around on the vehicle floor jumps abruptly from the vehicle and scrambles up the muddy slope, away from the foul swamp.

'Get back here,' demands Theodore swiping out at the insects with his hat as he does so, but it is to no avail. Vince, who has suffered from insect phobia since a chance childhood meeting with a Vespa Auraria on a golf course in Malaysia continues to scramble upwards through the mud.

It takes forty minutes to escape the perils of the valley and to return to the airstrip. With Kornilenko and the Armenian already aboard, the stairs leading up to the jet have been retracted. Theodore, Benedict, Mark and Louis disembark the truck and begin to wave frantically to get Kornilenko's attention.

Theodore noting that the rain is now little more than a persistent drizzle announces, 'the weather will break soon then we can film again.'

'It's over,' remarks Benedict despondently, as he takes off his shirt and begins to ring it out.

'I tell you it's not it will be sunny soon,' says Theodore.

Louis following Benedict's lead removes his own shirt and says, 'Benedict's right, that lagoon's unfit for human habitation.'

Theodore does not reply and instead begins to wave hysterically in the direction of the jet once more.

Mark remarks, 'that body of water is worse than that Vietnam rat pit in The Deer Hunter, have you seen it Benedict?'

'Yeah with Meryl Streep, De Niro and Christopher Walken,' replies Benedict abjectly.

Theodore, his eyes bulging alarmingly, points at Benedict, Mark and Louis in turn and then declares, 'We need to get rid of the insects.' He then reaches into his pocket and takes out his mobile. Mark, Louis and Benedict look at each other in disbelief. Miraculously the mobile is still working and there is a signal. Theodore selects Antonio Manuelos's number from the address book and with a trembling finger presses the phone button. There is a long delay followed by an answering machine message. Theodore cursing loudly hangs up and then selects the Marbella City Council office's number from the phonebook. After several rings the call is answered by an operative with the words, 'cargo público de buenas tardes Marbella.'

'Antonio Manuelos,' orders Theodore.

'dispénseme,' replies the confused operative.

'A-n-t-o-n-i-o   M-a-n-u-e-l-o-s,   land   registration department.'

The operative takes a few seconds to digest the information and then replies, 'he a nota here.'

'Listen Pedro put me through to his department now it's an emergency.'

'Okayaa,' replies the operative, pressing the transfer button.

Theodore runs his left hand continuously through his soaking hair as he waits. Eventually a voice says, 'hello who is this.'

'This is Mr Miller you don't know me I'm an associate of Antonio's and who am I speaking to?'

'My name is Alegria Torres. I am the manager of Marbella's Land Registry department,' says Alegria in faultless English.

'Great to speak to you at last, I've heard so much about you from Antonio,' lies Theodore in a vain attempt to flatter her.

'What is it that you are phoning about?' responds Alegria curtly.

'A sprayer,' blurts out Theodore.

'Excuse me.'

'A light aircraft equipped with a sprayer and insecticide,' continues Theodore.

'Why?' asks Alegria, quite taken aback by this request, the most bizarre she has come across during her twenty years at the council.

'I'm in the Tranquilo Valley, we're doing err a building project and there's an issue with mosquitoes.' Theodore immediately regrets using the words, building project.

'This is not possible,' states Alegria emphatically.

'Construction is not permitted in Tranquilo.'

'For now yes but that's going to change when Manuelos's uncle wins the election, so why not face the inevitable today.'

'That's as maybe,' replies Alegria. 'But until that time it's protected.'

Theodore blurts out, 'If you help me now I can do anything for you, money, favours, anything you want.'

'Mr Miller,' replies Alegria. 'Our coast has already been violated with the blood and vomit of you English. Are you now suggesting the same for our interior?'

'It's not like that, Tranquilo is top end…'

Alegria hangs up before he can finish the sentence. Theodore shaking his fists in the air yells loudly. The others watch him in alarm. A few seconds later Benedict pointing towards a dot in the distance exclaims, 'Look, there he is.'

'Bravo, it's Vince,' says Louis.

Vince, his hands still flailing at the now imagined insects is running towards the airstrip.

Rays of light are beaming downwards upon them through the gloom and in the distance the sky is a bright blue once more. Theodore yells, 'The weather's breaking.' The drone of the Gulf Stream's engines startles them. Theodore turning in horror runs to the front of the jet, waving his hat frantically in the air to get Kornilenko's attention and then pointing at the clear weather in front of the plane.

'They're going to leave us behind, the bastards,' remarks Mark.

Vince arrives breathless, collapses to the ground in front of them and mutters, 'it's the worst day of my life.'

'Don't worry it's over.' says Benedict. 'Well, almost.'

'Worse even than when I missed the cut for The Qatar Desert Classic last year,' continues Vince, struggling to catch his breath.

The engine stops, the jet's door opens and its stairs begin to descend towards the ground. The group, looking up in unison, see the large Armenian beckoning them with an outstretched hand. Grabbing the equipment the four of them run towards the plane, Benedict and Mark shouting 'Thank you!' to their driver as they run. Within seconds they have ascended the steps, lugging the heavy equipment behind them. The Armenian hands each of them a pile, consisting of clothes, a large towel and a bin liner; Vince's pile has a sick bag atop of it. They are made to put their wet clothes in the bin liners on the stairs outside by the Armenian, and then with towels wrapped around them, they are admitted. The cabin attendant hands them each a shot of vodka as they enter the plane. Benedict, one hand clutching the bin liner and clothes, the other the vodka, looks up to see Kornilenko, his usually cold expressionless features contorted in mirth. Only his pale blue eyes, which continue to bear a sinister unexplainable ferocity, remain unchanged. The four of them thank Kornilenko forthrightly and head towards the bathroom to change.

Theodore now at the top of the steps peers around the large Armenian into the interior, smiling maniacally as he does so, at the same time pointing out at the brightening sky.

'Sasha the weather's turning lets finish the shoot.'

'Niet,' replies Kornilenko, the expression of mirth disappearing instantaneously at the sight of Theodore, as the cold inhumanity descends upon him once more.

'But please,' pleads Theodore with his hands outstretched in a praying motion. The Armenian pushes Theodore back just as he is about to wriggle around his gargantuan frame and into the jet's cabin. Theodore falls back; tumbling down the first few steps but manages to grab the railing which prevents him hurtling all the way down to the ground. The door closes and the steps begin to retract, Theodore clings to them with a grim resolve, yelling all the while, but it is to no avail and he is forced to release his grip and fall to the muddy runway below. Rising from the mud he begins to wave and jump up and down to get Kornilenko's attention. The engine starts again and the Gulf Stream begins to move along the runway. Theodore grips the axle of one of the back wheels and hangs to it. As the jet accelerates he is forced to release his grasp and is left forlorn in the mud. Moments later the plane ascends into the sky.

The rain has stopped and a rainbow arcs across the landscape, the bands of colour refulgent in the moist air. Theodore lying despondently on the airstrip becomes aware that the prospect of salvation has ceased and that his position is terminal.

Twenty

Adrian, along with a hundred or so other guests is standing on the lawn of Somersham Gardens, champagne flute in one hand, minted cucumber and feta hors d'oeuvre in the other. Sri, the final speaker of the day, is standing on a small podium in the centre of the lawn regaling the audience with his poise and charisma. The subject matter is horticulture, specifically the Encore Azalea, the evergreen low maintenance member of the Azalea family. The topic surprises Adrian somewhat, having assumed that Sri's chosen subject would either be spirituality or The Kerala appeal itself, perhaps even a fusion of the two. Never did he suspect, despite the location that flowers would be on the agenda. He is already somewhat familiar with azaleas, due to his mother's passion for horticulture. The knowledge he possesses includes the fact that azaleas' penchant is for acidic soil, preferably with a Ph value of between five point five and six point five, in addition to the fact that they generally bloom more than once a year. However he is astonished when Sri states that the Encore Azalea is the only patented brand of azalea to bloom in spring, summer and autumn.

As the talk continues, he becomes aware that the subject matter is somehow entirely relevant to his own circumstances; that this notion of continual flowering is in fact a message about life being cyclical. As Sri in all his serenity explains and motions, Adrian identifies his own current existence with a spring Encore Azalea, who previously was Charles Middleworth, an autumn incarnation of the very same plant. He marvels at the simplicity of the message and Sri's ability to use the Encore Azalea to illustrate a lesson on the meaning of life, without actually specifically stating so. Perusing the crowd and noticing their concentrated features and bright alert eyes, he wonders if they too have come to the same conclusion. He suspects that they have.

The mobile phone vibrates in his trouser pocket signifying the arrival of a text message. Annoyed at this intrusion on a rare tranquil moment, Adrian mutters 'Benedict' under his breath, then takes the offending item from his pocket and presses read. The message says, 'Disaster at Tranq! See u in approx 2hrs.' Momentarily Adrian wonders what might have occurred and then returns his attentions to Sri.

At the conclusion of Sri's talk, the guests congregate in small groups on the sun-soaked lawn, talking eagerly amongst themselves whilst taking occasional sips from their drinks. Adrian is keen to speak to Sri, but as he is surrounded by a large circle of people, he concludes that this is not an opportune moment. Instead he wanders across to the wooden table situated next to the podium, from where Sri had delivered his talk. On the table is a large pile of leaflets with the title Kerala - Urgent Appeal in a font Adrian is unable to discern. He picks up one of the leaflets, briefly examines it, then places it back on the table and ambles over to the large flowerbed, complete with several varieties of azaleas, at the far end of the lawn. Meredith, Sri's secretary, is standing in the midst of a small group of people next to the flowerbed, conversing animatedly. Noticing Adrian, she greets him. Adrian takes this as an invitation to join the group. Topics ranging from azaleas to the Kerala appeal are discussed. No mention is made of reincarnation.

Two flutes of champagne and three minted cucumber and feta hors d'oeuvres later finds Adrian standing next to a rhododendron bush at the entrance to the car park, waiting for the ABC mini cab, ordered some minutes earlier. Having enjoyed the relaxed proceedings of the afternoon, his current disposition is a contented one. Stretching upwards, he yawns widely, pleasantly weary from the cumulative effects of sun and champagne. The mini cab arrives soon after. Adrian clambers in, reminds the driver of the destination and they depart. Turning out onto the congested A19, the tranquillity of Somersham Gardens seems a world away.

Adrian's face is pressed up against the glass of the window beside him. Furrows appear across his brow, as his eyes flit nervously from side to side. With one hand he secures a resolute overhand grip on the armrest to his right whilst the other fiddles nervously with the Nokia in his trouser pocket. The cause for this obvious concern is not immediately apparent. For with the torrent of traffic, the mini cab is travelling at a slow, non-threatening pace and far above the sky remains an unbroken expanse of blue.

They have travelled a little over a mile when Adrian, his face now covered in beads of sweat, begins to murmur continuously. Moments later he sits bolt upright and stares at the back of the seat in front of him with bulging fearful eyes, all the while murmuring incessantly. If one were to lean very close, one would hear that he is muttering, 'thirty-nine-years, ten months four days,' repeatedly, in a frenetic fashion. After a while he falls silent and the only sound audible aside from the sound of the engine is his breathing, which comes in harried gasps. Sometime later Adrian begins to whisper, 'thirty-nine-years, ten months and four days,' repeatedly once again, at an ever increasing pace.

'Thirty-nine-years, ten months and four days. Thirty-nine-years ten months and four days, thirty-nine-years ten months four days thirty-nine-years ten months four days...'

Thirty-nine-years, ten months and four days is Adrian's own age as of today, which on its own holds no particular significance. The reason for this sudden fixation with today lies rather in its connection with his former self, Charles Middleworth. For Adrian has just come to the realisation that it was at this exact age, thirty-nine-years, ten months and four days that Charles Middleworth had met his demise in the car inferno. He is astonished that he had never considered this correlation at a prior point in time.

Pulling down the sleeve of his cotton shirt, he glances at the screen of the Casio Mudman. The time is 16:09:33. His heart beat resonates through his body and his breathing becomes yet more agitated, such is the concern that seven hours, fifty minutes and twenty-seven seconds remain of the day. Despite being in the confines of a car however, Adrian can detect no immediate threats to his current existence. The speed dial is wavering around the twenty-four miles per hour mark; a speed that offers little threat of a fatality when travelling as he is, in the back seat. Adrian checks his seat belt is fastened correctly and then tightens it somewhat. Taking a deep inhalation through his nasal passage, there is a modicum of relief that the odour of smoke cannot be detected. He repeats the exercise to make sure and gets the same result. After which he concentrates his auditory senses until quite certain that there is no rattling noise being emitted from the back of the car. Leaning forward in a brace position, identical to that recommended in cases of emergencies on flights, Adrian attempts to convince himself that the journey poses no risk. A number of facts appear in his mind to support this. One of these is that this mini cab is a Ford S-Max, recently voted the safest vehicle in the MPV class.

The suffering is alleviated considerably on arriving back home and exiting the mini cab. Having paid the rather bemused driver, Adrian walks up to the house and unlocks the front door. Standing motionless in the dim light of the hall, he surveys its interior. The only sound is the barely audible ticking of the Thomas Turner grandfather clock. Walking into the study, he slumps into Colin's chair, before taking several gulps from a half empty bottle of Evian mineral water on the mahogany desk in front of him. Once more he checks the time; it is 16:23:55. Barely a second later he has calculated that seven hours, thirty-six minutes and four seconds remain of the day.

Selecting the stop clock function on the Casio Mudman, he enters a minute and then proceeds to measure his pulse with the first two fingers of his right hand. It seems like an eternity until the beeping signifies that the minute has elapsed. Though the pulse rate is twenty beats faster than its normal rate, ninety as opposed to seventy, it remains far below a speed that could potentially signify an impending cardiac arrest. Adrian sighs with relief and takes another gulp of water.

His attentions fall on a framed photograph on the far wall. It is of a funeral procession; a youthful looking Colin at its helm. Adrian is unsure whether the picture is his father's first working funeral or perhaps even the funeral of his own grandfather. For some time he gazes at the picture, once again acutely aware of the futility of his efforts to escape the Raven family's close association with death.

In the familiar surroundings of the study, Adrian begins to relax somewhat. Gradually the pace of his breathing subsides and his pulse returns to close to its normal rate of seventy throbs per minute. By the time the Thomas Turner grandfather clock has completed its final chime for six o' clock, Adrian has concluded that his own existence is not in jeopardy and that there is nothing consequential about having reached the age that Charles Middleworth had, at his time of death. Despite this, he remains eager for the day to draw to a close.

The sound of a car pulling to a halt outside the house can be heard, followed by the sound of doors slamming shut; the noise of which startles Adrian. The very next moment, his auditory senses are accosted by argumentative voices. They are instantly recognisable as belonging to Benedict and Natalia. Through the closed door of the study Adrian hears the front door open, followed by an angry tirade from Natalia, as the two of them pass through the hall, into the sitting room and then out onto the veranda.

Adrian remains in his seat for several further minutes then stands up, walks out of the study and through the hall, before continuing through the sitting room and the glass door at its far end, onto the veranda.

'Adrian,' greets Benedict. Natalia turns her back to them and departs haughtily, bearing an acrimonious expression whilst cursing loudly in Russian. Adrian moves very slightly to the side, to allow her the space to fit through the half open door.

'What a day you won't believe what's happened,' says Benedict in an exasperated tone.

'Well I rather feel that I was there in person, what with the continual text updates,' replies Adrian, reaching over and pouring himself a glass of wine from the open bottle of Chianti on the veranda's table.

'The project's finished,' continues Benedict despondently.

'Basically when we got...'

'Please explain why you are wearing a t-shirt with 'I love Sochi' emblazoned across it,' interrupts Adrian. 'To the best of my knowledge you've never been to the Black Sea.'

'My clothes got sopping wet in Spain,' replies Benedict, shuddering at the memory of the foul lagoon. He then begins his monologue, starting with the words, 'it's a long story.' For the next ten minutes Benedict relays in the most intricate detail the events of the day. On finishing he expresses his concern that it might be rather difficult to secure the return of their loan, as he is suspicious that Theodore's financial position is tenuous. Several minutes later, he concludes that he should have followed Adrian's advice and abandoned the project. Benedict apologises unreservedly for having put them in a position where their money is now at risk and for pressurising Adrian to be involved, against his better judgement.

Adrian sitting on the teak bench taking sips from his glass of Chianti feels both sympathetic towards his brother, and determined to secure the return of the loan. He wishes to explain to Benedict about Middleworth and his concerns over today, but is acutely aware that this is neither the time nor place, particularly with Benedict so distressed. Instead he suggests only half seriously that they should rent the mini crane from the local building supplies company in Falgate, drive it to Ramsbottam Hall and remove the Venetian black marble balls from the columns at the top of its drive and hold them as collateral.

21:00 - Theodore is walking dejectedly down Ramsbottam Hall's drive. The wretched ordeal at Tranquilo has been followed by an arduous journey, littered with obstacles. Having dragged himself from the muddy airstrip, he had walked for several hours, the sodden fabric of his trousers chaffing painfully, before eventually stumbling across the highway. There after numerous failed attempts, he had
hitched a ride on the back of a poultry cart, huddled in his sodden clothes between the cages, tormented by the incessant clucking of the chickens. Exiting the vehicle at the transit stop on the outskirts of Marbella, Theodore's muddy travel suit plastered in white down, he was a deplorable state. The final five kilometres to the airport were travelled on foot.

Refused admittance to the airport terminal by its security, who assumed Theodore was a homeless vagrant, he had purchased a flight to Heathrow over the phone on a budget airline that departed two hours later. He had withdrawn his account's remaining ten Euros from a cash dispenser outside the terminal. After which he headed to the local Clothes-Depot outlet, situated on the opposite side of the highway. It was his first visit to the multinational retailer, having previously always viewed the shop contemptibly from the interior of his car. On entering the store Theodore is distressed by the thought that this may not be his last.

Weaving melancholically up the aisles clustered with holiday makers of the budget variety, he scanned the cheap fabrics either side of him with dismay. Even here misfortune reigned supreme, for with only ten Euros at his disposal, it seemed he was unable to finance the purchase of a t-shirt and shorts, let alone socks. However if only for the most fleeting of moments fortune smiled upon him and he stumbled across a wide cage of about waist height. Ravenous shoppers were bent over it, rummaging through the items, as if they were pigs at a trough. Reluctantly he too had begun to sift through the fabrics it contained. Sometime later near the bottom of the pile, he located two items of clothing from last year's stock that met his budgetary requirements. A pair of the vilest fluorescent green and orange board shorts he had ever had the displeasure to witness and a brown t-shirt with pastel lime stripes. It was a size too small and had 'I Love Clothes-Depot Marbella' scrawled across it. Momentarily he considered shoplifting something marginally more upmarket from the prestige range on the other side of the shop. However on noticing the large security panels at the doors, he had decided against it. Changing in the shop's car park and binning his trousers, shirt and beige travel suit jacket, he had returned to the airport and awaited the flight home.

The flight was a wretched experience, a window to a frightful new world that had already descended upon him. Travelling with a grade of holidaymaker he loathed above all other. Their drunken jollity and antics antagonised his morbid predicament yet further. By the end of the flight, Theodore had concluded that the loathsome company of his previous travel companions the poultry were preferable to these. From Heathrow, two public buses at a cost of six pounds eighty brought him to within an hour of home. Trudging disconsolately in the encroaching darkness along the side of the road, one regret tormented him ceaselessly; the intervention of Adrian on his life.

For despite the hopelessness of his predicament and the knowledge that Ramsbottam Hall would soon be repossessed by the bank, the belligerence remains and he does not look inwards for the reason for his failure. Not once did he consider the prior warnings his dreams had offered him. Instead he blames Adrian as being the catalyst for the events at Tranquilo, convinced that had Adrian not brought up the matter of the planning permission in Vince's presence, then the Tranquilo shoot would have been a success. For it would have taken place days earlier when the weather was fine, resulting in the avoidance of the lake and at any rate the insects would have been dormant in sunny conditions.

Theodore is clutching the final twenty pence he possesses in the world in his palm on arriving at the hall's front door. On entering the house, Anastasia, sitting at the top of the spiral staircase views her husband with contempt. She need not enquire about the outcome of the trip, as it is obvious on examining Theodore's bedraggled appearance and ghastly multi-coloured apparel. Her mind flits back to her first acquaintance with fluorescent garb of this ilk. It was during her childhood, shortly after the collapse of the Soviet Union. A number of Nizhny Novgorod's inhabitants', previously only familiar with the drab uniformity produced by the communist era factories, had embraced the new multi-coloured world with ill-conceived attempts. Shocking gaudy outfits, so repugnant that the memory of them had stayed with her to this day.

Noticing her on the landing; Theodore begins to ascend the stairs, complaining bitterly about the events in Spain that have transpired against him. Anastasia ignoring the morose monologue turns her back to him and walks down the passage to the dressing room, slamming the door shut behind her. Theodore attempts to open it but the key turns and the door is locked, leaving him alone in the corridor.

Standing on tiptoes, Anastasia opens the top cupboard and pulls out the eight large Versace suitcases. They tumble to the ground. As she begins to neatly fold items of clothing and place them in the suitcases, there is sadness at the imminent departure from the house and its Ming Dynasty wallpaper, Georgian furniture and carefully manicured lawn. She considers her future existence with the colostomy-bag-wearing Earl in Abbotsford Manor House, seven miles away near Fordingham. Anastasia can hear nothing now, despite her husband's tyrannical shouting from the corridor, and she smiles contentedly, as Abbotsford's indoor swimming pool complex, complete with waterfall and sauna, appears in her mind's eye. So real in fact, that she can almost reach out and touch them.

Eventually Theodore stops shouting and goes through to the master bedroom, where he hurriedly puts on a pair of corduroy trousers and a sleeveless Musto shooting jacket. After which, he walks down to the basement, takes the safe key from the hook behind the boiler and opens the gun cabinet. He examines the shotguns, running his fingers along their polished barrels as he does so, before selecting the twelve bore Purdy with a Turkish walnut stock and inlaid gold lettering. With the shotgun in one hand, he reaches down and picks up a box of Eley twenty-eight gram sporting cartridges from next to the basement's freezer. He inserts a cartridge into each barrel, a further six in his pocket and goes upstairs. In the kitchen Theodore peers out through the glass door that leads to the courtyard. The only sign of life is a solitary robin chirping animatedly on the white carrara marble-topped table.

Meanwhile back at the Raven household, Benedict and Natalia have started bickering again on the veranda. Even several rooms away in the study, the noise is a mild irritant to Adrian. He glances at the screen of the Casio Mudman and then calculates that four hours, twenty-one minutes and forty-two seconds remain of the day. Resting his elbows on the mahogany desk, he returns his attention to the online blog. The blog is written by a young female lawyer, who claims to have been reincarnated. At least, she had been employed as a lawyer until being dismissed on account of her reincarnation assertions. She is currently in the process of suing her former employer for unfair dismissal.

The volume of Benedict and Natalia's arguing is such that neither of them hears the sound of a vehicle parking outside the front door. Noticing Theodore approaching the veranda, Benedict exclaims, 'What are you doing here?'
Seeing the shotgun held casually in Theodore's left hand, surprise turns to alarm. Benedict and Natalia look at each other, unsure as what to do. Theodore, who is now standing alongside them asks, 'Where's Adrian?' in a calm yet authoritative voice. Benedict does not respond. Theodore repeats the question.

'Why?' asks Benedict in a timid voice.

'Because I'm going to shoot him.'
Benedict stares at Theodore unable to speak, his pupils dilating with shock. Some seconds later he asks 'Why' again.

'Benedict you're a clever boy I'd have thought you could work that out all by yourself,' replies Theodore in a patronising tone. 'He delayed the trip and that's what killed the project.'

'That's ridiculous,' blurts out Benedict in a quivering voice. 'I won't tell you where he is.'

Theodore's eyes narrow threateningly.

Adrian having heard the commotion has crept into the sitting room, where he now stands out of sight, pressed against the wall on the other side of the veranda door, watching in horror as the situation unfolds.

Natalia pointing at her husband with a perfectly manicured finger says, 'it because Benedict, if no Benedict no Adrian and no problem.' Benedict stares at his wife incredulous but does not respond.

'Congratulations Natalia,' says Theodore smiling broadly, baring his teeth. 'Not only have you just constructed virtually an entire sentence, your also correct for once.' He then slowly and very deliberately begins to raise the gun towards Benedict, who though attempting to speak is unable to vocalise any words.

At the very moment the shotgun reaches Theodore's shoulder, Adrian peers out from through the partially open veranda door and calls out, 'Tranquilo.' A demonic roar emanates from Theodore as he swivels the gun towards him. Adrian slides the door shut just as the first shot is fired; it is followed swiftly by a second. The glass cracks but it does not shatter, behind it an unharmed Adrian peers out. Emitting a single frightful yell, Theodore charges at the door, smashing it with the butt of the gun several times. He then hastily begins reloading it with trembling fingers.

Swiftly sliding open the door with his right hand, Adrian takes one step outside and punches Theodore in the ear with his left hand. The gun and cartridges spill to the ground. Theodore collapsing to his knees grabs Adrian's legs, screaming maniacally as he attempts to wrestle him to the ground. Sprawling, Adrian forces his considerable bulk down on top of Theodore, who in spite of struggling ferociously is soon prostrate on the ground, still screaming, his eyes bulging menacingly as froth forms at the corners of his mouth. Adrian places his knee on Theodore's back, pinning him down. Natalia flees around the house and up the lawn, headed for the safety of her sister at Ramsbottam Hall.

Benedict inconsolable with shock says, 'She tried to have me shot, why?'

Adrian ponders the question from his new position, sitting on the prone Theodore's back and then replies, 'Life Insurance Policy.'

'How can you be so cynical,' howls Benedict, before becoming aware that Adrian's answer is most likely correct. Theodore, continuing to struggle with ever feebler efforts, offers no comment.

Benedict takes his mobile from his pocket and telephones the police. The two brothers then wait in silence on the veranda for their arrival. Theodore twisting his head towards Benedict proceeds to make a desperate plea to be released, excusing his actions as a momentary loss of control and reminding him that he is 'after all still family.' However his influence over Benedict is at an end and his protestations go ignored.

Ten minutes later, three police cars, sirens blazing, screech to a halt outside the house. Within seconds a procession of police officers are surrounding the veranda. The most senior of the group, a female detective sergeant records details of the alleged crime in an Evidence in Action booklet. Meanwhile two burly police officers lead Theodore away in handcuffs to one of the cars. With the arrogance and belligerence now gone, he seems to Adrian much smaller than before. The gun and cartridges are placed in separate transparent plastic bags, and then they too are taken away to be examined by ballistics. Adrian and Benedict sit in silence on the teak bench, both in deep thought, though on very different matters, watched over by a female and male police constable, who have remained behind for the purpose. Some minutes later they too are led away to the remaining police car. Unlike Theodore they are not placed in handcuffs.

Arriving at Fordingham police station, Adrian and Benedict decide that it would be advisable to contact their father's lawyer, a Mr Elliott Wilson, the same lawyer who had prepared the Tranquilo loan document. Forty minutes later Elliott arrives. Benedict and Elliott go through to the interview room. Adrian sitting on a polypropylene chair waits his turn in the waiting room, drinking tea from a Styrofoam cup. A short while later three figures appear in the corridor that leads out from the far end of the waiting room. Looking up from his tea, Adrian sees that it is Theodore, flanked by two policemen. Having been photographed, had his DNA collected from the inside of one of his cheeks with a swab and his fingerprints taken on the Live Scan machine, Theodore is now on his way to the cells. Momentarily, Theodore and Adrian make eye contact. Adrian notices the dullness of Theodore's eyes, the malignity having deserted them.

Theodore finds himself standing on the cold and slimy stone floor of the basement holding cell. The reinforced metal door slams shut behind him. Hanging from the ceiling is an exposed flickering twenty watt bulb, the room's only source of illumination. The persistent drone of a single mosquito is discernible as it circles the light relentlessly. Sometime later, Theodore, slumped dejectedly against the peeling paint of the cell's damp wall comes to the realisation that his dreams were offering him a premonition that he chose to ignore, resulting in his dissolution.

Meanwhile upstairs the continuing deluge of bureaucracy means that neither Adrian nor Benedict have time for pensive introspection. Once the formal statements have been taken from the two of them, they are required to fill in a multitude of forms whilst a plethora of information is relayed to them. Several hours' later the process has been completed and Adrian and Benedict are allowed to leave.

They are strongly advised to remain in the locality for the next week, as they may be required to make another appearance at the station.

Several minutes later, Adrian and Benedict are sitting in the back of an ABC mini cab. Benedict lowers the electric window and the brothers thank Elliott one final time for his assistance. As the engine starts, Adrian pulls down the sleeve of his cotton M&S shirt and checks the time. One hour, ten minutes and forty-three seconds remain of the day. He checks that the seat belt is secured and then tightens it slightly. A short time later, satisfied that there is no sound emanating from the rear of the vehicle and that no odour of smoke can be detected, he looks pensively out of the window beside him.

The mini cab is turning into the lane when Adrian looking across at his brother asks, 'What about Natalia?'

'I'll drop her stuff off in front of Ramsbottom Hall tomorrow and that'll be the end of it,' replies Benedict. Several seconds later he adds, 'I can't believe you risked your own life to save mine.'

Adrian turning his head towards Benedict again replies, 'the risk was minimal.'

'What do you mean?'

'The veranda door is security glass.'

'So what?'

'Through a process known as lamination, a polycarbonated material is layered between the sheets of ordinary glass. The polycarbonate was able to absorb the pellets ... '

'That's enough,' interrupts Benedict, only mildly annoyed.

By the time they are turning into the drive, Adrian is concluding that the intervention of Middleworth in his life seems now to have been a warning about a threat to his mortal existence, which with the detainment of Theodore has hopefully passed. In addition to this encouraging theory, is the bonus that Natalia has with any luck been permanently removed from the family. Adrian waits until the mini cab is stationary before unfastening his seat belt and reaching for the door handle. He is satisfied that he is now ready for an imminent return to London and more determined than ever to achieve attainment amongst the clouds, once his current existence is complete.

Benedict having paid the fare is putting the change in his pocket when he asks, 'What do we tell father?'

'That we will pay for the damage to the glass,' replies Adrian.

The End

Printed in Great Britain
by Amazon.co.uk, Ltd.,
Marston Gate.